CHANCE FOR
RAIN

CHANCE FOR RAIN

A NOVEL

TRICIA DOWNING

FRONT STREET
PRESS

Chance for Rain
Published by Front Street Press
Denver, CO

Publisher's Cataloging-in-Publication data

Names: Downing, Tricia Lynn, author.
Title: Chance for Rain / Tricia Downing.
Description: First trade paperback original edition. | Denver [Colorado] : Front Street Press, 2018.
Identifiers: ISBN 978-0-9984302-3-2
Subjects: LCSH: Fiction - Romance. | Disabilities Fiction. | Paraplegics—Fiction.
BISAC: FICTION / Women.
Classification: LCC PS370-380 2018 | DDC 813–dc22

QUANTITY PURCHASES: Schools, companies, professional groups, clubs, and other organizations may qualify for special terms when ordering quantities of this title. For information, email info@frontstreetpress.com.

This book is printed in the United States of America.

Patricia Skates
1938-2011

This book is for you, Mom.
"A mother is someone who dreams great dreams for you, yet
accepts the dreams that you decide to follow, and will always
love you just the way you are. Thank you for being you and
encouraging me to be me."
—Unknown

CHAPTER 1

WHOEVER SAID IT'S BETTER TO HAVE LOVED and lost than to have never loved at all was full of shit. I am sitting on the patio of my childhood home with my father; together we are a testament that it doesn't matter whether you once had a great love or never had one at all. Between the two of us, we have experienced both, yet here we sit—on the same playing field of loneliness—spending time together while lost in our own worlds.

Sunday mornings with my dad have been a tradition ever since I moved out of our family home and got a place of my own. It's our *quality time*, if you can call it that. He's got his nose stuck in the *New York Times*, and I'm scrolling through Facebook on my iPhone.

"Rainey, I just read an interesting article about how more

people are breaking the smartphone habit and reconnecting with each other face-to-face," he says. I can tell he's looking at me and waiting for me to glance up, but I only respond, "Uh-hmm," as I'm thoroughly glued to the screen of my personal electronic device, reading Jenny's status update and wondering exactly what she's referring to when she says how crazy last night was and that "what happens in Vegas stays in Vegas." I make a mental note to text my high school friend for more on this juicy gossip and perhaps even consider my dad's commentary and schedule a face-to-face lunch date to catch up.

This weekly get together and inanimate exchange of conversation is my father's and my attempt at keeping our family together. I use the term "family" loosely because I'm not convinced that two people alone constitute a family. But, it's all we have left. Our inattention isn't because we don't like each other. On the contrary, I love my father more than any other person on this earth. Yet, our conversation is hollow, as are our hearts.

Today, the Colorado sun feels like it is shining especially bright, and I experience an intense sensation of warmth as it falls directly on me, accompanied by a certain crisp feeling in the air. It's the end of August, and though the daytime temperatures remain balmy, with each sunset comes a burst of chilly air, seemingly cooler than the day before—a sign from Mother Nature to begin preparations for a change of season. I know the signs by heart and realize in a few short weeks the leaves on the trees will begin to turn and autumn will arrive.

As I sit on one of the new wicker chairs my father and I purchased together at the beginning of the summer, I close my eyes and tilt my head back to face the sun. I glimpse upward to bathe in the glow. Not that of the actual fiery orb, but the rays of compassion radiating down from my younger sister Sunny, who I imagine is looking upon me at this exact moment, wishing she could send me the love that has been missing in my life ever since she and Mom died. It's been seventeen years since my father and I lost the loves of our lives, and you'd think we would have moved on by now. I suppose we have—in most ways. But how do you recover from something so precious being taken far too soon? Now, we're left with a void in our lives that we've never been able to fill. I don't know ... maybe we haven't tried. Maybe we never will.

I look at my father lost in his thoughts and wonder if he is thinking of my Mom. Every once in a while, I see that sparkle in his eye, but then as quickly as it comes, it fades to black and vanishes. Even as a kid who knew nothing about love, I could see how my father's eyes followed my mom's every move. He is an unbridled, starry-eyed romantic. For as long as I can remember, at our house when the candles came out and the lights were dimmed, Sunny and I would be shooed along to the neighbor's house for pizza and a movie. And there wasn't a week when he didn't come home with flowers in hand. He referred to my mom as his *everything* because in his eyes she truly was. "Without her," he'd say, "little else matters." You've never seen a man as in love as he was. In my teenage vernacular, I believe *lovey dovey* was the mocking phrase I used to refer to this state of infatuation.

Hence *my* problem—never to have truly loved. They

say most girls fall for men like their daddies. If that's true, I may never find the man who exudes love, affection, and romance like my dad did with my mom. His attention and thoughtfulness rivaled the leading men in the best chick flicks. The one we all yearn for but intuitively know couldn't possibly exist. Except for the fact that I witnessed it. A love so complete between my parents, it belonged on the big screen. It was not only the perfect model of love, but it seems now to be a curse—because I'm convinced there is no other man like my dad. That idyllic mold of suitor seems to have been broken with him, though his example was strong enough to become seared in my mind. I still dream of finding the perfect man, to whom I could be an *everything*—not merely a *something*, a *plaything*, or *not-much-of-anything-at-all*.

My dad has always been my hero. When I was younger, and Sunny was just an infant, summer evenings and Sunday afternoons with him were my favorite hours of the week. He and I would "get out of Mom's hair" and head to the racetrack. As he tells the story, he was born behind the wheel and worked his way from driving karts as a kid to racing cars professionally in his twenties, until he met my mom and gave up the oval for the suburbs and ditched the champagne sprays on the victory stand for children. I'll never understand how he gave up such a promising racing career, but I guess it's the power my mom had over him. As a result of his former status as a pro, he became a celebrity at the local track and still managed to stay involved with the sport, whether it was participating in the weekly race series, mentoring up-and-coming drivers, or tinkering on cars. And though he probably wanted to pass on his love for racing to a son instead of a daughter (which he vehemently denies), I took to it without an ounce of coercion. In fact, while many of the parents in our auto sports community started their kids in go-kart racing by the time they were five or six, I had to beg to get behind the wheel as an eight-year-old. Once my dad gave me the green light I quickly became addicted to the speed and thrill of the track. And when he wasn't teaching me driving skills, he was letting me ride shotgun in some of his local races. I'd spend hours hanging out in the garages watching (and sometimes assisting) the mechanics and learning cars inside and out. By the time I was thirteen, my father and I together had rotated tires, installed radiators, changed carburetors and rebuilt engines.

My need for speed was obvious from the beginning. I fell in love with the stimulation of the racetrack and couldn't wait until the day I would be behind the wheel of a true Indy car, but that desire became even stronger after the day that changed our lives. I've always turned to my love for speed to awaken my senses and delve into that corner of me where passion lives. Unfortunately, after the accident, my dad's devotion to racing never fully returned. He went through the motions on occasion, but he set aside the fevered buzz of racing and retreated into his own world. I, on the other hand, embraced it wholeheartedly. Going fast, whether at the track or down the ski hill, made me feel exuberant, yet numb, all at the same time.

Some people saw it as a reckless disregard for life. Ms. Henry, my Sunday school teacher, who never approved of my father's racing hobby and the fact that at a young age I aspired to follow in his footsteps, once said to me at church, "Speed kills, you know?"

Interesting point, I thought, because one does not have to be going over 100 mph for death to be involved. In fact, I'd say we were probably going in the neighborhood of twenty-five.

It was a Saturday at the end of March. The day had been unusually warm for the time of year. My dad took us out for dinner—family-style Italian. Sunny and I pigged out because the night was for us. Nothing big, but our mid-semester grades had come in the mail, and both of us had earned straight A's. It was no surprise for Sunny because even as a fourth grader, we could tell she was going to be the brains of the family, but in my second semester of high school, it was a nice, possibly lucky, surprise that I should have perfect marks. And with a college professor for a dad and a schoolteacher for a mom, one can imagine how important schoolwork was in our family. Good grades that reflected our hard work were cause for celebration. After dinner, we went to Lick's Ice Cream Parlor to choose from a rainbow of flavors. Although Dad didn't have a sweet tooth and Mom was always on a diet, Sunny and I, being allowed two scoops each, were in heaven.

After getting our cones from the server at the counter, we raced each other across the sleepy neighborhood street to where our car was parked along the curb. Once Mom caught up with us, she opened the back door behind her front passenger seat. Instead of taking our usual seats, I dove in first and scooted across the bench seat behind the driver's seat and let Sunny sit on the side closest to the open door, so she wouldn't spill her ice cream as she crawled over the upholstery. As we drove, I looked over at Sunny. She had blonde hair that was spun gold, a result of the time she spent in a pool. A competitive swimmer, she spent countless hours every week in the chlorinated water perfecting her strokes. During the summers especially, her hair turned another three shades lighter from the sun, while her skin was a perfect shade of bronze. As Sunny walked down the street, people stopped to admire her. She was too cute for passersby not to take a second glance. I could see her being in an old-time Coppertone commercial before the Surgeon General issued warnings about skin cancer and a deep, dark tan was a coveted accomplishment. It didn't matter how much sunscreen Sunny put on; the rays were attracted to her skin, and she was constantly glowing. I think a lot of her radiance had to do with her outgoing personality and contagious optimism. Even though she was my younger sister, I looked up to her and admired her for those traits.

From the moment we got in the car, Sunny was running her mouth—one of those kids who verbalized every word of her inner dialogue. She began, "Daddy, I want to be an astronaut. Do you think I could go to astronaut school?" The innocence of her eight-year-old questions was endearing as her monologue continued, following her own train of thought. "Do astronauts have to do a lot of math? I hope not. Math isn't very fun. Don't you think it would be fun to take a rocket into outer space? I do!"

"Honey, why don't you concentrate on eating some ice cream before it ends up a sticky mess in the car?" Mom said.

Sunny took a big circular lick around the glowing green mint chocolate chip in her cone and then asked, "Are there any girl astronauts?"

While Sunny was pondering the farthest reaches of outer space, my mind was a million miles away in another direction. I wished my dad would step on the gas and get us home.

"Dad, why are you going so slow?" I asked him in a snotty teenage tone. "You only have to go twenty-five when children *are present*. Can't you read the sign? You can go thirty-five miles per hour now ... probably forty because no one is looking. Geez, I drive faster than this in my go-kart!"

"Patience, sweetheart," my dad replied sarcastically.

Even though Dad was a race car driver, he was a strict proponent of following speed limits on the street, because he wanted to set a good example for us to be able to separate the speeds he drove on the track from those on the road. He didn't condone speeding outside of the racecourse and warned us that even if he was a good driver, not everyone on the road had similar skills behind the wheel.

It was almost nine o'clock, and I was anxious to get home. My new boyfriend—again, a term I use *loosely*, since I was only fourteen at the time and had never been kissed—was going to call at 9:08 p.m. Gabe and I chose that time to talk each night because it was exactly twelve hours after the first time we lay eyes on each other every day in our third period English class. I didn't want to miss him or our special time.

We drove along the tree-lined road that wound past Sunny's elementary school. As the car crawled past, we could see the playground where Sunny spent her daily recess. She pointed to her favorite play spot. "Mommy, Daddy, look! Do you see the cool ladybug in the middle of the playground? It's the new jungle gym. You can climb all over it, and it's my favorite. You know why? 'Cause ladybugs are for good luck."

Her innocence was endearing, but before anyone could utter a word in response to the ladybug, her time was up. Those were the last words Sunny ever spoke. Coming from the north was Suzy Simmons, a drunk driver who'd had a little too much wine at the afternoon wedding shower she'd attended. Perhaps she overindulged to soothe her discouragement at not being the one getting married—always the bridesmaid, never the bride. But, no matter the reason, she blew right through a stop sign and directly into the passenger side of the car where my Mom and Sunny were sitting.

Suddenly we were bashed around as if on a broken carnival ride. The sound of the impact, the crushing of the car, and the shattering of glass boomed in my ears. I can't say what was more vivid—the screech of metal against metal or my memory of Sunny being flung into my lap as her side of the car was smashed so hard, it collapsed in around us, wrapping us like a constrictor. The more I tried to move, the tighter it seemed to get. It took a few moments for the pain signals to reach my brain. As they did, I discovered that not only could I not move, but I didn't want to.

I screamed as my eyes focused on Sunny lying lifeless on my lap with blood gushing out of her head. And then just as suddenly, everything went black.

I tried opening my eyes, but my eyelids were like lead. They fluttered several times as I struggled to get control. When they finally opened, a flood of fluorescent light made me want to shut them again. With a moan and a burst of strength, I got my eyes open, but that was the only part of my body I could get to move. Lying on my back, I had little perspective of my surroundings. I looked up at the ceiling and then through my peripheral vision, around the room. My father was wilted into a burnt orange vinyl chair in the corner. The only color in the entire room. I tried to pick up my arm, but it didn't have any strength. My eyes quickly darted around the room, machines, and tubes coming in and out of focus. A steady hum came from a machine next to my shoulder. Tubes draped from the apparatus to my arm, and I watched the slow and steady drip of clear liquid seeming to come from the machine, through the tube and entering … where? I looked down at my hand, and there was a needle protruding from my vein. Afraid to move, my breathing became heavier, and I began to whimper. I tried to scream, but no sound came out. Startled, my dad looked up, and in one giant leap across the room, was at my bedside. His eyes filled with tears as he grabbed my hand, leaned down, and gave me one long kiss on my forehead.

"Daddy?" My voice came out in a gravelly whisper. "Daddy, what's happening?" I was so frightened.

He put his hand on my head and smoothed my hair. His eyes filling with moisture, but not spilling a tear.

"Baby you've been in an accident," was all he could say.

"But … I was with you. Me and Sunny were eating ice cream. And then …"

And then the memory started to come back. The loud sound of a crash echoed in my ears. Sunny's limp body landing on mine. I remembered being bounced between the front and back seat. The pain was searing and the screams piercing.

My heart began to pound, and an internal chill penetrated my body.

"Where's Sunny?" It came out more like an accusation than a question. "Where's Momma?"

"Honey, relax and close your eyes," my dad said as his voice trembled, and his white-knuckled hands grasped the side rails of the hospital bed.

"Daddy, where are they?" I asked again. I wanted an answer, but my gut was already telling me.

"Baby ..." he said as his voice trailed off.

"No, Daddy. No. Please no!"

"It was a very bad accident."

A shiver seized my body, and the tears came fast and fierce, followed by uncontrollable sobs. I couldn't catch my breath, couldn't swallow. I was drowning in sorrow and my inability to get enough air into my lungs.

Although I was awash in my own grief, watching the tears slip down my father's face and his shoulders visibly shudder, for the first time in my fourteen years, made everything seem so real. It was alarming to me in my delicate state. I panicked.

I made a sound that could only be described as a squeal of pain—emotional more than physical in that moment—and must have caused a loud enough commotion because a nurse came running in to find my father and me creating a waterfall of tears together.

"I have to go home. I have to get out of here!" I said with as much force as I could summon. I tried to sit up, and nothing happened.

"Honey, you mustn't try to move."

I began to throw a tantrum, but as I attempted to kick my legs, they didn't respond. I could feel my eyes widen as I looked at my dad. His shoulders slumped, and his legs looked like they might buckle. He turned away. Lucy, my day nurse who was standing on the opposite side of the bed, grabbed my hand and said, "I'm so sorry, dear."

"What do you mean, you're sorry?" I demanded.

"Thom," she said to my father, her one-word statement suggesting he be the one to elaborate.

"Sweetheart, in the accident … you … broke your back." He stumbled over the words.

"Well, how long until it's better? I want out of here. I'm going to run so far away and never come back!" My voice was small, but I could tell Lucy had picked up on my fury.

He sighed in response as his lip trembled. "Sweetie, that's the problem. You can't run."

"Obviously, I can't right now. My back is broken," I said spitefully.

"No, you're not understanding me. I don't think you'll ever be able to run again. You have a very severe condition … a spinal cord injury. The nerves in your back that control the rest of your body have been severed. You don't have the use of your legs anymore. You'll need a wheelchair when you leave here."

"A what?" I said defiantly because it was the only thing I

could think to blurt out. Half of me couldn't process what he had said, and the other half didn't want to.

Only my dad came out of the accident with no physical injury. Only later, as I looked back at him through the eyes of a grown woman, would I realize the emotional toll the accident had taken on him. He had lost the love of his life, his "peanut" (his pet name for Sunny), and would have to endure the pain of watching his eldest daughter navigate a life-altering injury. It was heartache times infinity, leaving him at a loss for how to heal the emotional devastation while maintaining a steel-coated exterior to hold his remaining family together.

CHAPTER 2

MY INITIAL DAYS IN THE HOSPITAL WERE FILLED with visitors, stuffed animals, and chocolate. None of it helped. Every one of my teachers came to see me. Classmates poured in and out, even ones I barely knew. I saw the looks of pity in their eyes. Sometimes, it seemed, they came more for curiosity and to witness the devastation that had hit within our tight community. Regardless of their motives, it was nice to have company, but as they flowed in and out of the hospital, the one person I had expected to see remained absent. Day in and day out, I waited for Gabe to walk through the door. Even in my broken and depressed state, I pictured it—the perfect opportunity for him to arrive as my knight in shining armor, wielding an armful of roses and ideally a white horse, to take me away from this place. I imagined how it would feel to have him show up, scoop me into his arms in a loving embrace, and give me my first real kiss. But a week went by and then two, and Gabe never came. The pain of his absence and the shattering of my teenage heart only added to the list of my other losses.

By the third week of my hospital stay, my condition had stabilized, and I was finally able to get up from the constraints of the bed and sit for short amounts of time in a hospital wheelchair. It gave me a change of scenery and allowed my dad and me to take short walks through the corridors of what felt like a prison.

It was Thursday of that week when sitting alone in my room, I heard a knock on the door. Unable to move myself in the wheelchair and not knowing who was on the other side of the door, I replied to the knock with an invitation to come in. The door opened tentatively, and on the other side was Gabe. Dressed in ratty blue jeans and an untucked flannel shirt, he entered with his eyes glued to the linoleum floor. As his gaze rose to meet mine, we locked eyes, and his attention returned quickly to the floor. I wasn't sure if it was from shame or the sight of me, clad in a back brace, hair matted to my head, and legs, which we all knew by now, would remain lifeless. He mumbled a barren apology for not showing up sooner. He said he was scared to see me. Didn't know what to say. I looked at him with scorn, knowing it didn't matter anyway, since a few days prior, Jenny told me he had already started *going with* one of our other classmates.

Eventually, we both spit out a few words, but the conversation lasted mere minutes before he let out a sigh, slouched further, and gave his final goodbye to the floor and turned around to leave. Not only would his departure in my time of need be permanently etched in my mind, but also his expression and mannerisms would stay with me for years. Not that our romance was one for the storybooks, but in my young mind, I thought he cared about me. In the innocence of teenage life, I believed our relationship meant something. Instead, he made me feel small and insignificant. It was Heartbreak 101. It also created within me an insecurity regarding relationships that would follow me into adulthood.

Fortunately, there was one person I could always count on who never made me feel like I had become something less, despite what had happened to me. The one individual who was there because she genuinely loved me and treasured our friendship—my BFF Natalie—the next closest person to me beyond my family. We met as three year olds in a preschool class and have been joined at the hip ever since. I've always considered her a sister more than a friend. More so after Sunny died. People even tell us that we look alike, which I love since I think she's stunning—a Kate Hudson look-alike, most people say. It was almost as if we were twins, with matching blonde hair and green eyes. At five-foot-ten, Nat has two inches on me, but even as kids we were both taller than most of the boys at school, having hit growth spurts early before the boys could even contemplate puberty. We dressed and acted alike, sharing our clothes and rarely spending time apart from each other. If I ever lost her, it would be like losing my right hand. I've always known that no matter how the roads of our lives diverge, *home* would always include Natalie.

Nat and her mother, Cecile, had been the first to the hospital, after receiving a frantic call from my dad as he sat in an ambulance at the scene of the accident. She and Cecile, my surrogate family, were there to see me off into surgery and were there for me as I returned from the operating room, witnessing moments of which I have no recollection. Once I woke up from my drug-induced coma, Natalie was a permanent fixture by my side. She gave up her life outside of school to spend time with me. She'd even ditch a class here and there to keep me company. Of course, the teachers knew, and they let her get away with it anyway. She'd bring me Big Macs and chocolate shakes, to escape the doldrums of the hospital food. I'd perk up when I saw the latest issue of *Teen Beat Magazine* under her arm, and then I'd slump down when I saw my homework underneath it. When I was allowed to sit up in bed, she would brush my hair, which fell slightly past my shoulders. Sometimes Nat would French braid it down the back of my head, so that I could feel pretty like a girl instead of a spiritless patient. Weeks of bed baths rather than showers made me feel offensive, like the time Mom, Dad, and I went on a four-day waterskiing, fishing, and camping trip and only bathed in the murky waters of the lake. Even though it helped us remove the surface dirt, it was the pond scum that seemed to have permanently attached itself to our bodies. I'll never forget how heavenly it felt to take a shower in the luxury of my own bathroom.

Each evening, Nat stayed in my room way past visiting hours, and sometimes she'd even crawl into bed with me, circle her arms around me, and spend the night. In the darkness of my hospital room, I could shed the tough exterior I tried to hold together for the benefit of my father and friends; the truth was, I was terrified. Everything in my life had changed in an instant, and I wasn't sure what my future would bring.

One night, with tears streaming down my face, I finally uttered the words. It was the first time I had said them to anyone.

"Nat, I'm scared," I whispered to her. "I can't walk … and Mom and Sunny are gone. It's only Dad and me now, and I feel like I'm not even all the way here. I feel like half of me was taken away."

She looked at me and wiped the tears away. "I know, Rainey. You've had a big change and, to be honest, I don't know what I can say that will make it better. I have no idea what happens next. But I do know, no matter what, I will be here by your side … always. Even though I can't be Sunny, and we're not related by blood, I'm your sister, through thick and thin. I promise. We'll figure it out."

She went beyond what a good friend would do. She was the best. I had other close friends who visited too—Jenny and Christine, our high school clique—and though I knew they still cared, their visits started to become fewer and further in between as my days in the hospital dragged on. Natalie was the only one who visited religiously during the four months I was in recovery. She never missed a day. Not one.

<hr/>

After the accident in March, I spent almost a month in the hospital going in and out of the operating room, addressing my injuries—a broken leg, arm, collarbone, and surgery on my back to mitigate the damage to my spinal cord. Once the rods were surgically placed in my spine, my pain came under control, and the back brace became unnecessary, I was transported to a specialized rehabilitation hospital, where I would begin the long road to learning my "activities of daily living," as my therapist would say—which included things like feeding myself, bathing, and dressing. I worked out with three pound dumbbells to get my strength back and learned to navigate a wheelchair.

Nothing could have prepared me for how much work my daily life had become and each day brought on another new challenge. If it wasn't learning how to pull my clothes on while lying on my back or sitting in bed or mobilizing the strength to exercise by pushing myself up and down the hospital hallways, then it was transfers, which seemed to be the hardest part of all. The "transfer" was the cornerstone of being able to get around. Without learning that skill, I wouldn't be able to get from my wheelchair to the bed or the shower chair. Or the opposite, from the shower chair or bed, back into my wheelchair. It was a skill of strength, agility, courage and, in the beginning, extreme focus. It was an acrobatic stunt I would have to master in order to become independent. With one hand on my chair and one on the bed, I learned to push up with my arms, lifting my rear end off of the chair, do a quick swivel move to get my body aimed toward the bed and then gently let myself down. It was a difficult skill to learn and one that I would have to modify each time I found myself transferring onto or off of a seat, whether the car, couch, bed, chair, shower bench, or floor. The transfer from the floor back to my chair was impossible at the start, and even after seventeen years still commands a full effort. No more free rides. I would have to work for everything from getting dressed in the morning to navigating throughout my day. Everything, and I mean everything, seemed to take a monumental effort. The struggles continued 24/7. I quickly learned that there is never a break from being paralyzed.

After I dressed each morning, my therapist worked with me on the skills I would need when I left the hospital, such as being able to open a door, and maneuver along sidewalks, and up and down the curb cuts. There was no limit to the things I would have to do differently now that I was unable to use my legs and core muscles. And the more I could do independently, the less I would have to depend on my father. As a teenage girl, I was mortified by the thought of my dad having to help me with my personal care needs. Those fears were my incentive to become as independent as possible before leaving the rehab center.

Even with the determination of a competitor, which I knew myself to be, the drudgery of each day, staring at white walls, having nurses, doctors, and therapists breaking into my personal space, battling my demons and loss—every moment of every day wore on me. Time slowed, hours stretched. As I watched the wall clock, it seemed as if several moments passed in between each tick of the second hand. Endless repetition of movements I resented having to relearn made the captivity of the rehab center almost unbearable. The only highlights were the days I had my sessions with Ellis, a newly graduated physical therapist who made Natalie and me giggle with his proper British accent and the funny differences between his English and our American English. He described my sometimes-clumsy transfers as *rubbish!* Or if particularly coordinated—*brilliant!* He taught Natalie to assist me with the things that might come up in a world that wouldn't always be accessible, like how to get up and down curbs if there weren't curb cuts. And he took us in the rehab center van to the mall and taught me how to go up and down escalators in my wheelchair.

Most importantly, he taught us skills for getting in the car, as we expressed this would be essential when we passed our driving tests on our sixteenth birthdays, both a little over a year away. I learned how to transfer into the driver's seat and disassemble the chair by myself—first removing the wheels and tossing them over my right shoulder into the back seat, then lifting the body of the chair, up and over my lap to sit in the passenger seat. If we were to go in Natalie's car or if she was a passenger in mine, I'd leave the lifting and disassembling to her, and the chair would go in the trunk and out of our way so we could sit side-by-side in the front seats.

When mid-July finally came, it was time to say goodbye to Ellis and the others who had helped me in the healing process. I never looked more forward to anything in my life. That day should have been a celebration. I was leaving the captivity of the rehab center, but it was a bittersweet drive home. I didn't know who was going to cry first, my dad or me.

Instead, we both kept silent and stiff upper lips on the drive. We dreaded the emptiness that would greet us in our formerly warm and inviting home.

When we arrived, Dad wheeled me into a dark and quiet house that hadn't been cleaned for months, except in the spots where I could see that remodeling had been done to install ramps and widen doorways—all the things needed to accommodate my new situation. As I looked around at the changes, the magnitude of what had happened finally began to sink in. When I wasn't looking at the fresh modifications, I saw the rest of the house had remained untouched. I realized that once my dad left the rehab center each night and came home, he simply spent his nights holed up, surviving inside the shell of our former lives.

Everything was in the same place it had been before we headed out to dinner that March evening. Sunny's and my report cards were proudly displayed on the living room table. The wicker basket Mom had designated for mail was still in its place. The only difference was, instead of holding a handful of envelopes, it was overflowing and spilling onto the floor. It all seemed so useless now with Mom and Sunny gone. Nothing seemed to matter anymore. I wondered if Dad had even taken the time to read the mail or pay the bills. In a house typically full of color—flowers on the table, Mom's brightly colored outfits, Sunny's drawings on the refrigerator— everything now seemed to be in black and white.

For weeks after I arrived home, neighbors, church friends, and some of our extended family swarmed around us, checking in and bringing food, but eventually, the phone calls and dinners faded away as everyone went back to their personal realities and we attempted to cope with ours. The house was empty and lifeless. So was my dad. Fast food became a matter of course, the house fell apart, Dad did his thing, and I did mine. We lived day-to-day. More like hour-to-hour, merely trying to hang on to some semblance of normalcy. My father would greet me in the breakfast nook each morning, but his booming-voice greeting of, "It's a beautiful day!" turned into a meek assessment of how I was feeling and if I was able to get around the house sufficiently. My former life as daddy's girl, teasing each other and joking around, became strained. It was as if he didn't know what to say to me any longer. I wanted to be able to say something, anything, to make him feel better, but I too was at a loss for words. Where we used to go on trips to the auto store for supplies for our car projects, or to the doughnut shop to get a Saturday morning treat for the family, he now pulled out boxes of cereal, and we ate wordlessly at the table.

We moved around like robots, going through the motions. But in every direction I looked there were memories. My dad hadn't had the nerve to go back to sleeping in the master bedroom, so each night, he went down the hall to the guest room. All six feet, two inches of him crammed into one of the twin beds. I suppose he preferred that over a king-sized bed which was like an abyss without mom sleeping by his side. Eventually, all of his necessities ended up in the spare room and the bathroom down the hallway. After a while, I stopped seeing him go into their room altogether. He had everything he needed and said he wasn't ready to look at Mom's things again.

Over time, we became accustomed to this new normal at our house. When I was settled, and Dad stopped worrying about leaving me alone, he headed back to work at the University, and I practiced my independence as I got around the house in my wheelchair, trying to find things to pass the time while he was gone. While my dad lived in denial that his wife and daughter were gone, I tried to hold onto them—in each and every memory I could grasp. I went through Mom's jewelry box and tried on each necklace, bracelet, and pair of earrings. I quizzed myself naming the last time I saw her wearing each piece.

I cleaned up Sunny's room like I had so many times before. She might have been cute as a button, but her room-keeping skills left much to be desired, though it was a trait we shared. I could tell on the day of the accident, she couldn't quite figure out what to wear (shirts and pants flung everywhere), she ate half a Ding Dong (and left the other half wrapped on her desk) and Barbie had been given a bath (she was lying on the bed with her hair brushed straight up from her head and fanned out just a bit, to aid in drying). Barbie was also naked, but from the looks of it, she was going to be wearing a sundress that day and driving her beach cruiser, which sat on the floor near the desk chair. Sunny loved dress up, whether her Barbie dolls or herself. As I stopped to look around, I imagined how much I would miss her after-dinner fashion shows, when Mom, Dad and I would sit on the living room couch and be her audience as she walked down the catwalk, in fashion combinations that only her unique, visionary brain could create.

Natalie helped me pass as much time as she could when she wasn't working her part-time job at the mall. She and I spent afternoons on the couch watching movies or going for walks to help me build the stamina I would need to push myself around the school in my wheelchair.

But as the summer days got shorter and the school year closer, I started to feel nervous. *What would the other kids think of me in my wheelchair? How would I open the heavy door that led into the school?* No self-respecting high school student wants their parent to take them to school on the first day, but I was actually relieved when my dad suggested he accompany me. He walked me to the main office the day classes began, and I met with the principal to talk about strategies to reintegrate me into school life. As if being a teenager isn't hard enough, we needed to discuss how I would navigate the school campus in a wheelchair. I was assigned a resource teacher who would follow me around for the first few weeks to help me get to classes on time, get to the bathroom, and work with me on any other logistical issues that might come up.

I couldn't have felt more out of place if I tried. Even though I had spent three quarters of my freshman year at the high school, I now felt like the new kid. As I arrived on my first day, I got more blank stares than hellos as I pushed down the hallway. I reminded myself that I had had several months to get used to my new appearance, while the other students hadn't. I felt like I looked the same, but then I realized I was riding into school on a super colossal elephant and many students had likely never known someone who used a wheelchair. Especially one who formerly didn't use one. The discomfort of the eyeballs following me felt intrusive and heavy; I was relieved when my father and I took a left-hand turn and slipped into the door of the counseling office to meet Ms. Partridge, my resource teacher. I was only inches inside the door before she stuck her hand nearly in my face and introduced herself. As I tentatively shook her hand, I realized how far back I had to tilt my head to speak to a grown-up. She immediately fired a million questions off at me, none of which felt welcoming or apologetic. No, "how are you today?" or "I'm sorry you lost half of your family in a tragic accident just months ago." She was all business. In fact, she looked business too, with navy blue slacks, a white button-down blouse, and conservative navy pumps to match. She was actually a physical therapist, I would later learn, but she was a far cry from being the same brand of fun Ellis was. I could tell there wasn't going to be any laughing and joking around with her.

After the first week, when the awkwardness wore off, the other kids began to rally around me to help with my every need. The popular kids even invited Nat and me to their get-togethers. The boys would gather around and lift me in my chair down flights of stairs to get me to basement parties. I felt like I had a whole new group of friends, for a short time, but then the novelty of hanging out with the *girl in the wheelchair* seemed to wear off, and I began to feel like a burden. I couldn't do the same things they did, like run through the cemetery at night playing touch tag or ride bikes on the weekend. I had to sit in the special accessible seating at the football games, and everyone else wanted to sit squarely on the fifty-yard-line (as I would have last year—*before* the accident). They didn't want to change their plans to accommodate me. I was different, and at some point, they stopped making attempts to help me feel any other way.

I was left out and didn't want to take Natalie down with me. She was the kind of person who could mesh with any crowd, and everyone wanted to claim her as their own. She was bright and quick-witted with a magnetic personality. Everyone adored Natalie. Although I was afraid to let her go, I encouraged her to do stuff without me. I was the one in the chair, not her. I had the limitations—she didn't. "Live," I told her. "I'll be fine." At least that's what I told myself. I knew it was unrealistic to believe Natalie would be with me 24/7 and there were times she went with the other kids to do what "normal" kids do. But she never stopped being a true friend to me. If I needed her, one call was all I had to make. We still talked daily as we had done our whole lives. And as much as I wanted her time, I knew I needed to learn to navigate my new life independently.

When I wasn't with my friends, I was at home in my new family life which had become a floundering twosome. I found spending time at home with my dad was beginning to pull me down the rabbit hole I had been trying so desperately to get out of. I needed to get away from our demons and find a new contentment. Even as a fifteen-year-old, I could diagnose my father as being stuck in the web of his personal tragedy.

"Hey, Dad," I said one cold day in December. "Why don't we go check on the cars?" referring to his prized Corvette project car and the Porsche he used for club races.

"I don't think so honey, not today." It was the thousandth time I'd received a similar reply.

"Then which day, Dad? Mom and Sunny are gone!" I exploded. The moping, the sadness. I couldn't take it anymore. "But we're still here. And we have to live! I'm tired of you never wanting to do anything."

Before the words were completely out of my mouth, luckily, divine intervention stepped in. The doorbell rang.

My dad silently went to the door to answer it. I stayed a safe distance behind but wanted to see who was interested in talking to us at seven p.m. on a Saturday evening. When my dad opened the door, I recognized Mr. Powell, a man from down the street. I had seen him over the years, mostly in the summer, as I rode my bike. He was always tending to his garden, the most colorful and impressive one on the block. He never said anything as I passed, but he always smiled and waved. Seemed pleasant enough. But this was the first time I'd seen him in the winter—he was wearing a black down vest and red turtleneck, and his cheeks were pink as if he'd been outside all day. On this evening, I wondered what he wanted with my dad.

"Thom, I'm sorry to intrude, and I'm not sure if it's my place to butt into your business, but I volunteer for a local organization that coordinates weekly adaptive sports outings for kids with disabilities. We're currently entering our ski season, and I was wondering if Rainey might like to join us. We've just returned from the ski hill after today's lessons, but we'll be headed back up the mountain tomorrow. It's short notice, but I thought I would see if perhaps Rainey wanted to give it a try."

My dad nodded, looking like he was trying to pay attention.

Still in his months-long daze, I wasn't sure he wanted to admit he had a daughter with a disability. He seemed cemented in the denial stage, though I had moved past it months prior. He continued to avoid it in conversation, daily life, sometimes even in the logistics of our activities. After that first day at school, Dad never asked questions about how I was getting around at school (he'd ask about grades instead), or what it was like for me to spend my days using a wheelchair (but he wanted to know how I felt about Mom and Sunny). As I sat there, staring at Mr. Powell, staring at Dad and Dad staring back, Mr. Powell looked over Dad's shoulder and finally broke the silence.

"Rainey, have you ever thought about skiing?"

I looked down at my wheelchair wondering how the heck I was going to slide down a ski hill in it. I looked back up and must have had a blank stare myself.

"We can take you up to the hill and get you some lessons. You'll use a monoski, which is also sometimes called a sit ski. My nephew uses a wheelchair and has been skiing for years. He's sixteen, so not much older than you. The parents and volunteers drive the kids up to the ski area every Saturday and Sunday morning at six a.m.," he said, neither directly to my dad or me. "I have an open spot in my car tomorrow and would be happy to take you."

Dad turned to me and asked if I wanted to give it a try. I was so tired of being in the house, with the darkness and depression hanging like a fog between us, all I could utter was a simple, "Yeah." It didn't come out with enthusiasm, more like a sigh of relief.

The next morning Mr. Powell, who told me to call him Michael, picked me up bright and early. I wore the kelly-green snow pants and black parka my mom had bought for me in the eighth grade when my class went on a field trip to a local tubing hill. The pants were high-waters on me, but it was all I could do on such short notice. I wore my snow boots and a pair of my mom's ski gloves. I carried a brown sack lunch in my lap along with fifty dollars, for the day of skiing, in my pocket.

We drove two hours to the ski resort—Michael, his nephew Benjamin (who told me to call him Benji), and Benji's ski buddy, James. They talked the whole way up with Benji bragging about the "gnarly moguls" they had gone down the day before and how he was excited for the races today. I got the feeling from Benji's conversation he had been using a wheelchair since he was a kid, although I wasn't sure what his disability was. James was equally as "stoked," he said, to get in the race and told Benji to watch his back—he was coming for him. They sounded to me like the guys at the go-kart track, so it didn't take long for me to settle in with the boys in the car, and I looked forward to learning this new sport.

When we got to the ski lodge and entered the equipment room, I looked around and saw a handful of kids, who all looked like me. Each one was zooming around in his or her wheelchair throwing everyday clothes off, putting on ski outfits, and rushing out the door with volunteers and monoskis. I was apprehensive but hopeful. Michael guided me to the row of skis by the window and started to measure me to find the best fit.

I didn't know what to make of the contraption the first time I saw it. It was a fiberglass bucket seat on an intricate shock-absorbing leg that sat on top of one ski. Michael and my instructor Ken helped me transfer from my wheelchair to the seat, which fit me snug, like a glove. Ken then fastened me in, handing me two short ski poles with mini skis attached at the bottom. He told me they were called outriggers, which I would use to maneuver the monoski, and to assist me with balancing and turning, as well as pushing along the flats. That first day, and for the entire season, it was a challenge to figure out the harmony of balancing and turning, but after a whole winter of lessons, I started to get the hang of it. From that first day, I went every Saturday and Sunday without fail. Usually with Michael and Benji, but sometimes one of the other parents would drive me, and by the end of the season, my dad even took a few turns as part of the carpool. I immediately fell in love with the speed, skill, and courage required, not unlike kart driving. And not only did it get me out of the house, but I was with other kids in situations similar to mine. It was refreshing to have friends who could understand life in a wheelchair. It wasn't like high school where I stood out. Being part of the program helped me refine my wheelchair skills and the other kids demonstrated how normal life could be, despite our disabilities. I noticed how the parents and volunteers didn't treat us with kid gloves; they challenged us to rise to the occasion, build coping and problem-solving skills, and to see ourselves as equal to our able-bodied peers. In the comfort of my new community, I felt safe to ask for help when I needed it or get answers to questions my friends at school had no experience with. It was a growing experience for me, and I appreciated the mountain, a place where I fit in perfectly and saw it as my own private getaway from the *real world*.

Sitting in class at school during the week, I'd daydream— envisioning myself swishing down the mountain. Although it wasn't easy to learn to ski, I threw myself into the process of acquiring the new skill. Becoming a master of the sport was my goal, and it became my second nature. Skiing was the thing that brought me back to life. But the experience of being with other adults whose children had disabilities also helped my father to come out of his shell. It helped to make us both forget the chair, the accident, what was missing from our lives, and the stares of sorrow I received from many of those around me.

Over time, I could ski as fast and as well as the other kids in the program, and we skied as well as the able-bodied kids our age. I reveled in the confidence and fervor it instilled within me. Although my dad had given up his passion for racing cars, shattering our Sunday ritual at the race track, skiing became our common ground, and the trip to the ski hill became our new tradition. My dad never got on skis but was happy to watch from the lodge along with the other parents.

One day as I came inside from the crisp cold, I actually saw Dad talking to Nancy Marsh, the single mom of my ski buddy Melody. On the way home I pestered him about his conversation and told him maybe it was time he went on a date. That went over like a ton of lead balloons, and I quickly gathered it was too soon. In the relationship department, he was still stuck on the path to healing.

I stayed in the ski program for the rest of my high school years and my instructors saw promise in my ability, encouraging me to begin racing. I didn't have to be asked twice and found that through each success I had in competition, my self-esteem grew. On top of that, Dad and Natalie came willingly to every event. I think because it was the first positive thing in our lives signaling everything was actually going to be all right. I loved to hear them cheer as I came tearing down the mountain, crossing the red finish line painted in the snow. I became so good at it, I began to race competitively for a local team, and when I got to college I was able to race alongside the able-bodied students on the varsity ski team.

After my three long and trying years of high school, going to college was a much-needed breath of fresh air. It was finally my opportunity to start over. I could be someone new. Not just the girl-who-was-in-the-tragic-accident-with-her-family. Not the girl-who-used-to-be-able-to-walk-but-is-now-paralyzed. In college, I recognized the division of my life—the time before the accident and the time after it. Then and now. Once I left home and my high school friends, it seemed there were fewer and fewer people who knew me in the *then*, which somehow made me feel more normal. Most people didn't even consider that I had ever been any different, assuming I had always been in a chair. It didn't occur to them there was a substantial and tragic backstory to Rainey's life. As far as they knew, there was never a time when I had walked around as they did, blending into the world around me. It also forced me to break out of the protective shell constructed of Dad and Natalie's unconditional love, to attempt new friendships and bonds. With Dad forty-five minutes away and Natalie at a school on the other side of the country, I vacillated between freedom and insecurity.

Of course, my new circle of acquaintances still saw me as different. *Special*, some people called it, though it was more than obvious that that reference was not meant in a flattering way. Still, I built a close group of friends and experienced the satisfaction racing on the university ski team. I was the pretty girl in the wheelchair who was an academic overachiever and a badass on the slopes.

It was nearly a typical college experience, but while my friends were pairing off in their first relationships, whether young love or one-night stands, I realized where the edge of my confidence as an athlete vanished and butted up against the insecurity of a body that deviated from the norm, making me feel unattractive and afraid. Dating was, for the most part, a bust. I often wondered, *who is going to love me? Who will want me?* Even though college held so much reward for me academically and athletically, on an intimate level, I still frequently felt lonely and alone. I always thought college was the place where people meet their future spouses. Where the seedlings of love take root. But I was missing the partnership so many of my friends and teammates were experiencing. It wasn't like I never had a date. For a short time, I dated one of the guys on the ski team, but it didn't last long. More because of my self-doubt than incompatibility, but I kept waiting to find that someone who would accept and adore me like my father adored my mom. When I was with Nate, the skier, I wasn't much unlike my father when I encouraged him to go out with Nancy, the ski mom. When it came to love, we were both cautious and unwilling to take the plunge.

Like most kids do, I graduated college at twenty-one. I felt I had my whole life ahead of me and hoped for good things to come, especially in the area of romance. But now, as I sit here on the patio with my father, my optimism toward a fulfilling relationship is waning. I am drawn back to the fact that he once had a great love and lost it. At the age of thirty-two, I am beginning to believe I will never even find mine.

CHAPTER 3

"SOMETIMES GOING SHOPPING IS WORK," Natalie announces as we head back to her house after a morning at the mall. "You can't be creative when you've been jammed up in an office for five hours. You have to get out for new ideas to come to you."

"I love how you can rationalize almost any of life's indulgences," I say. Nat turns and winks in response to my playful smirk.

"Life is *too short* to deny yourself all self-indulgent behavior." The words hang in the air slightly, as we both know it was an off-handed comment, but our minds go immediately back to the event that reinforces her words.

"Yes, life *is* short." I say this in a way that reassures her that her comment was taken in the spirit it was said, rather than meant to dredge up bad memories. Though I can't help but elaborate on the subject. "Do you realize I'm only six years shy of my mom's age at the time of the accident?"

"Yep," Nat answers a bit too quickly. "I do. And I also realize something else. Your mom was thirty-eight, married to the love of her life and had two charming young girls." I quickly realize I have given her the perfect segue into a lecture that has been constructed, rehearsed, and delivered to me many times in many different iterations over the past ten years. Now, as if she is attempting an intervention while we drive down Colorado Boulevard, Natalie blurts out, "Rainey, it's about time we found you a man."

"Why? Are you getting tired of hanging out with me?"

"It's not that," she says. "It's just. That. It's time," the words spit out of her mouth. It's obvious she wants to punctuate her points. "You can't keep running away from it. You're an incredible catch—beautiful and charming to be around. Athletic. Everything most girls would die to be."

I know she is keenly aware of my resistance, but I get the feeling she isn't going to fall for it today. But I also can't ignore my feelings or my truth.

"Perhaps," I reply, "but the difference is, most girls aren't dying to be in a wheelchair, and most guys aren't dying to date a girl in one. It isn't in style. It's not sexy."

"Rainey, what does sexy have to do with a wheelchair? People aren't chairs. And people don't date chairs. People date people. Sometimes, those people might date someone who uses a chair, but it certainly isn't your identity … and I don't understand why you constantly have to see it that way. You act as if you're undatable. Why?"

"Come on Natalie. You live in reality. How often do you see women in chairs being referred to as enticing? Do you see them in the movies playing the leading role? Or celebrated on the cover of a magazine?"

"You're using that as an excuse, Rainey. If every woman judged herself only by what she saw in the media, we'd all be running an open tab at the plastic surgeon's office. We'd all be undatable. Face it. Those movie star looks are unattainable to most of us, so why even bother considering them? Rainey, you're beautiful. I know you don't see it, but when you're pushing your wheelchair down the street, you turn heads. And it's not solely due to your mode of transportation. Besides that, the person inside of you is phenomenal. I only wish you could see yourself the way I see you." Nat looks at me hard as we sit at a stop light. "Do you know how often I'm jealous of your looks when we get dressed up and go out? You have perfect hair, which always falls just right, sparkling white teeth, and radiant skin, which rarely sees a drop of makeup and doesn't need to. All of that makes you stand out in a crowd. And in fact," she says, "you do have a face that belongs on a magazine cover."

"What good does it do to have a face that belongs on a magazine cover, when the rest of me doesn't belong there?"

"Okay, you have a choice," Natalie says as she begins on one of her famous lists of options. "A – You can either choose to love yourself so that someone else will love you or B – you can wallow in self-pity for the rest of your life. But I can't sit by and watch you get in the way of your own happiness. I will always be your best friend, but there is so much you're missing by avoiding a true, intimate relationship. You're in your thirties for heaven's sake, and the last time you even *tried* dating was in college. Sure, it's hard to open yourself up and be vulnerable. It's scary to let someone in so completely that they know your most intimate thoughts. But it's a miraculous thing to know you don't have to explain every little detail in your mind, and he gets you anyway. It's fulfilling to be loved for exactly what you bring to the table, knowing your partner isn't looking for one thing different. But I can't make you want it. I can't make you do it. Someday, though, I think you'll look back and regret it if you don't at least try. Being single and free certainly has its perks, but ending up lonely and alone? You deserve more."

It is such a well-thought-out speech there is little I can say in protest. I want to mouth off and tell her that she is being a drama queen, but the truth is, she's right. When I lay on my deathbed one day, will I wish I had someone beside me to hold my hand? Will I wish I would have taken the risk to love and be loved? Although her nagging words are not new to me, I still choke on their bitter sting. I don't disagree. I only wish I believed it was so simple. But—it's complicated. For a moment, I am speechless.

After she is done with her lecture, Natalie turns her head and looks at me for a reaction.

"Keep your eyes on the road," I tell her. The truth is I feel tears welling up. I suppose when you've grown up with someone and they know every detail about you, they have the right to be brutally honest. And ... they know how to push your buttons. The truth stings sometimes.

"Are you going to say anything?" she asks.

"You make it sound like I've never even given it a try. What about when I dated Gabe in high school … or Drew the lifeguard?" Drew had been a three-day relationship at best, the summer between high school and college. "Or Nate?"

I hate to bring up Nate because Natalie and I both know I caused the collapse of that relationship. The truth is, Nate and I were great together. I loved skiing with him, and when we traveled to the other universities for races, we'd sit next to each other on the bus and talk for hours. During the ski season that we dated, I loved having someone to hang out with, study with, and have as a date to all the parties. By all accounts, it was a good relationship. But the problem was I could never get comfortable enough to truly open up to share my feelings. Sure, we talked, but it was about sports or school or current events. Beyond that, I was always self-conscious. I tried but couldn't seem to give him one piece of personal information. I never even told him the extent of the accident. I told him it was a car wreck and that was all. He had no idea about my mom and Sunny.

Nate and I were good together when it revolved around skiing or talking skiing because in that arena I was confident. I knew I was a good athlete and Nate respected my talent. But when it came to more intimate moments, when he tried to reach out to touch me, I recoiled. Not because I didn't want him, but because I was afraid he'd be disappointed. What would he think when he felt my legs, which, instead of being muscular and strong like the other skiers, were thin and atrophied. I was afraid to let him see me naked and the thought of him watching me move through my behind-the-scenes life—it was nothing close to fluid and graceful—made me feel insecure. Though he was always giving of himself, trying to get close, all I could do was drive him away. Somewhere in the back of my mind I knew I'd lose him someday. Why not push him away on my terms so it didn't catch me off guard or hurt so much? I can admit, but only in my own brain, that I sabotaged the relationship. To everyone else, I give the vague explanation of "It didn't work out. We weren't meant for each other," when I know he would have been perfect for me.

I suppose on some level I felt strongly about him, but I couldn't allow myself to truly fall in love even though the potential was there. Unknown to Natalie is the fact that the only two guys I have slept with are those I term *men of no consequence.* Not one-night stands, but not relationships either. And definitely not Nate. One was Ward, my first-year college chemistry partner. Friends with benefits, but only a couple of times at the end of the semester when I knew I wouldn't have to see him much longer. The other, one of Christine's college friends from Colorado State. Another "let's-just-keep-this-between-ourselves" hookup when I spent the weekend visiting her and Jenny, girls whom Natalie and I had been friends with from elementary through high school. As I think about this information I have withheld from Natalie, I feel a tinge of guilt. We've always told each other everything.

But the worst is thinking about Nate. It makes me sink in my seat to think how I pushed him away and retreated to my own bubble because I couldn't stand the thought of him possibly rejecting me, and in a small voice, I say, "Maybe I could start with baby steps—like find a good therapist."

"No, you should stop with avoidance," Natalie says. "I'm sure you'll find there are good guys out there and they aren't nearly as scary and judgmental as you have them pegged to be." This from Natalie with the perfect life, perfect figure, and perfect husband, Seth.

"Okay," I sigh. "What do you suggest?"

"I have an idea, a way you can start small with something that's not too intimidating. You can even stay nearly anonymous … at least to start."

"Such as?" I ask with curiosity.

"MFEO dot com, Baby," Nat says with a shit-eating grin.

"What? I don't even know what that is."

"Rainey, where do you live? Under which rock? It stands for *Made For Each Other*. It's a dating website." I hear the exasperation in Natalie's voice.

I shake my head in disbelief. Online dating?

"Listen lady. He isn't going to come knocking on your door. Well, unless he's the UPS man. And actually, while I'm thinking about it, my UPS guy is pretty hot … if you discount the brown socks. Eewww. I just got a thought. Imagine having sex with a guy who is totally naked, except for his brown socks."

"Gross, Nat!"

"Okay then, it's settled. That does it. MFEO is the answer," she says.

"Let me think about it, and I'll get back to you," I tell her. "Now can we change the subject?"

The rest of the way home we catch up on a little gossip

and make a side trip to the drive-thru at Scanlon's Coffee House to pick up a couple of lattes. Minutes later we end up in her driveway, where my car is waiting to take me home.

Natalie gets out of her BMW, and I sit there for a moment in silence as she circles back to the hatchback to pull out my wheelchair. I wonder how I got so scared of dating. I am a grown woman, for heaven's sake. I remember back to when we had the accident. I was a boy-crazy teen then. But afterwards, I became a terrified shadow of myself, always wondering what people thought of me and believing they assumed the worst.

Natalie brings my chair around to the passenger side of the car, so I can transfer out of the front seat. After I get out, she says, "I really wish you'd try. I know you would argue if I told you that you're still screwed up from losing Sunny and your mom, but eventually you have to unlock that tight exterior of yours and love somebody again."

"I do love somebody," I reply. "I love you."

"I know you do. And I love you too. But Rainey, honestly … you need more. You need action! And you need to learn to open up again. It's not going to be perfect or easy. But it isn't easy for anyone. I certainly kissed my fair share of toads on my way to Seth. But it was worth it. You were there for the late-night teary phone calls, the fits and heartbreak. It'll never just happen. You have to start the ball rolling. I will always be your best friend, but you have to learn to trust … in yourself, in a man, in a relationship. You use your wheelchair more as a dating excuse than a way to get around. You and I both know you have never let that thing get in your way. You ski, you work, you drive, you do anything anyone else does. Yes, some people will look at you and see only your chair, but if they do, they're not the right person for you anyway. And you *will* have to have thick skin, but you won't find what you're looking for and what you deserve if you don't put yourself out there. Will you try? For me? I want you to be *truly* happy." She nearly begs.

"I am happy," I tell her as I hug her goodbye.

I turn and push myself down her driveway; I put my head down and roll to my car. *Why do best friends have to be so honest?*

CHAPTER 4

DRIVING HOME FROM NAT'S PLACE PUTS ME IN A reflective mood. I know Natalie only meant well, but her words make me think about all that has transpired since the accident and makes me wonder if she's right. Am I truly stuck in a rut?

It's been seventeen years since the accident, and it seems so much has changed and yet so much is the same. Dad and I remain half a family, with neither of us making a move to add a significant other to our closed-off worlds. My life still revolves around skiing and, when possible, racing my car at the local track. Christine and Jenny remain my go-to for a single-girl's night on the town. Natalie and I have stayed as close as ever, and I see or talk to her daily, but our paths have been our own.

While I stayed close to home for college, attending the University of Colorado, Natalie fled to a school as far away as she could go—to the lights and action of the Big Apple to attend New York University. I always knew Nat had a flair and desire to be in a fast-paced world, to be in the spotlight or at least around the people who were. Following graduation, she landed a super internship in public relations, which turned into a full-time job six months later.

Three years after graduation, during a night out at the bars with friends, she met Seth—an NYU law school student with aspirations to become a big-time sports agent. They were perfect for each other—big personalities, big dreams, and a big desire to take the world by the horns. Natalie loved being in the mix of the city, getting invited to parties, film premieres, dressing to the nines, and mingling with everyone who's anyone.

She and Seth fell fast in love and married four years ago in a grand wedding, held at the Waldorf Astoria. They had to save for several years to make it happen, but because together they don't do small (nor have I ever seen Natalie, herself, not get something she had her mind set upon), their dream became a reality.

Natalie's life had fallen perfectly into place, and she and Seth were happy with their city life—until she got the call. Cecile was diagnosed with cancer, and Natalie, an only child with her father out of the picture, came home to care for her mother. It was hard for Nat to give up everything she had established in New York, but it wasn't worth missing the precious time she had left with her mom, so she and Seth packed up and headed west. Returning to Denver was like landing in a small cow town for the two of them, but it didn't take Nat long to return to her roots and break into the work and social scene back at home. In fact, I think she enjoys it because of her New York experience. She is now a big fish in a small pond.

The good news is that Cecile—whom over time I have come to refer to as Mom—is in remission. Still, I know Natalie will not leave her side until the end, whether that's months or years from now. I hate to sound selfish, but it's insurance for me that I will have her around for a good while to come. Although I know she feels somewhat limited, she has found her niche. She loves the public relations agency she works for, and Seth is busy traveling around the country landing deals for professional athletes. It's working for both of them, and they seem happy.

In my post-college path, I followed in my mother's footsteps and returned home to teach at the same elementary school where she taught. I received my teaching certificate and could have a classroom of my own, but I currently only work part-time as a teacher's assistant. It allows me to keep my schedule flexible so I can take the needed time off to continue to ski competitively.

In the world of sports for athletes with disabilities there are opportunities to compete at the highest levels. The competition is stiff, and it requires the same dedication able-bodied athletes put into Olympic training, which means I have little free time outside of my workouts and competition. During the summer, I follow the snow to other parts of the globe to get as much ski time in as I can. While my friends back home don bikinis and spend weekends at the pool and summer nights at outdoor barbeques, I continue to wear ski clothes and huddle by firesides.

In the winter, I travel back and forth from the city to the mountains and fit in work where I can. Fortunately for me, I have sponsors, team funds, and a savings account—all of which get me by without having to work full-time. I do love having the opportunity to continue with my job because it gives me a much-needed break from the intensity of my training and helps keep life in perspective. Skiing is important to me, but so is molding young minds and giving them the tools they need to grow up and reach their own dreams.

If there is a silver lining to my accident, it would be that I have found a passion and talent in my athletic endeavors, and as a result of my hard work, I've earned the opportunity to travel the world with Team USA. I never expected to grow up and become a skier. I always thought I would be behind the wheel of a car and maybe even securing a place as one of the female pioneers on the Indy Racing League Circuit. But now my athletic talent has taken me around the world and allowed me to compete for my country. And it's not only been rewarding, but it has been a diversion that has kept me from focusing on meeting the man of my dreams, settling down with the white picket fence, and the American average of 2.5 children.

If there's one thing I know for sure, it's that life takes detours, and if I hadn't opened my eyes to skiing, I might have gone off the deep end after the accident. Even the several years of therapy I endured during the balance of my time in high school wouldn't have brought me back to life the way skiing does. Hurling your body downhill at speeds of over seventy miles per hour requires equal parts fearlessness and tenacity. It's a dizzying mix of being able to let go while having faith that you will make it to the bottom of the hill unscathed. Your body takes over from your brain, and the primal instincts kick in. It's almost like taking in a big gulp of air and descending on that single breath until it's over. When I'm on the course, I use Sunny's presence to boost the trust I have in myself, my skis, the mountain. She is my rock and my guide. With each run I take, I want to make her proud. She is much of the reason I have never given up. Every time I am in the start gate, I envision her on the starting block of the swimming pool. Even as a young kid, she had that look in her eye, while she was waiting for the race to begin, that said, *this is my world. Watch yourself.* In her short career, I never saw her lose a race.

But while racing for Sunny lit the fire within me, my dad's flames were doused. His dreams died the day of the accident, and he has never been able to resurrect them. He quit going to the track and put his cars in storage. I think they reminded him how life used to be, and the memories were too painful. Instead, he has spent his time doing his thing at the university, hiding behind books, and student meetings—anything not to have to think about my mom. He does have a lot to show for it—he's received many accolades for his work, and it seems like every other month he's taking me as his date to another rubber chicken banquet dinner. But just as I long for love in my life, I wish that for him too. I know he considers it now and again because he makes comments about how he doesn't get out enough or how maybe it's time to give the house an update. To me that means he's either spent too much time in those four walls, or he is beginning to consider the thought of moving on. Sometimes I wonder if he's held back on finding a relationship because he is afraid, like me, or if he's worried that he will hurt me, cementing mom's place in the past. I know it would be difficult for us both, but it pains me to realize the vibrant and happy man I knew as a child never returned after the accident.

I have a good life now. I can't deny that. Things have turned out much better than we all expected during those horrendous days I lay hollow in the hospital. I have learned how to live again, and even how to thrive despite my disability. I have done all of the things I think I could have or would have done—and more—had the accident not happened. But Natalie's words still ring in my ears—I want you to be *truly* happy.

On my way home the word happy gives me something to ponder. I decide this—it's not that I'm sensationally happy or despairing over how my life has turned out. I just am. *Is there anything wrong with that?* I don't think so, but there are times I look at other people and think maybe there is more to life, and I'm the one missing out. Sometimes I think, *maybe I will be happier later … when I do find the man of my dreams or have 2.5 children.* But I've read the self-help books and they all warn against saying *I'll be happy when.* I can see the printed words in my mind. *Don't wait for events, landmarks, or love,* they say. *Be happy now. Right where you are.*

Sitting at a stoplight on the way home, I think to myself, *my life is satisfying as it is. Right?* I look at the drivers around me and begin to take inventory—a happiness assessment of each of them to compare my life to.

For instance, from the middle lane where I sit, I look to my right at the girl driving in the car next to me. Her window is rolled up, but her hair is blowing from the breeze of the air-conditioning. She has long caramel-colored hair with highlights, and she looks like one of those swimsuit models on the beach with a fan on her for effect. Looking at her I feel pangs of jealousy flowing through my body, and I tell myself it's because my air-conditioning is currently on the fritz, and on this August day it's eighty-five degrees, and I've got a stream of sweat flowing down my back. It's then that I see the giant diamond perched on her left hand, and I think how lucky she must be to have someone who adores her and thought enough of her to purchase two carats worth of brilliant diamond when he asked her to marry him. Happy, she must be.

Then I look to the guy on my left, and he's bopping to the music. *Why is he so happy? Or is he?* The realist comes out in me. Appearances can fool. Maybe that girl said yes because the diamond was breathtaking, not because she was in love. Perhaps the guy next to me isn't bopping. Instead he's fidgeting because he has to go to the bathroom, and he's still five miles from home. Looks can be deceiving. But appearances account for a lot, which is why I do think about what people conjure up in my presence. I realize that there is looking happy and then there is being happy. Somehow in our current world, those two things have become confused, and it now seems more of a priority to look happy than to be happy. And I know this from experience: when others look at me, they aren't envious. They don't even entertain the fact that I could be happy. Instead, they look at me with giant puppy dog eyes filled with sorrow, thinking, "She can't possibly have a good life in that wheelchair. Poor thing."

But it wasn't always this way, I know, which carries me to a new train of thought. *Everything can change in an instant, and suddenly there is a new frame of reference by which to measure happiness. Or despair.* Like the moment your wife dies or your mom announces she has cancer or you get hit by a car. All of a sudden, things are totally different, and you didn't get any say in the matter. Life is fragile, and as much as you think you are in control and making the decisions, they are being made for you. All you get is to decide the next move. Which is why I know I shouldn't envy another based on appearances or presumed happiness. I shouldn't want to be in someone else's shoes because I have made the assumption they have it better than I. Because, in the next moment, anything is possible. Intuitively, I know these things and try to be happy about who I am, where I am in my life, and to appreciate every instant. But sometimes, for one moment, I want to try being someone else, to see if the grass is, in fact, greener. We all have our worries, downfalls, and weaknesses. Most people simply have the benefit of hiding them from the world, whereas, my differences are out in the open for others to scrutinize and make assumptions about how they may or may not affect my happiness. And unfortunately, in my case, a wheelchair seems to be the epitome of *worst-case scenario.*

CHAPTER 5

DESPITE ALL MY THOUGHTS ON THE WAY HOME about being content with where I am, I decide to try being someone else for a little while. And this new person I am going to become is about to assemble the courage to go home and put an ad on a dating website.

I pull into the drugstore down the street from my house, park, and get out of the car. I take a big breath as I enter the store with one goal in mind. I'm going to become someone new. I head to the far-left side of the store and roll silently through the hair color aisle. That's one of the best things about the wheelchair. It's quiet. Rolls without even a purr. I can sneak up behind people without them hearing me. No loud footsteps, no forewarning, and suddenly, Bam! I'm right there. I used to sneak up behind my teachers all the time and scare them. I didn't even have to yell out "Boo!" I simply appeared when they weren't expecting me. Good for eavesdropping. And how could they be mad? It's not my fault my wheels roll silently. Of course, on rainy days, it didn't work as well. That's when I became the proverbial squeaky wheel. Dead giveaway.

As I roll down the aisle looking at all the hair colors and the flowing locks that adorn the covers of the boxes, I think about whom I would like to emulate. Or at least whom I would enjoy looking like. I scan the plethora of colors on the shelf and wonder what a flaxen blonde like myself might pull off. But before I can give it much thought, the box draws my eyes right in—the fluorescent lights of the store shine down and accentuate the picture of a gorgeous model on the box, with hair the color of 'chocolate dream.' If it were edible, I'd say it sounded downright delicious. If blonde is synonymous with fun, I think it's the brunettes who corner the market on seductive.

The chocolate dream color I now hold in my hand reminds me of a summer in high school when I had my first foray into hair dyeing. It was two years after my accident and I was still struggling to find myself and, really, what high school student isn't struggling with that? One of my therapists from the hospital suggested a program to help kids deal with loss. When she proposed the idea, I envisioned myself lying flat on a couch, staring up at the ceiling, and listing out a string of problems to a therapist. But it wasn't like that. It was a summer acting therapy class, or dramatic play, as they sometimes called it, where we sat around in a circle and role-played different scenarios and talked about them afterward. *How did that make you feel? What is going through your mind right now? Did that bring out any emotion in you?*

Apparently, my role-playing was downright good acting because one day the therapist introduced me to her friend, a summer theater director. The play her group was performing that year was *West Side Story*, and this forward-thinking director thought having Maria in a wheelchair would add an extra flair to the production. For lack of anything better to do, I went along with it and surprisingly loved performing, mainly because a handsome boy from one of the neighboring high schools played opposite me in the role of Tony. Of course, I had emphatically hoped our onset romance would go beyond acting, but it never did. What it did do was land me my first kiss—and although it was only a stage kiss, it is something of which I have always been proud. But, sensing a theme here, I did enjoy stepping outside of myself and being someone else for a while. With acting, I could be a whole new person. I could forget about the chair and be the enchanting and sought-after Maria—with jet-black hair.

When I colored my hair for the part, my friends were astonished that a towhead like me could dye her hair the color of a witch and still manage to look far more optimistic than the mopey looking Goth kids at school. Even though I am a natural blonde, my skin color has a tint of mocha, thanks to my mom's deep olive skin mixed with Dad's Midwestern undertones.

As I examine the box in my hands, I make the decision. I will become a chocolaty, dreamy brunette for a while. See how that goes. I set the hair color in my lap and push off to the register without looking back.

⟨⟩

When I get home, I head straight for the bathroom. Quick look-over of the directions and off I go. Let it sit in for the recommended twenty minutes and then into the shower for a rinse. When I get out, I glance in the mirror and can't believe what stares back at me. *Holy dark hair, Batman! Wow, what a difference a little color makes.* I stick firm to the thought that I am doing the right thing, and then I will it to dry a shade lighter. Regardless, I don't care. I know I can pull it off … and if anyone doesn't like it, well, meet my new rebel self.

I dry my hair, pull out all my weapons of mass styling, and get to work. At this point, I have decided that since I'm going to take a photo of myself and post it online, I want it to look nothing like me. I like the idea of doing this on the sly and staying anonymous for a while. Of course, I want to look pretty, but I don't want to look like me. As I finish, I apply a little makeup, grab my phone, hold it at arm's length in front of me, and click. Instant portrait. Or should I say *selfie?* I lay the phone on my lap and push myself over to the computer, reaching directly for the on switch. *Deep breath*, I whisper to remind myself of my need for oxygen as I ready myself for my new dating life. It's time to meet Prince Charming … or Mr. Right … or Mr. Right Now. I type in: www.mfeo.com.

The home page starts off simply enough. *I am a*—and then a drop-down menu appears. Only two choices: Man. Woman. *I'm off to a roaring start.* Then *looking for a*—again, pretty easy. *I am looking for a man,* I state emphatically to the computer screen. Next up—age preference. This I have to think about. Since I'm thirty-two, I think I can go a couple of years younger, maybe down to say twenty-eight, and perhaps an even bigger handful of years older, so I put a range from twenty-eight to thirty-nine. No specific reason for capping it at thirty-nine. It's not because I think that forty is old or anything, but I don't think I'm ready to make the jump to a new decade quite yet. I put in my zip code and hit enter. I answer a few more questions about me: username, password, and I'm in. Account created!

Just then a whole slew of options come up for me. Initially I have 2,038 possible matches—that means actual men— in my zip code and surrounding area who have declared themselves eligible. I'd say discount that five percent—those who say they are eligible but might be stretching the truth. *This is great.* I click on "customize search." Next pops up a big fat man menu. It's like ordering up dinner. What height would I like? Faith? Ethnicity? One who smokes and/or drinks? How smart does this guy have to be? High school education? PhD?

I'm feeling pathetic that I'm even doing this, but I stick with it. I never thought I would look for love on my computer, but it is the twenty-first century, and this is not uncommon, I remind myself. At least that's what the commercials say. One in five marriages originates online. We'll see about that. Let the man shopping continue.

Body type. I choose athletic and toned since sports are so important to me. Eye color. I'd love to gaze into a bright blue pair of eyes day after day. Hair color? Definitely dark brown. After I have put in every possible thing I could ever want in a man, I come up with zero matches. The big goose egg. Talk about fast—2,038 to zero in sixty seconds. A message comes up on the computer. No one is perfect. Refine your search and keep an open mind. *Wow, I feel like I got reprimanded by the Love God.* But, that very sentence stops me in my tracks.

What have I done? I have done exactly what I fear. I have been narrow-minded and shallow. Isn't this what I have been worried about all along? Having a man look at me, judge me, and see only a wheelchair? To be labeled as less than perfect because I don't fit the mold of the ideal woman? A man who sees something different than the norm and turns the other way? I feel it everywhere I go. I've even heard it whispered about me behind my back. *Such a waste of a pretty girl. Too bad she's in a wheelchair. Unfortunate she is disabled.* But inside I don't feel like a waste or that I'm less than anyone else. I have a disability, but it doesn't define me. And it certainly doesn't mean I'm not full of promise and potential. I have feelings too and, if I don't say so myself, I am a good catch. At least that's what those close to me say. *Certainly, they wouldn't lie only to make me feel good, would they?* Besides, I can hold an intelligent conversation, I'm often complimented on my looks, and I'm always game for having a good time. I realize this attitude of the so-called search for the *perfect* person has to change and it's going to start with me. I decide that *He*, whoever *He* is, doesn't have to be athletic and toned, a race car driver, a masseuse, a good cook, and sensual lover with blue eyes and brown hair. Instead, I should be looking for someone who is open, insightful, adventurous, caring, and understanding.

As I begin again, my list gets shorter and becomes less superficial. Instead of picking out certain physical traits, I need to be able to look inside, like I want someone to do with me. I change tactics and decide to take a break from the *man menu* for a few minutes. I begin to read what the guys have to say for themselves. I read a few profiles, but realize I end up on the opposite side of the spectrum. I could only get through the first sentence, at best, with most of them.

I've got two free tickets to the gun show ...

When I'm not at work on the construction site, you can find me in the gym working out. I love my body and want you to love it too ... Bob the Builder987

Sci-Fi and High-Fi

Far out films and rock n' roll ... that's what I like. Will you join me in an out of this world romance? ... Stuey

If I roll my eyes anymore, I'll end up cross-eyed looking out the backside of my head. *You can't be serious,* I think in disbelief. I decide to switch gears and get back to my profile. At least maybe I can approach this a little more intelligently than Bob and Stuey. I skip again to the next step and decide maybe it would be easiest to start with who I am and what I'm looking for. Then I can go back to reading more profiles.

What I find when I put my hands on the keyboard is the business of profile building is no easy task. I want to make sure my personality comes through in my words because, as they say, you only get one chance to make a first impression. Then, aside from that, is the whole time I am staring at the computer, my heart is nearly beating out of my chest. My palms are sweating. I'm as terrified about finding someone as I am about not finding someone. As much as I hate to admit it, Natalie has me pegged in the love department. She knows me better than anyone else. Yes, I am deathly afraid to bear my soul. Getting close to someone scares the crap out of me. I am so scared of loss. I fear judgment. Sometimes I think I don't even know how to be loved. I can't be the only one who feels this way. On the other hand, I believe there are people who meet online all the time. *How hard can it be?*

What I fear the most is being evaluated by my past. To most people, a disability is the worst thing in life. Especially when it involves a wheelchair. But I know that while it has caused some amount of challenge in my life, it has also brought with it a fair amount of perspective and positive traits—creativity, perseverance, and flexibility. It's also the thing that makes me unique. But it doesn't matter how it has affected me in a positive way, the problem is what most people see when they look at me. My differences. Not how ninety-eight percent of me is the same as most other thirty-something women. I want all the same things—hope, health, happiness, a nice handbag, preferably Coach—but I can compromise. Not to brag, but I have been told over and over that I am pretty—sometimes I even get the word gorgeous thrown at me. But that is often overshadowed by the looks of pity or the exclamation, "You're such an inspiration!" *And why am I inspirational?* I ask. To most people, getting out of bed or getting to the grocery store is inspirational for someone in a wheelchair. Instead, it seems they believe I should be at home on the couch waiting for my life to end. So yes, these are things I worry about when it comes to dating. Will there ever be a man who can look past my appearance into who I am as a person? I'm not sure. People are tricky the way they label each other.

This is one reason I love my job working with my kiddos. I can escape these preconceived notions. Unless they have been taught otherwise, kids are open-minded. On the first day of school, they are intrigued and interested in this teacher in a wheelchair. I sit them down, tell them my story, and open up the lesson for discussion. I let them ask every question under the sun, and I answer them as thoroughly and honestly as possible. They are so genuine and curious. "Ms. Rainey, is being in a wheelchair like driving in a car with the top off? Can you do wheelies and cool tricks? What happens if you get a flat tire?" The innocence in their questioning is charming, but after the first day, I never hear another word about it. I think they actually stop seeing the chair altogether. I don't know if they don't quite grasp it or if it simply doesn't matter. It's a novelty at first, and they want to touch it and push me around in it or take a ride, but then it's about me—as their teacher—an adult who listens to them and who cares. When they come in crying from recess, I put Band-Aids on their boo-boos. I teach them new words and open their minds to new ideas.

In elementary school, kids think their teachers are rock stars. It's incredibly rewarding. I never even give it a second thought. But adults are a whole different story. They are jaded, opinionated, and sometimes downright scared of people who are different from them. If they were as uncensored as the kids, they would blurt out the things that only get whispered behind my back, "Do you think she can still have sex?"

This is what makes online dating much more appealing than simply putting myself out there. Maybe I can have a part-time boyfriend. *Half-real and half-whatever-I-want-him-to-be.* I decide I like the idea and continue with my profile.

Name. I stare long and hard at that first descriptor because I'm not sure if I should use my real name or an alias. I decide to go with a little bit of both and type in May. It's not an out-and-out lie. After all, May is my middle name.

Yes, it's true; Rainey May is what is on my birth certificate. My mom, one might surmise, was a hippie and also quite literal. I was born on a rainy day, the eighteenth of May, with a stormy disposition. Sunny was the opposite. When she came around, she lit up our lives. She didn't even have a middle name. I mean, how do you follow up Sunshine? With a name like that, what more do you need? I envision a thirty-something version of Sunny, and draw courage from what I imagine would be her inner certainty and charisma. Snapping out of my own self-defeating thoughts, I return to filling in a few more details on the profile:

Hair Color: Dark brown (at least for today)
Eye Color: Green
Height: 5' 8" (though I actually sit just about four feet tall)
Build: Athletic
Interests: Sports, reading, outdoor activities
Sign: Taurus
Relationship Status: Never been married

But then it asks for a headline and the nitty-gritty. A paragraph about me and what I am looking for. *Oh boy.* I feel my lungs expand as I take a deep breath. I pause and then decide to take a break. Splayed out next to the computer on my desk is Rufus, half in and half out of a slumber. One eye opens to look at me as if to check on me, knowing what I am doing is somehow important, yet sensing my strain and apprehension. But then his eye slowly slides shut again—my cat's interest in online dating shifts from slim to none. I look at him and envy his life for a moment. Sleep, eat, drink, cuddle. He doesn't have to wonder if he's lovable; I believe I have answered that question for him as I've showered him with love over the past five years we've been together. I remember clearly the day I went to the shelter, all metal and cement, dogs barking, cats meowing, and me thinking what a miserable place for a little guy so new to the world.

As I pushed past the kennels of cats, Rufus had his head shoved up against the metal grate that kept him captive in his cell. He extended his front paw to me as if to say, *please choose me. I'm the one for you.* It was such a simple gesture, yet so direct; I immediately had no doubt he would be the feline who would accompany me home. And when the shelter employee pulled him out of his cage and set all two pounds of him on my lap, he didn't hesitate to curl up and begin kneading my spongy fleece sweatpants with his tiny, white, cotton ball paws. It was love at first sight. Five minutes later, I was in the adoption office filling out the papers to take home my three-month-old, palm-sized snuggle bug. Young and needy, Rufus didn't stray far from my lap and quickly learned that if he simply sat still, the wheels on either side of him would take him to and fro across my ranch style house. He grew up with this wheelchair and has never been frightened or intimidated by its presence. I think how nice his indifference to it is. To him, it's a part of the package that has become his home. And I am the one he goes to for comfort and affection.

I ponder this as I push to the kitchen, pour myself a cup of hot Earl Grey tea, carry it to my desk and begin again.

As my fingers hover over the keyboard, I think, *What I am looking for is this*: I want that feeling when the sight of him makes your breath go away, where three hours alone together isn't enough time, or when you can talk about anything or nothing and it's still a perfect night. Does that exist or is it only in the movies? I take a deep breath and start pounding away at the keyboard.

Treading Lightly in the Sea of Love

About me: *Some people would call me impatient and intense. I love driving fast, downhill skiing, and anything involving speed. I am competitive and driven. But I have another side to me that knows when to slow down because I am an elementary school teacher by profession, and impatience and intensity don't have a place amongst my first graders. In the classroom, I have learned to take it slow, and that patience truly is a virtue. I have to be quick enough to keep up, but slow enough to appreciate the innocence of childhood.*

Although with most things in life I am not afraid to jump right in, dating, for me, is where I put on the brakes. I don't know why I am confident careening down a mountain or driving at speeds that will get you put in jail, yet I can't wrap my head around falling in love or even the thought of it. Love is really so similar to sports: daring, adventurous, and with an element of danger. At any time, you could get hurt. Both sports and love can change the course of your life.

What are you looking for in a relationship?

I'm looking for two different sides of one coin. I want someone who makes me smile and makes me laugh. Who can make the load on my shoulders feel lighter and make me feel like I've taken a breath of fresh air. I am looking for conversation that is captivating and takes me places I wouldn't ordinarily go. I want to feel emotion—maybe ones I have hidden away for one reason or another, and to be with someone who makes me want to share those feelings. I want to open my mind and my heart and be with a guy who is intriguing to get to know, who will let me in and be the best friend I've ever had. I'll know when it's true because there will be a connection and electricity you can feel yet can't define. I am looking for a man who, in turn, can be vulnerable and strong. Your infectious sense of humor, generosity, and kindness are traits on which all of your friends would agree. I also love to be with someone who is spontaneous and can switch gears and turn a romantic night out for dinner into a crazy all-nighter of bar hopping or go to the movies on one ticket and sneak into five other theaters (I know, juvenile, right?) or take off to who knows where on a midnight, moonlit bike ride.

On the other hand, I am looking for someone who offers stability. Who can be a rock when I feel like I need something solid against which to lean. I want to meet a man who isn't afraid to say "forever" if or when the opportunity to speak the words "till death do us part" comes about, and can truly mean those words. I seek comfortable, unwavering, trusting love. I want to love someone with his flaws, quirks, and differences, and I want to be loved for mine.

I am not in a hurry. I don't want to meet for drinks tomorrow night or a quickie next week. I'm not rushed for love, and my clock isn't ticking. I want the suspense to grow as we unravel the mystery of each other through our words and thoughts. I think it's much easier to reveal yourself online, with the anonymity it provides, and that is where I would like our relationship to begin. For now, I don't want to see you, hear your voice, or know where you work. I want to know what makes you, you. If you are game to play by these rules, the ball is now in your court.

I sign it May Belle. Adding the Belle on the end makes me feel like a princess. It reminds me of my childhood because it was the nickname my mom picked for me when I was a young girl. And to spell it out on the screen takes me back to a time in my life when simply the presence of my mother brought forth the feeling of true, unwavering love.

Prior to Sunny's birth and before Disney made it into a movie, my mom used to tell me the story of *Beauty and the Beast*. It was my favorite book, and I would ask her to read it over and over again. Eventually, she began to get bored with the main storyline, so she started adding in sidebars to keep things interesting. As she told me the story of Belle, my idol, who was so lovable and kind, Belle began to take on new attributes, like how she was a perfect little girl who was cheery and bright and who happened to clean her bedroom every day. This was at a time in my young childhood when she and I were having power struggles over my room—I'm not quite the neat freak my mom was—and I wanted to be as gorgeous and sweet as Belle. When I would clean my room, my Mom would say, "Thank you, Belle." Or, "Nicely done, Belle." I could hear and feel the satisfaction and pride in her words, and it made me feel a deep-down happiness that comes from unconditional love and acceptance. My mom knew how important her approval and affection were and used this name as a true term of endearment. She knew how much it meant to me.

I sit back and read what I've written. *Not half bad*, I think. With that checked off the list, I navigate back through the "man menu," careful to be less absolute in my preferences and 547 profiles load. I don't know how I can possibly choose between that many men, but I scroll down until I find a warm, inviting-looking smile on Brian85. His headline and description encourage me to take a step forward into his world.

Looking for a Great Adventure

About me: Some people are voted most likely to succeed. Some, class clown. My high school classmates voted me best listener. I have invariably been the mediator—the one to hear both sides of a story and draw conclusions based on what he said and what she said. I've always been interested in hearing each point of view. I want to know what people think and what shapes their personalities. We all have stories to tell, whether happy or sad, funny or serious, and I enjoy hearing them all. I am a curious person by nature, which is why I became a journalist. I wanted to learn other people's stories, write them down, and savor them. My parents raised me to open my mind and my ears. Getting to know and understand people is what I perceive to be one of my strengths. Some would say my curiosity is a coping mechanism to take the spotlight off of me, which may or may not be true. I'm not sure, but I maintain that I find others' stories are more interesting than my own and I love to hear them.

But aside from my love for stories and my inquisitive nature, if I had to pick one word to describe me, it would be adventurous. When I'm not delving into research or an interview, I spend my free time enjoying the outdoors. I don't like to be still, and it's almost impossible to get me to sit down in front of the television. An occasional movie, maybe, but I enjoy cycling, snowboarding, or rock climbing. I'm not the gonzo thrill-seeker type, but I like to have fun and stay in shape. I have a long history of competing in sports from being on the cross-country team in high school and college to the occasional mountain bike race. I am competitive but also enjoy sports for the sake of physical and mental release.

What are you looking for in a relationship?

I am looking for someone who wants to go on an open-eyes and hearts journey. I want someone who is athletic and adventurous ... who likes to play hard but cleans up nice. I don't want someone who will try to change me, so I'm a take-me-as-I-am kind of guy. I like a woman who enjoys her independence and lets me enjoy mine, but we can still come together to be a cohesive unit. I like a low maintenance woman, natural in her beauty, who doesn't come with a makeup bag bigger than my suitcase.

In my personal life, family is extremely important to me. Eventually, I hope to meet a woman who will be my other half, complementing my strengths and helping me grow in my weaknesses. I love kids, but only time will tell if I will have my own someday.

I am looking forward to a woman who is willing to share her story and be open to hearing mine.

Brian85

As I read his description and study his picture, I imagine staring across a candlelit table at the man with chestnut brown hair and piercing blue eyes. The thought makes my heart palpitate, and a hot flash of excitement or nausea (I'm not sure which) comes over me. I decide it's time to take the plunge and connect.

Dear Brian:

As I sit down to write you, I wonder how one begins an online relationship. On the one hand, it seems complicated. In all of my dreams of searching for "the one" not a single scenario began with looking through a catalog of men on a computer screen. I always imagined staring across the room, eyes locking and magical chemistry pulling two beings together. With that said, I still imagine this message is much like a first date. This is my singular opportunity to make a connection, and if I can't capture your imagination with what I have to say, I'll likely never hear from you. Is that how it would work had we met in person? We go out; you buy dinner, I don't laugh at your jokes or put out. You never call again? Is that it? Or is there a longer warm-up period online? I will admit, I'm unsure of the etiquette.

Regardless, with certainty, I can tell you this— I'm gun shy when it comes to relationships. I'm thirty-two and have never been in love. Is that weird? Whether it is or not, I don't know, but one thing I am sure of is that I have declared this online dating an experiment. I want to know if I can open up to someone—and connect on a deeper level. I have to know if I even have the heart to get involved. My best friend says I'm too scared to be in a relationship and become intimately involved, because I'm afraid of loss. She says I don't let myself get wrapped up in attachment because the uncertainty kills me. I wouldn't believe a thing she says, because she surely isn't a shrink, but she does know almost everything there is to know about me. Therefore, my question, can I actually do it? Get to know someone and let them know me? I want to, I promise, but I have to take it slow. I hate to say it, but I'm going to be that annoying woman who says, "I just want to talk …"

I'm not sure if it's because I haven't found someone who brought those feelings out in me or if I didn't want to let them go. I feel wound tightly when it comes to emotion and hope that online, I can be free. I want to let someone get to know me, but for me this isn't simple. So, I want to know who you are first and have you get to know me before going any further. I won't give any details that will help you track me down, and I don't want to know where you work, your last name, or your phone number. I want to write about feelings and insights and who you are and have us accept each other first, on the deepest of levels. That's why all the ground rules.

If I have scared you off by writing all of this, then I know you are not the one for me. But if you are intrigued, the ball is in your court. You make the next move.

Sincerely,
May Belle

I read it over and over again before I send it. It feels heavy as I analyze my message. But I figure it's better to let it all out now. Lay my cards on the table. I'm not sure it's the right strategy, but it's all I have. I want to be as honest and straightforward as possible—at least where feelings are involved. There's so much that needs to wait until later.

After I hit send, I call Natalie to share the news.

"Hey Nat. You're gonna be so proud of me."

"What'd you do?"

"I got on MFEO dot com, set up a profile, and responded to one personal ad already."

"No way! I've got to see this. Hang on. I came into work this afternoon, so I've got to close my office door. Okay ... how do I navigate this site? Where do I find your profile? Heavens, I'm glad I'm not single. No offense, but how, exactly, do you wade through all of these men? Okay ... I'm not finding you. I typed 'Rainey' in the search box, but you didn't pop up. Seriously, how many people named Rainey do you think are on this?"

"Well, there's one small detail. I didn't use my real name. Or, I did use my real name, but it's my middle name."

"Why did you use May?"

"I actually used May Belle." Natalie already knew the story behind that, so I explained my desire to remain anonymous, for self-preservation sake. "And besides," I add, "What if that creepy science teacher at my school, Mr. Ryan, is on MFEO? I could see him sending me gross, inappropriate messages."

"Okay, Ms. May Belle ... what is your last name?"

"You don't use your last name. Search under May Belle."

"Oh, you're a piece of work," she says as I hear clicking around on the keyboard.

"Here it is. May Belle." And then there is a very pregnant pause on the phone. "Wait. What? What is this picture? Rainey this isn't even you! You don't have brown hair."

"Oh, you're so three hours ago! Clearly, you haven't seen me since one o'clock."

"You dyed your hair? Are you eff-ing kidding me?"

"Nope."

"Why on earth would you do that? Oh wait, don't tell me. To remain anonymous."

"Nat, you know how sometimes my picture turns up in newspaper articles after a ski race. I'm not ready to go all the way yet. Besides, blonde seems so vanilla. So, All-American. Brunette says mysterious, deep."

"Don't get me wrong ... you don't look bad, just ... different. Rainey, you don't look like yourself."

"Sure I do. I only look different than you're used to."

"But I've known you for twenty-nine years and for twenty-eight years and fifty-one-and-a-half weeks you've been a blonde. How can you tell him you're a brunette?"

"Because I *am* a brunette ... until further notice."

"Oh my."

I can imagine her crossing her arms and scrunching her nose.

"What happens when you finally meet this guy, and you have to come clean about all the lies you've told him?"

"I haven't told him any lies. I do have chocolate-dream-colored hair at the moment, and everything I said in my profile is true. Besides, if he is absolutely *the one*, he'll forgive me."

"Or maybe … if he is *the one*, you shouldn't have to lie."

"Come on, Nat. You know how I feel. If I totally come clean … thirty-something blonde woman in a wheelchair looking for a date … the only thing that will fill up my inbox will be cobwebs."

"You don't have to say it like that. How many times do I have to tell you there's more to you than that chair?"

"Yes, you and I are aware of this, but if I show it in the picture or put it in my description, it will be the end of my dating career."

"I don't think so. But do it your way."

"How many times have we been told that we look like sisters? Yet, when we go out to bars, who's the one turning heads and collecting phone numbers? Not me. I'm the poor sidekick in the wheelchair, and it doesn't matter how I see myself. I don't look at my chair … and it has never stopped me from doing the things I've wanted to do … but let's face it … there is a stigma associated with a disability, and we both know it. I can be beautiful with a great personality, but if a person isn't willing to look past that first downward glance, I'm done. You can call me insecure, but these feelings didn't come out of nowhere. They came from experience. Yes, I'm as kooky as any single thirty-something woman, but I have an added layer of challenge in my situation." I end my soapbox lecture.

"Oy. What else did you tell him?" she asks as she reads my profile.

"Likes to ski, drive fast, take risks … except in love … blah, blah, blah."

"Okay," she says. "Not bad. But eventually, you have to come clean. Don't let this go on for so long that you can't go back again."

"I won't," I promise. But in my mind, I'm not so sure.

CHAPTER 6

NATALIE AND I HANG UP THE PHONE, AND I GRAB my sports bag and head off to the gym. Even though fall has only just begun, I need to remain focused on the upcoming ski season, which is right around the corner.

As a teenager, when I first took up the sport, I did it because it was a diversion. It took my mind off of how awkward I felt at school or the fact that since the accident I had an overwhelming feeling of being different and had a void in my life that needed filling. But when I was in my ski and on the hill, I felt invincible. It was the mountain and me. The only challenges I had to face were navigating the terrain, staying upright, and getting to the bottom of the hill. That was easier than navigating a high school social life. It gave me something to look forward to, a place where I could be myself and concentrate only on the task at hand without worrying about what people thought of me. No one felt sorry for me on the racecourse. In fact, they looked up to me. I was powerful and talented. Very much the opposite of how people perceived me at school or pushing down the street.

One day a ski coach approached me and told me about the competitions available to athletes with disabilities. As it turned out, I could race against other wheelchair athletes and go to national events, the World Championships, and even the Paralympic Games. Just like the Olympics, the Paralympics take place every four years in the same venues, and the best of the best in the world show up and contend for gold, silver, and bronze medals.

I was flattered the coach saw so much potential in my talent, and I was excited to be considered for the U.S. Team. After college, I committed to go full bore into skiing, and eventually reached the pinnacle of the sport—my first Paralympic Games. Four years later was a disappointment because even though I probably would have made the team, I had a shoulder injury and had to take time off. My goal is to try to make the team one last time before I retire and move on to whatever comes next. This upcoming season, I want to be in the best shape ever.

Skiing, for me, is way less complicated than online dating, where there can be some gray areas, like how I presented myself in my profile. Skiing is a lot more black and white. Results don't lie. You're either fast or you're not. You win, or you don't. How do you tell who wins in dating? I don't know the answer to that, but I do know if you lose, you're left holding shattered pieces of your heart in your hands and wondering what to do next.

⌒

When I return home from the gym, my immediate instinct is to make a beeline to the computer. I don't want to be overcome by my hopefulness over whether Brian has written me back, but I am. I toss my workout bag aside, glide across the hardwood floor, and head straight into my office where I left my laptop earlier this evening. I turn on the computer, log onto MFEO, and am suddenly breathless when I see what I had hoped to see. Brian85 has promptly responded to my first message. I click on his reply waiting in my inbox.

Well, Ms. May Belle:

I understand your hesitancy regarding the online dating rules. I admit to you; I don't know them either. Was I supposed to be more patient in writing you back? Sort of like how you're supposed to wait the requisite three days after a date before calling the woman again? I'm not sure, but I'm taking my chances by writing right away. I can tell I like you already. In your profile, you said you were looking for two sides of a coin, and it sounds like you possess both of them too—the lively, spontaneous woman and the slower more discerning one. Maybe everybody has those sides, I don't know, but I get the feeling spending time with you wouldn't be dull.

I've also learned that you are direct and to the point. No messing around here. You strike me as the kind of woman who calls it like you see it. I like your style and ground rules. Let's do this the old-fashioned way and get to know each other first. Okay? Play ball.

As you read in my profile, I am a journalist. I won't tell you where or I might risk breaking Rule #1, and from my impression of you, there would be hell to pay. I have never been married, but I have been in love. It didn't end well, so I haven't tried it since, but as my friends start coupling up, the young single life has less appeal. That doesn't mean I am in a hurry to get hitched; it means I'm testing the waters.

I like sports, both playing and watching. During the weekends, I usually spend my time camping, mountain biking, rock climbing, or hanging out with my friends. I am a Colorado native, and all of my family lives nearby—Mom, Dad, and two older brothers. I am the youngest and the only sibling without kids—but I don't mind. Not ready to jump in the waters that far, but I am proud to be an uncle. In fact, it's one of the most important roles in my life. I am especially close to my fifteen-year-old nephew, Casey. I've considered stealing him from my brother on many occasions, but Charlie (my oldest brother), says if I want one, I have to make my own.

What about you? So far, I know you're intense and introspective, but there has to be an easygoing side to you, right? What do you like to do for fun? I have to start making notes, so when we go on our first date, I know what to plan. It wouldn't do me any good to take you on a camping trip if you wear high heels and carry a Coach bag, now would it?

You've got my attention, though, and I'm intrigued, wondering what you'll say next. Tell me more about you. (Sorry, that sounds more like a job interview than getting to know each other, but if we don't ask questions of each other, we won't get very far, will we?)

I'll leave it there so you can tell me anything that comes to your mind. I want to read any words you are willing to put down.

I look forward to getting to know May, the mystery woman.

Hope to hear from you soon,
Brian85

I like how he's taking the mystery part in stride. I even think that after only one message and a profile, I like him too. He's perceptive—I'll go with the intense and introspective. I've been accused of that before. It's also a good sign he asked about me. Some guys would get online and talk about themselves, but he asked and seemed genuine in his inquiry. And the kicker—he mentioned a first date. That prospect both excites and scares me at the same time. With a smile, I log off the computer and head to the bathroom to brush my teeth and get ready for bed.

As I lay down, my thoughts go a million miles an hour. All

I can think of are dating disasters. My mind takes me back to how I felt on prom night, when I had agreed to go with Steven Kinney, or more correctly, he had settled on going with me because his best friend had asked Natalie, and by senior year in high school, all of our classmates knew that Natalie and I were a package deal. The guys made reservations, keeping the restaurant a surprise. When we arrived, and were being shown to our table, the hostess took us over to where we were to be seated. Separating us from the table were three steps. I asked if we could be reseated because I clearly couldn't climb those steps, but the guys protested. Said our table was prime real estate. From the platform, not only did we have the perfect view of the restaurant, but of the mesmeric waterfall cascading nearly from the ceiling to the atrium below. So instead of honoring my request, they grabbed my chair on either side and hoisted me up. Everyone in the crowded restaurant turned to watch the spectacular display of the girl in the wheelchair being "chivalrously" lifted to her table. As they set me down on the platform where only five tables took up residency, the entire restaurant began to applaud, as if it were pure enchantment. Steven, the savior, bringing the disabled classmate to the prom. Inspiring! Unless, of course, you were me. Then it was only a reminder of my lost independence, my seemingly undesirable nature, and confirmation that I had become a "charity case."

Later that night, as I hurried out of the restaurant to avoid further humiliation, I led our group to the car, but on the way, the front caster wheel of my chair hit a small pothole in the parking lot and launched me into mid-air, crashing on the ground. As I landed, my dress bunched up over my knees, Natalie and the guys ran over to me, scooped me up and put me back in my chair. It was all I could handle. I asked to be taken home immediately in an effort to avoid the dance, and what I was sure promised to be additional embarrassment. And that was the night Carly Saxton lost her virginity to Steven.

Obviously, there was someone else he would rather be with. I was purely a *favor* to his friend. I guess his valiant deed paid off because at the end of the night he got what he wanted. I, on the other hand, got a glimpse of what my future dating blooper reel might look like.

I try not to think about my past disasters and focus on the potential positives of having a boyfriend, but it's hard to ignore all the what ifs flooding into my mind, squashing the excitement.

In the morning when my alarm goes off, the first thing that pops into my head is Brian, his profile photo, and most importantly, his message. I feel the urge to write to him before I leave for school.

First things first, though, I head for the shower. Before transferring over to my shower chair, I plug in my iPhone and blast some music to get my eyes open and my brain engaged. The first song that comes up is AC/DC *Shook Me All Night Long*. It makes me smile since it's one of my favorite throwback songs and perfect for my morning shower. Listening to it takes me back to Natalie's wedding reception. As she gathered all of her girlfriends, from every period of her life—childhood to college—onto the dance floor, she requested that song specifically, and when it came on we all went wild. It was a boisterous, let-your-hair-down, scream-the-lyrics type of song, and all of the girls kicked off their high heels—except me. I could dance in my shoes since, in my wheelchair, they'd never touch the ground. It was one of the rare instances where I actually attempted "wheelchair dancing" without the insecurity and self-consciousness of feeling like a circus act. We danced until our faces were flushed and sweat ran down the sides of our cheeks. Our wedding hair and makeup were on the downslide, but we didn't care. It was one of the most festive occasions I have ever attended.

Admittedly, it was also a bittersweet night for me. I was delighted for Natalie but worried our friendship would never be the same. It was the first time I realized that even if we were friends forever, there would always be someone else there vying for her attention. It made me wish I had someone by my side like Natalie had Seth. Although in the past I'd had a million reasons to envy Natalie, it wasn't until her wedding night when I truly felt the pangs of jealousy. Not because she looked like a stunning model in her wedding dress or because her life was unfolding like a storybook. It was the fact that she seemed so complete like nothing was missing in her world and nothing she couldn't do. After all the years since my accident, one might think those thoughts would go away, but every once in a while, they would show up and haunt the back of my brain. In the past, Natalie's good fortunes made me happy for her, but her marriage was much harder to accept. I felt like she was making a giant leap forward and I was getting left behind. We would no longer be two single best friends, partners in crime, doing everything together.

That night I was paired off as her Maid of Honor with Seth's college buddy, Jacob, and at the beginning of the night, I thought I might have an opportunity to experience some male companionship. He was humorous to hang out with as he spent the night doing stupid magic tricks … many of which were less mysterious the more he drank. We hit it off, each of us having a sarcastic sense of humor and enjoyed a constant flow of conversation and joking before the wedding and during the sit-down dinner reception. Things were looking good. But after that, he made a straight line for another of Natalie and Seth's college friends, Sage. And with that, the magic was over. Literally and figuratively. I think those two actually ended up married. And I ended up, once again, being a placeholder for a more appropriate contestant. I knew I shouldn't have taken it personally, but knowing my dating history, or lack thereof, it was another indication I was only great for a night of conversation—not to be confused as actual dating material. My life was becoming a broken record of near misses.

I tried to put the rejection I associated with Jacob out of my mind, and, following my shower, I set those memories aside and opened a new screen to return Brian's message.

Well, Bri (can I call you that?):
    You can rest easy because although I do have a Coach bag, I'm more often carrying a

sports bag. I am active and a competitor, and any opportunity I have to go fast, I take it, whether it's driving, snow skiing, waterskiing, or riding a bike. (I debate adding the part about the bicycle because of its two-wheeled connotation. I do ride a bike, but mine has three wheels and is called a handcycle. Same concept, but I'm certain it's nothing like what he is picturing in his mind). I crave an adrenaline rush. But I do have a more refined side too. I love to dress up and go to the theater. My favorite nights involve going out to dinner with a small group of friends and talking way into the night over good food and a bottle (or two ... or three) of wine. But most of my free time is spent working out and staying in shape. That is truly my passion.

I was born and raised in Denver, and it's been my home my whole life. I went to the University of Colorado and moved right back home after school. Not that I'm a homebody, but I figured my dad needed me to be close. Our family consists of just the two of us, so I don't know if I could leave him even if I tried. My only other family is my best friend, Natalie. She and I have been inseparable since we were three-year-olds, except when she went off to college in New York City. She's back now too, and is the person with whom I spend most of my free time. I should also mention I have an extended family—aunts, uncles and cousins—but they're all out of state, so when I refer to "family," it's Dad,

Natalie, and me. Nat is married, so you can throw Seth into the mix there too, but he's just an extra part of the package. I also have an extensive group of friends ranging from high school, to my current job, to the other athletes I train with. And even though I manage to stay busy between all of my involvements and obligations, I completely understand where you are with friends pairing off, having kids, and acting like grownups, when I feel anything but. Oftentimes, I wonder if maybe I'm missing something. I'm hoping getting to know you will help me answer that question. I don't know if it's proper to share the fact that I enjoyed the anticipation of hearing back from you, but I did, and it sent a new little spark up my spine that I haven't felt in a while (*no pun intended, I thought to myself*). I will also admit, I wouldn't mind if I could feel it again. If you're so inclined to write back, tell me more about you, your friends, your job— anything really.

Enjoy your day.

May Belle

As I get in my car to head to work, I find myself whistling and wonder where the heck that's coming from. I never whistle. I mean, never. But I go with it because I know it is a new part of me coming out. A piece I thought had gone missing, a piece I don't mind having reemerge. I feel lighter believing, right now, somewhere in this city, there could possibly be a man, thinking about me. It brings a smile to my face, though my stomach feels like a washing machine on spin cycle.

When I get to work, I realize all of my daydreaming has gotten me slightly off schedule, and suddenly I'm in a hurry. I burst through the doors of the school and give the rims on my wheels a few exuberant pushes, and then I get it—one of the most annoying phrases a wheelchair user can hear. Mr. Ryan, the creepy teacher at work, sticks his head out of his doorway and says, "Watch it, speed racer, you're going to get a ticket."

There's something about using a wheelchair that makes people feel compelled to open their mouths and let the most ridiculous things roll off their tongues. As if I haven't heard those words shouted at my backside a million times as I've moved quickly past someone. The speeding ticket comment is among the most annoying, but every time someone says it, they act witty and smug as if they are the first ever to utter those words. All I want to do is yell and say, "Do you realize how many times I have heard that?" *Wheelchair-isms*, I call them. The dumb things people blurt out when they don't know what else to say, and when a simple "hello" would suffice. If I had a dollar for every "ism" I've ever heard, I could afford to live in a mansion next door to Kim Kardashian and Kanye West. Not that I'd want to, but still.

I get to my classroom and fling open the door to find twenty adorable cherubic faces looking up at me in anticipation and my team teacher, Lisa, standing there keeping a watchful eye on our firsties—that's what we call the first graders—so they don't get out of line. I am grateful she has arrived punctually, opened the door, gotten the kids settled, and kept me from looking like the irresponsible adult who was late to work because she was busy oohing and ahhing over an online romance. I am beaming in my appreciation for Lisa, until my attention is diverted to Mrs. Cornwall, one of our classroom parent volunteers. As if she weren't already annoying (she is!) my body tenses as the dreaded words come out of her mouth, "Wow, Rainey, you did that so well!" she says as I arrive in the room after coming through the door. I close my eyes and pause for a second, asking for strength not to punch her for actually complimenting me on my ability to open a door. This is exactly what I am referring to, where a simple hello would suffice. But alas, another wheelchair-ism. Cha-ching! Another dollar in the bank.

As I go through my day, I get a handful of wheelchair-isms and only two comments on my hair. You'd think my coworkers, by now, would see beyond the chair. But I believe it is always there, in the back of their minds. In the back of mine. It's on this day I realize how much people pay attention to my chair and how little they pay attention to the person using it. More ammunition to use against Natalie, I think, when she hounds me about delaying my in-person meeting with Brian.

I'm exhausted by the time I get home. For some reason, the kids have worn me out today. I think it's because I've gotten too used to working part-time during the ski season, but until the snow flies and I begin traveling to competitions, I put in mostly full days, and the kids keep me going full throttle. It makes me realize how exhausting it must be to raise a child 24/7. I begin to wonder if that's something I will actually do when I meet this elusive Mr. Right. *Let's not get ahead of ourselves. I'll cross that bridge when I get to it.* Alas, there are many bridges to cross between here and there.

When I get home, I go straight to the computer to see if I've heard back from Brian85. As I wait for the screen to light up, my heart races into overdrive. I don't know if I'm more scared to hear back from him or to learn that maybe he hasn't written at all. Either option gives me anxiety. Even so, when I open my inbox and see his name, a smile creeps across my face.

Dear May Belle:

I know this is only my second message, but I am reveling in anticipation of coming home to you and reading what you have to share. It's suspenseful being in that place where anything can happen. It's my most treasured relationship stage because optimism rules. I don't know what's in store for us, but my mind keeps taking me to good places. I hope it continues. It made me smile to know I didn't set off any red flags in my first message and you wanted to write me again.

I'm not sure where this conversation is supposed to go or what I should share online, but, if you don't mind, I am going to start with my day. It was a backbreaker. Not physically speaking of course (I am a writer), but mentally draining. There are financial issues with the company I work for, and I don't know how much longer the organization will stay afloat. With that in mind, while I am attempting to think positively, I'm also a realist. So, tonight I am going to spend some quality time with my resume. I'm feeling uneasy about this process, since I've never had to look for a job before. Straight out of school I did an internship, which turned into a job and was followed by an offer from another company. I accepted the position and have been there ever since. It has been a perfect position for me, so if it goes by the wayside I will undoubtedly be disappointed. It's my favorite kind of journalism—writing in-depth features on my subjects.

Like I said in my profile, I like to get to know people. Finding out what motivates a person to do what they do and be who they are is a journey into a new world with each interview I do. Sometimes I think I should have majored in psychology, but my goal isn't to change or fix someone, only understand them. I think we all deserve understanding in our lives, don't you? And it's pure satisfaction to sit back and craft my subjects with words. Spill them out on the page and see what I've learned. When you take the time to listen to other people, you learn lessons about yourself. Maybe a particular quote from a subject opens you up and makes you see your life in a new light. I enjoy the people who aren't afraid to be an open book and let me in to gain insight, teaching me things I didn't already know. That being said, I also want my writing to grip the reader and touch his or her life also. It's a dream job for me, at least at this point in my life. Where will I go next? Perhaps we will find that out together (if you stick around, that is) because it is yet to be seen but will likely reveal itself much sooner than I'll be ready.

But enough about me. You're a daddy's girl? If I am ever to meet your father, should I worry about dating his only daughter? Does he carry around a shotgun? What's he like? What does he do for a living? I don't know if I am overstepping my grounds, and please let me know if I am, but what about your mom? Can you tell me about her?

I believe I've filled you with your dose of me today, however, I look forward to sharing more and getting to know you and learning more about you too. You have me intrigued. I look forward to the day we meet. Until then, mystery woman.

Your friend, Bri

We're off to a good start. We're friends now. I like that. And I appreciate what he says about relishing the opportunity to get to know people and understanding them. It makes me feel optimistic—perhaps I have a chance. He doesn't seem the judgmental type. Open and laid back. I like it. The question is, can I trust my instincts? Can I trust him? Will this be the guy who becomes part of me and my world and accepts me as I am? I wish I had a crystal ball, but only time will tell.

My immediate reaction is to write him back, but the more

I try to rush this, the quicker we'll run out of things to say online and then I'll have no choice but to meet him in person. Instead, I re-read his message three more times and force myself to shut down the computer and head off to the gym. It's the only thing I can think to do.

On my way home from the gym, I stop by the grocery store to stock up for the week. Food shopping is one of my favorite things to do because I love to cook. I won't say I'm an expert since I only got a few years' training in the kitchen before my mom died, but cooking reminds me of her. It's one of the activities that keeps her memory alive for me. When I pull out a recipe written in her handwriting, I try to envision her when she was my age—married with a family. I don't know how she did it. I can't imagine having two kids right now. Heck, I'm still working on getting my head around even falling in love and ultimately getting married. But she did it with such finesse like she was born with a perfect mothering gene.

I remember her clearly as a thirty-two-year-old because she had Sunny when she was thirty, and I have vivid memories of celebrating Sunny's birthday two years later. My mom insisted we make a big deal out of it, so we made an elaborate birthday cake of layer upon layer of flavors until it was literally a foot tall. Mom and I decorated it like a castle. We found figurines of a prince and princess at the hobby store and decorated the base layer of the cake, imagining an enchanted forest. I couldn't understand why she made such a production out of a two-year-old's birthday cake, but it finally dawned on me years later. The cake wasn't simply to acknowledge Sunny's birthday—after all, she was never going to remember or appreciate it—but it was about me. I was beginning to grow up. Although only nine years old at the time, I sense now my mother knew my childhood wouldn't last forever. Those days in the kitchen would soon be replaced with me running out the door to be with my friends. I suspect she wanted to hold on to my childhood innocence and at the same time look forward to her years raising Sunny. With seven years between us, it was hard to find common ground and things Sunny and I could both do and enjoy together, but the cake making kept Sunny entertained in her highchair as she watched us work, and Mom taught me some valuable kitchen skills in the process.

As I comb the aisles of the grocery store, I am reminded of what a lonely prospect it is to cook dinner for one and wonder what Brian likes to eat—and if I'll ever have the opportunity to cook for him. Even after all those memories of Mom and the thoughts of the meals we cooked together, in the end, cooking for myself alone seems less appealing. I do an about-face from the food aisles and head to the prepared foods section of the store, pick out the healthiest choice I can find, grab a few more staples, and head for the register.

When I get home, I eat and think about answering Brian but decide I'm not yet ready to answer his questions about my mom and Sunny. That will have to wait until tomorrow when I have more energy.

Saturday morning, I wake up to a storm of beeps and whistles from my phone. I look at the clock and wonder who is texting me relentlessly at 7:30 a.m. Christine has left an obnoxious string of messages. Apparently, last night at the bar, she met "the one." The six-part text tells me the whole story in detail, from what she wore to the bar to how he has just left her house to go to work at the hospital. HE'S A DOCTOR, she says in all caps, as I can envision her rubbing her hands in delight about how, as his wife, a larger credit limit would be available on her Nordstrom card. I crack a grin at her elation and materialistic fetish, and then hit silence on my phone as I know from experience that everyone Christine meets is "the one." That is until things fall apart and she has her radar out for the next in line. I roll over and return to my slumber.

When my phone rings at 9:00, I realize both that I had better get out of bed, and I should acknowledge Christine's message. Her last one asked if I wanted to meet for lunch. I text in reply, "time and place?" and receive word to meet at Maxwell's at 12:30. I send her a thumbs-up emoji and begin to mentally prepare myself for what undoubtedly will be a long lunch analyzing Christine's love life. Not that I don't want to hear about it, but while I consider myself looking for love, she has kidnapped cupid, stolen his bow and arrow and is prepared to hunt it down for herself. I decide I will wait until this evening to write to Brian, hoping there isn't an expiration time that comes with answering messages.

"Hey, Rainey," Christine greets me as I pull up and park in Maxwell's lot. "Always the rock star parking," she comments, as I have taken up residence in the spot closest to the door.

"The lucky perks of wheelchair life, right?" I say to her. My friends always comment on the luck of the disabled parking tag, as if parking close to any venue is a fair trade for the challenges of navigating the attitudes, stereotypes, and the complications of disability. While I've been able to find the positives in my situation, close-proximity parking doesn't nearly make up for the adversity I've experienced in the course of my life.

Christine opens the door for us, and as we go in, we're greeted by a middle-aged woman in a too-short-for-her-age straight black skirt, and sweater vest with fall leaves on it. Her top says elementary school teacher (I know because my coworkers often wear similar sweaters branded for the seasons) and her bottom says, meet me at the bar later.

"Two for lunch, please," Christine requests.

The woman grabs two menus from the hostess stand, looks around at the half-populated restaurant, turns back to Christine, and says in a slightly elevated, and slow-talking voice, "where do you think she would be most comfortable sitting?"

"Uh, I don't know," Christine replies. "Perhaps you should ask her. She's a grown woman. And by the way, you've got your disabilities mixed up. She's paralyzed, not deaf."

The woman looks at me in shock and mumbles for us to follow her.

"We'll take a booth, thanks," I add.

Christine takes a seat in the booth, and I scoot out of my chair onto the bench across from her. "Okay, spill it."

"I met the greatest guy last night at the 15th Street Tavern. His name is Thad, and he's a doctor at Denver Health. He was out last night with a bunch of co-workers celebrating a birthday, and we spotted each other from across the bar. It was like … instant … connection."

Christine always has a flair for the dramatic, but as she tells me of this first meeting, I think how simple dating must be when your differences and quirks don't shine like a beacon on a foggy night.

Dear Brian:

I apologize for the lapse in communication … it's been thirty-six hours since my last message. Have I missed the imaginary timeline for replying? It's funny to me that technically speaking, we could be connected 24/7 since I can read your messages from any one of my personal electronic devices at any time of the day. Instead, I prefer the suspense and anticipation throughout the day and having something to come home to at night. As much as I could monitor your responses on my phone during the day, I appreciate the attention I can give our communication from the comfort of home. And for some reason, the introspective part of me comes out more when the sun goes down, when I'm alone, relaxing, and have time to think. And, with your latest question, I knew the mood I had to be in to give you a complete and honest response.

As I sit there and write in my pajamas and slippers, with a hot cup of tea in hand and Rufus spread across my lap—curled in a ball, eyes closed, utterly oblivious to the human condition—I think about the fact that above him, on my laptop, I am writing to an unknown reader, who could possibly be the man of my dreams or an ax murderer, and I'm about to share the story of my life.

First, let me say, I'm sorry to hear that your job may be ending shortly, but I have a hunch this is life throwing you a new adventure you wouldn't have created for yourself. And I suppose the upside is, you know it's coming, and you can be prepared. That's better than being blindsided, in my opinion. I will keep my fingers crossed and think positive thoughts for you. I would be honored to be your sounding board, your cheerleader, or an impartial ear to listen. I don't know how it is with guys, but some of my girlfriends are more than willing to give advice—a little too much advice—whenever it is that I'm trying to make big decisions. In fact, I might as well come clean. It wasn't my idea to get online to find a date, but I was nearly handcuffed to the computer by Natalie, who twisted my arm to create a profile. Okay … it wasn't that bad, but it was highly encouraged. And here I am. You want to know the good thing, though? I don't regret it one bit. Receiving a message from you, once again brightened my day. Thank you.

I will tell you about my mom and my sister, but to preface it, I am okay to write about it and you haven't upset me by asking. Sometimes when people ask, and I tell them the story, they immediately wish they hadn't inquired, and the situation gets awkward quickly. My mom and sister, Sunny, were killed in a car accident seventeen years ago. My father and I were in the car but on the opposite side of the impact. I was in ninth grade, and it has since defined my life in many ways. Mostly because they were my world. I wasn't the typical rebel high school kid. I didn't go through a period where I was ashamed of my parents or the fact they existed at all. On the contrary, my mom was one of the best people I knew. And besides that, I don't think it matters how old you are—you never get used to losing your mother.

A mom, I think, or maybe I am generalizing, is the one person on earth who loves you more than all others. If you're ever to be loved unconditionally, I reckon it comes from the woman who gave you life. At least that's how my mom was. She was always there to back me and give me courage in anything I did … from sports, to school, to making friends. She held me when I was unhappy and picked up the pieces when I fell.

My mom was a captivating beauty, and I dreamed of looking like her when I grew up. Her parents—my grandparents—were a couple of hippies who raised her to value peace and tolerance. She was the youngest of three children and was a fun-loving, free-spirited kid. I don't know what attracted her to my father—a Midwestern, blue collar, race car driver—or how they ended up settling down in the suburbs, all of which seems to me a contradiction. But that's how the story goes. She always believed she could make a mark on the world, which was what led her to teaching. She wanted to touch lives, one at a time, and help a new generation find its way.

When she gave up her white hippie smock dresses, beads, and flower headbands, she dressed fashionably, but not prissy, and was glamorous without the crutch of a makeup palette. She was kind and outgoing, and I never ran across a person who didn't like her. I had her long enough to know how much a kid could possibly need her mom and how painful it can be when she's gone. And it wasn't only my mom who was great. It was who we were as a family. My parents were so in love; it made us incredibly close.

And then there was Sunny. My little sister, who was seven years younger, and was everything to me. I would have given my left eye to protect that kid. In fact, I would have given my whole body if it would have saved her the night of the accident.

In the beginning, right after the car wreck, I would lie awake at night and wonder why it hadn't been me sitting on the other side of the car. It shouldn't have been Sunny. She was such a bright spot in everyone's lives. And, as siblings, we rarely had a fight or a disagreement. We were a team.

Ever since that night, there's been an underlying drain in our world, keeping my father and me pulled down so that neither of us, it seems, has fully healed. My dad skims through the days, like a rock skipping across water, but not touching enough to get wet. I think he's content, but he hasn't found the happiness he had with my mom. In fact, he hasn't even tried looking. She was his universe, and once she was gone, it was hard for both of us to pick up the pieces.

Natalie insists my family tragedy is why I'm afraid to open up to become close to anyone, and perhaps she's right. Who knows, though, maybe it's a cop-out, or I simply haven't found the right person. But life goes on, and not one of those days goes by where I don't think about my mom and Sunny.

The one bright side in this stormy tale is that the accident has kept my father and me tight. He has done the best he can, and I appreciate him more than anyone in the world. I know he wanted to shut down and fall off the edge of the earth, but he kept it together for me.

And to answer your question, he doesn't own a shotgun, so I think you're safe there. As dangerous as he gets is a pocket protector full of pens and maybe a textbook he could throw at you. He's an engineering professor. It's a job, which, I believe, keeps him busy and guarded from his emotions. Like father, like daughter, I have been told more than once.

I hope I haven't put too much of a damper on our exchange, but if you want to know me, you'll have to take the bad with the good. As long as I can remember, since I was a child, my greatest fear was losing my parents. I don't know where the fear came from, but I find it ironic that it's exactly what came to pass.

Well, with this conversation off my chest, I get to ask you a question. Tell me, Brian, what is your biggest fear?

May

Sitting at my desk, I slip into a hypnotic state, where my mind takes over and recalls images of my mom from the far reaches of my imagination. The more time passes, the fewer I have to choose from. Sometimes I'm afraid it means one day I will forget her altogether, but maybe I just keep the best ones around for the reruns. The cake baking event is definitely one of my favorites, but a close second is when I was eleven years old. At the time, Sunny was a high maintenance four-year-old, captivating the attention of my mom and dad, which meant I was on my own to entertain myself much of the time. However, one unfortunate day at the playground, I fell off the monkey bars, landed hard on the ground, and broke my wrist. Before I knew it, the playground aid had whisked me off the ground and handed me over to my teacher, who took me to the nurse's office. They put ice on my wrist and called my mom to come and get me.

Not knowing what she would find, Mom dropped Sunny off with the neighbor and came alone. The whole way to the hospital, she held my hand as she drove, singing along with the songs on the radio. She had the rare talent of being quick-witted enough to make up new words in perfect time to go with the melodies. She'd sing songs so funny—it wasn't long before I was doubled over with laughter, and had my mind fully off the pain. The twenty-minute drive was over in a blink. It was a full afternoon event of getting my arm set and casted, but instead of rushing directly home to cook dinner for Dad and Sunny, Mom took me out for ice cream and some one-on-one time. Outside of the shop, we sat on a red, wooden bench with a wrought iron frame and armrests, watching as the sun set, a frosty pink and electric orange. I talked her ear off about everything from the relentless teasing by the boys at school to debating if I should become a Girl Scout. I remember trying to talk fast to keep the flow of conversation going so she couldn't butt in and tell me it was time to go home. I was on a roll when at last she gently tapped me on the leg as a signal it was time to go. Time was up, and I was going to have to go home and share her again with Sunny. Life seems so unfair, especially when you are young— that a moment so wonderful, like my ice cream, was gone. I often look back on that day and know I would give anything to be able to sit and have a conversation with her again. I keep a running list of things in my mind I would ask about—her childhood, her first love, motherhood—subjects I would never have dreamed to ask as a kid, but now, as an adult, I realize there is so much wisdom and insight one gains from a mother.

I drift off to sleep thinking about the satisfaction I felt that day as we drove home and I soaked up the last few moments I had with my mom, like warm rays coming through the window on a summer day. Not that I am biased or anything, but I know I had the best mom in the whole wide world. And despite the pain and frustration of my broken arm, I remember wanting that day to go on forever.

When I wake up, my first thought is of my mom, and then I remember what, or rather who, triggered that memory. *Brian!* I hustle out of bed and over to the computer. I touch the power button, and as it's booting up, I wriggle in anticipation. Logging into my inbox seems to take forever, even though it's only five seconds. I scan the new messages and … *nothing.* The big goose egg. I've already scared him away. *See what I get for telling the truth? Some people can't handle it.* Maybe Brian is one of them. But he did ask the question. With a sinking feeling in my heart, I get in the shower to get ready for Sunday brunch with Dad.

I feel glum, having not heard from Brian, and my mind instantly goes back to my days in rehab. Dealing with the death of my mom and Sunny, and the look on Gabe's face when he came to see me the one and only time in the hospital.

And remembering how on that day, when I was still learning my transfers and becoming independent—I had to have a nurse in the bathroom with me at all times—I transferred into the shower, held the shower hose above my head and ran the water down my face so that it merged with my tears as they trickled down my cheeks. Those days were full of *why me?* Everything that was happening was bad and it was happening all at once. Today's sinking feeling is reminiscent of that time. Why does Christine get to meet the perfect, brilliant heart-surgeon-in-training, and I can't even keep an online conversation going past the second message? I reach for my towel, drying off and getting dressed, so I won't be late.

Today Dad has agreed to do some fall cleaning in the garage. Our activity has been spurred by my desire to find some of the books I collected in college and saved with the intent of using them in my classroom one day. I can envision the contents of the box clearly in my mind, but can't for the life of me find it at my place, so I assume it's in the garage at the house. I know this search through items of our past is an anxious subject for my father, but he promised to help me sift through boxes since most are stored up high, beyond my reach.

When I arrive, the garage door is up, and Dad has his car parked on the street. He's busily sweeping, which looks to me as more of a way to calm his nerves than a necessary chore. I park and get out of the car, and he waves at me as I push up to greet him. "Hi, honey," he says cheerily as if he is taking this day in stride. I wish I felt cheery. Without a message from Brian, I'm not in the mood to talk, and honestly, I just want to get to business.

"Are you ready for a bite to eat before we get to work?"

"Sure Dad," I try to match his enthusiasm, but truth be told, I believe his zeal is as fabricated as mine would be, had I decided to make the effort. This show of false feelings has become a pattern of habit between the two of us; I believe more as a coping mechanism than anything else. We both feel the burden of the compulsion to be eternally positive, even when our insides are crumbling and upbeat is the polar opposite of our true emotions. Between the two of us, we are good at ignoring it. But today, I'm fixated on my non-message from Brian and Dad is likely dreading revisiting the boxes in the garage, which haven't moved since Grandma and Grandpa (Mom's parents) helped pack up her things. Some went into storage, some to the local second-hand store.

I follow him into the kitchen, and over small talk, we scramble eggs, toast bagels, and then carry our breakfast to the table.

"I thought I'd pull some of the boxes off the shelves for you to go through while I wash the car in the driveway. How does that sound?"

"Works for me, Dad. Thanks for being willing to help. I know that box is in there somewhere."

It's a struggle for either one of us to get the momentum of a conversation going, but as usual, we continue to piece our communication together, at least to get caught up with each other. But, as I look at him, the lines of worry on his forehead, a tight smile, I am struck, on this particular day, what a departure this Dad is from the one who took me to the race track every Sunday when I was a kid. I can't help but think I want more for him. For us.

In the garage, Dad pulls down a collection of boxes and hands me a box cutter to retrieve the tightly sealed contents. It would be a lot easier had the boxes been labeled, but I imagine at the time Dad and my grandparents were going through things, they just wanted to get it put away. After about ten boxes, I pull one onto my lap, open it up and bingo! Exactly what I was looking for. But out of the corner of my eye, I see a smaller box on the floor and on it is written my name in my grandmother's writing. Curious, I put my college book box aside and open it. Inside is another box, slightly larger than a shoebox. It is pink and orange, my favorite colors, and as I open the lid, my breath is shallow. Underneath is a collection, my mom's collection, of mementos from my childhood—homemade cards I had given her for Mother's Day, my birth announcement, a picture of my mom and I holding hands on the lush green lawn of this very house, which my parents purchased when I was three years old. It's clearly a box of keepsakes meant for her to give me … when? College graduation? Engagement? Wedding day? She trusted in the future and saw it with optimism. Everything in this box means she believed she would be there next to me on the important occasions of her eldest daughter's life. And Sunny's life, for that matter. So much has changed. Such an unexpected path our lives have taken. I look up to see Dad rinsing his car; I quickly reseal the memories of the story of the life I was supposed to lead.

CHAPTER 7

MONDAY MORNING COMES, STILL WITHOUT word from Brian. My laptop slept next to me in my queen-sized bed in lieu of a companion, and my inbox was the first action of the day, beyond silencing my alarm. With no message from Brian, my day starts off at an all-time low. It is a chore for me to extract my body from the comfort of my bed and ready myself for school. Getting ready feels like the strain of a marathon and as I look in the mirror, my eyes are dull, and a frown settles on my face. It's not just Brian, but my mother's memories and the thought that once again, I'm not sure how to handle the curve balls of my life. I opt to forgo the eye make-up today. I can't be sure it won't run down my face as I'm likely to weep through the day.

When I get to work, I am fully centered on Brian and

whether I should have been so upfront about the tragedy of my life. Thinking and overthinking has me preoccupied, and I act edgy with the kids. I've made up a million scenarios about why he hasn't written back yet, and none of them are good. He doesn't want to get involved with a girl with baggage, or he met someone better online last night, or I scared him away like I knew I would.

Fine, I don't need him anyway. Although I know, it's a lie. Even though we've only had a couple of exchanges, I've begun to like the company. And after getting the story of my mom and Sunny out in the open, I felt like maybe I could start to open up even more. That is if he hasn't shut the door on me already.

Today, I'm glad I have a video planned for my students because I'm not in the mood to teach anything new. I put in the DVD and head back to my desk and computer. I want to avoid opening my email at work, and I already turned off the automatic alert on my smartphone. I will not let this dating thing distract me from my day. I need to focus fully on the things I do—work, workout, spend time with friends. I don't want my mind wandering. But as I sit there watching the video, I am distracted by my efforts to be undistractable.

It's a quiet drive to the gym for my usual afternoon workout followed by dinner for one and a solo night on the couch watching my favorite TV show. I'm starting to see how there could be something to this relationship thing. *What if I had the guts to see Brian in person?* I imagine us in the kitchen, on a cold winter night, cooking up a pot of stew and fresh biscuits. The kitchen would fill with the scent of comfort foods, and we would feel the closeness of creating something together. We'd take our bowls to the living room floor, spread out a blanket in front of the fire, and have a picnic as we share stories from our childhoods—laughing at the good ol' days. We'd clean up together and cuddle on the couch to watch movies. I can imagine the warmth of him spooning me and letting the very shape of my body mold into his. I haven't been held that close in so long, I don't even remember what it feels like to experience such intimacy and the ability to let go and be oneself. *Please*, I beg silently to the universe or whomever else might be listening, *let Brian be that special someone. Don't let me have scared him away.*

My self-pity is interrupted by my cell phone ringing. It's Natalie.

"Hi." I answer the phone in an exasperated monotone.

"Geez, what's up with you, Ms. Grouchy-Pants?"

"I told Brian about Mom and Sunny and haven't heard back from him. I knew this wouldn't work. My life is tragic. No one wants to be swallowed up in my baggage."

"Whoa, whoa, whoa! How long ago did you send that message?"

"Saturday night."

"Don't you think you could be overreacting a bit? That is a lot to dump on someone you don't even know. How many messages have you traded so far? Two, three, four? Give it time. I know you're not the most patient person, but really. Take. A. Deep. Breath."

"You're right. I know. It's just … I see Gabe. The face he made when he saw me for the first time. It's like the image is seared in my brain. I went from seeing stars in his eyes to looking into the black hole of his pupils where I felt he couldn't or didn't want to see me at all."

"You were both fourteen! Give Brian a break. He's a grown man and men need time to process. And it never happens on a woman's timeline. That much I know. Go easy on yourself and go easy on him. If it's meant to happen, it will."

"Yeah, I know. Sorry to dump my insecurities on you. I'll give it more time. But for now, I've got to try to get some sleep. I have work tomorrow."

"Okay. Text me when you hear from him."

"Will do. Goodnight, friend."

"Night, Rainey."

It's nine o'clock when I hang up with Natalie, and I realize if I don't get to bed, morning is going to come much sooner than I want, so I lock up, turn off the lights, and head to my bedroom. On the way there, I divert to the guest room, which I have turned into my office. This is my favorite room in my house because it's the one where I throw all rules of conservative (proper) decoration out the window. With a combination of tangerine orange and bold pink walls, it's both cheerful and whimsical. Most of the décor are the brightest pieces I have collected from my trips around the globe—figurines, wall art, and other accessories. They dot the room with the colors of turquoise, light greens, and pale purple. A white desk sits in the back of the room, with a photo of our four-person family framed in just the way I want to remember us, wearing black t-shirts and jeans, sprawled out on a beach blanket in front of the clear blue ocean. My mom, Sunny and I, all with fresh tans and long, blonde hair blowing in the breeze. My dad sits in the middle, proud and protective of his "girls." It's so stellar, so perfect. One might have thought Annie Liebovitz took it for an issue of *Vanity Fair*.

Nothing about my office feels ordinary. I wanted it that way; to create the impression that living outside the lines was an okay way to live. It's how I feel about the way my life has been handed to me. Nothing about it says inside the box. But sometimes, I think maybe it's too different for others even to understand me. Perhaps I'm too far out of Brian's comfort zone. *Humph*, and we were just getting started. I conveniently pass my computer desk and decide to give my messages one more check. Braced for the worst, I am relieved when up pops a message from Brian85.

May Belle:

I'm sorry I haven't responded to your last message. I feel badly to have left you waiting, not one, but two days. I wanted to write, but I simply didn't feel I had the proper words to say. I can't say I know how you feel, or relate on any level, and that made me feel ... well ... helpless. And if you know men at all, you know dealing with that emotion is not our forte. Regardless, I'm glad you opened up to me. It made me feel a connection to you, and I am honored you felt like you could expose the real you and be unguarded with what you had to say. It takes courage and strength, which I admire. It also helps me understand you better and your fears of opening your heart to someone. I can imagine with a loss like that, it's easy to stay distant.

It's also frustrating to me that, while we can share words, we are still so new to each other it's hard for me to know how best to show you I am sympathetic to your loss. That I am a real, live, breathing, feeling person on the other end of this computer, thinking about you and wishing I could offer a condolence with which you could feel my sincerity and how I genuinely care. That might be something to wait until we meet in person.

With that said, your assumption is right. Your email did take the words out of my mouth and gave me quite a pause. I am sorry to hear you've experienced such a tragedy. What I am not sorry about is asking you about your mom because May, I want to get to know you. And how else can you get to know someone if you're not willing to ask and answer the hard questions? The strength you showed in sharing it at all exposes your vulnerability. And honestly like that is what makes relationships work. If we hold back all vulnerability, we can't truly connect. And I don't know what it is, but I already have a feeling about you; a feeling you are someone with whom I could relate and appreciate. You make me smile, and you make me think. You're genuine and passionate. I can't put my finger on it, but I like you. You make me feel like a sponge, and I want to soak in everything there is to know about you. So how about telling me about your dad?

And since you've lain so much out there, it must be my turn. But do you have to go straight to the jugular and ask me, a man, about my fears? Aren't you aware, fear is a four-letter word and to admit I have one (or multiple), by definition robs me of my masculinity? Men aren't supposed to be fearful; we're supposed to be invincible. We're supposed to be strong, and stoic, and able to fix things. But you, you're not one to beat around the bush, are you? Trying to steal my man card the first time out. For the sake of getting to know each other, and because I get a hunch I might like you, I'll tell you.

My biggest fear is not being good enough. I've always felt, in my family, I have big shoes to fill. My father is a talented and sought-after surgeon. My older brothers have successful careers in scientific research and software development. I might be way out of line because I look up to them, being the youngest, but I have always felt I didn't quite fit in. It seems like everyone in my family has achieved recognition in his pursuits, and I feel like I'm still finding my way. I've always been the dreamy kid, artsy in a world of left-brainers. I'm in right field by myself. I love art, writing, and finding the next great feature story. Suffice it to say, my greatest fear is letting people down. Letting myself down. I'm a perfectionist, at least in my work, and it makes for a difficult existence. I try to relax, but it's hard. I've pushed myself a lot. I love what I do, but I always wonder what other people think. Do I measure up? I'm not even sure how to tell. Is it a feeling or does someone tell you when you've gotten there? How do you know what *there* truly means and when you've arrived at success? If you have the answer, I'd love to hear it.

I must sign off for now because I'm headed out to play a late-night pickup basketball game with the guys. I'm looking forward to meeting you and hope it won't be much longer!

Bri

I read his message and can only think he's genuine and transparent—he's passing all the right tests.

I pull out my phone and text Natalie.

He wrote! ☺☺☺☺☺☺☺☺☺☺☺☺☺☺☺

I knew he would, Rainey. You just need to relax.

I know, but I can't! I'm in serious 'like.'

She returns with a string of hearts. Now don't seem too eager. Give it the night and write him back tomorrow.

The voice of reason has spoken. And I promptly ignore it.

Brian:

To me, success should be strictly personal. What you work hard for, achieve, and which fulfills you is success. Unfortunately, society tells us it's the person who has the most money, the biggest title, or the gold medal around his or her neck that is the mark of success. I say this because I struggle with it myself. For so long, I have been an athlete and had to fight with my brain to believe I could still be considered a success even when I didn't end up with the win. And when I look at the people around me, who I look up to, they all display different versions of the same concept. My dad used to be a top race car driver when he was young, and we have pictures all over the house of him holding trophies overhead. But he has told me a million times that marrying and having a loving family, even though the experience of the four of us together was short-lived, has brought him complete satisfaction and a feeling of success. There's no way to measure it, but you do have to have the strength to know, whatever you do, and whatever makes you happy and helps you believe in yourself, *is* success, regardless of what name anyone else might give it. No, you may not end up the richest in your family or amongst your friends, but money or accolades in your profession need not be the only measuring stick for success. There are a lot of people in the world who look incredibly successful on the outside, yet are empty on the inside. Can it truly be called success if you simply move through the paces without finding what you are passionate about? If you go home at night and you don't have a feeling of accomplishment or true happiness? If you drown yourself in a bottle of whiskey? If you ask me, the revelation of finding what you love doing, and doing it well, means you've already found success. I admire that about you, and I don't even know you well yet. If nothing else, perhaps what I've written will give you something to ponder.

On to your next question, about my dad. I've told you a little bit, but I will complete the story for you. I adore my dad, but I've seen life take a toll on him. He used to be vibrant and happy all the time. He's the kind of person who wears his emotions on his sleeve. Maybe he thinks he can cover them up, but it's not hard to know exactly what he's feeling. He was over-the-top in love with my mom and having a family was a dream come true for him. He was challenged and satisfied by his career as an engineer, but on the weekends, he was all ours. We'd do stuff as a family all the time, whether it was skiing and sledding in the winter or swimming and camping in the summer. But after my mom and Sunny died, I saw a new side of him. It was new for him too … I could tell. He wasn't used to not being able to find joy in his life. The eternal optimist was replaced with, not a pessimist, but a doubter, and he dove into work like it could save his life. He's still been a great father and is always there when I need him, but I can tell something is missing. Maybe it's what is missing in both of us. Neither of us has found the means to fill the holes left in our hearts after the accident. I wonder sometimes if the void can even be filled ... by a person or a thing. Perhaps over time it scars over and you finally forget. I don't know what to believe, though each day I wonder and search.

But, Brian ... this I am sure of—I love to hear from you and read your messages, and am hopeful one day, when we meet, perhaps you can be part of what fills my emptiness, completing me and making me whole.

Thank you for making me smile, Brian.

As I sign off, I let my imagination take me away to a place where dreams come true, and I can be anyone I want to be. I giggle at the thought that pops into my head. I am standing in front of his house in only a satin robe. When he opens the door, I flash him a grin and a sneak peek of my sexy lingerie underneath. All I am wearing is a thong with two candles tucked in the string at the side of the undergarment. He grabs me and kisses me deeply. I am whole. I feel love. The only problem is, this isn't the real me. It's the imagined me. The one who doesn't sit in a wheelchair. The one who could actually be sexy. The one I'll never be.

My smile quickly turns to a frown. I hit send and head to bed with a pit in my stomach.

May:

It's midnight and I'm getting home from playing basketball with the guys. I sheepishly admit I was distracted the whole time. All I could think about was you—my mystery woman. I keep wishing I could know more about you. I knew you were going to bed early and because I am a guy, I couldn't help but wonder if you're the kind of woman who wears a sexy little number to bed, an oversized t-shirt, or nothing at all. Since I'm also a gentleman, or at least do my best to be, I will stop at that and let my mind continue to wonder. Goodnight, May. Thank you for giving me something to look forward to, and may my teammates not have it out for you for taking my attention away from the game.

This wondering about the person on the other side of the computer is invigorating. It's peeling away the layers of you that will keep me coming back over and over. There is still so much to know. I realize that I don't know your favorite color, the last song you downloaded to your phone, your favorite food, or where you'd spend your time if you had a Saturday to yourself. Or maybe *you* should be telling *me* the questions I should know answers to? In fact, there are a million things about you I don't know. But you are a person I want to get to know and a person with whom I'd like to share my world too. May, you have quickly charmed me and enhanced my world.

My question tonight: Do you believe in soul mates?

I hope you sleep with the angels.

Brian

I open the message as I am getting ready for work. Instead of feeling excited that he had been distracted by the thoughts of me, I feel glum. Memories of the brief moments last night when I had my able-bodied fantasy. How long am I going to go before telling him the truth? Of all the things he mentioned that he didn't know about me, never in a million years could he have thought of the enormity of my omission in our conversation. The one that will be immediately apparent the second he sets eyes on me. Natalie was right. I can't let this go on forever. He's thinking about me and getting the wrong picture. The thought makes my stomach turn, and reading those words makes me start to sweat and itch all at the same time.

As I think about Brain throughout the day, I decide my best tactic is avoidance. I will pretend he didn't ask the question about what he should know about me. And I always find the best way to respond to a question when you don't have an answer is to ask another question. Therefore, when I get home and boot up my computer, I dodge the bullet with a question of my own and answer his question about soul mates.

Dear Brian:

You are as big of a mystery to me. Is there anything about you I should know?

Soul mates. Yes ... and no. I believe you can find the love of your life who is not necessarily your soul mate. And—I think you can connect with your soul mate and have a disastrous and even destructive relationship. Then I think there are those few lucky people who find both. But it takes so much more than love and connection to make a relationship work—consistency of character, trust, respect, support, 'all-in' feelings. I like to think that's what my parents had. At the same time, you're probably asking the wrong person. I haven't found my soul mate, the love of my life, or even a date for Saturday night.

So, Brian, my question to you—what makes you smile?

But in less than thirty seconds, my plan backfires on me. An instant message pops up on my screen, and it says,

May, *you* make me smile.

As I read his simple sentence, my heart nearly jumps out of my chest. It feels like for the first time there is actually someone there, on the other side of this computer, to whom I can actually talk. In real time. In person, too, if I weren't so chicken. I feel nervous. My stomach churns, but then I smile to myself and again get lost in the fantasy of Brian and imagine a time when we've already met, the awkwardness of the wheelchair has come and gone, and all he sees is me. And he does think I'm attractive. And sexy. I love this fantasy, but not long after it begins, I am jolted back to reality as my phone rings.

"Hey, doll." It's Natalie. "Listen, I'm on the guest list tonight for the grand opening of a hip new sushi joint called Koisuru. It's supposed to be all the rage. Totally fab. Gonna be full of movers and shakers, and there might be some hot single guy kickin' it at the event."

I wonder where this new lingo is coming from. Natalie didn't use to describe things as all the rage or totally fab. And kickin' it sounds to me like dying is involved.

"Besides that, you need to get out of the house and away from that computer and have some real live person-to-person interaction," she reminds me. "I know you like the simplicity of talking to a guy who says nice things and has no idea who you truly are, but it's time. Step. Away. From. The. Computer. Rainey, you've turned into a hermit who stares into a box on your desk for hours a day. I'm picking you up at seven."

I try to turn her down, but that's not how it works with Natalie. She is not accustomed to being told no. She's persuasive and charming and gets her way more than any other person I know.

"Nat, you kill me!" I exclaim, and then immediately back down to her unavoidable charisma. "What am I wearing?" I ask as I shake my head, not believing she has talked me into this.

"You know that new strappy little black dress we picked up at Nordstrom last month? Wear that. It shows off every single hard-earned muscle in your arms and back, and you look hot. I know you hate it when people envy your build, but you have to admit, you look stunning."

She's right. Another "ism." How often I have heard, "Wow, I wish my arms looked like yours." In response, the first thought through my head is ... If you had to push yourself around in a chair everywhere you went, your arms would look like this too. But, more importantly: Get off your lazy ass, walk your able-bodied legs to the gym, and lift some weights. Now there's a thought. I know that sounds harsh or maybe bitter, but it does make me crazy for people to envy me over something that they are too lazy to work for, even though they have every bit of ability to have the toned upper body I have. For me, it's an inevitable part of my life situation. For others, it's merely a lack of motivation.

"Okay, for you, I will go. See you at seven."

I turn to the computer and am whisked back into my online world where Brian has told me I make him smile. I pause for a second to soak it in, then look up at the clock and realize Natalie has given me precisely ninety minutes to transform myself. My relationship has reached a new level with real-time communication, and I have to go eat sushi? I suppose there are worse things, so I write back:

Thank you. I love to hear I make you smile. You have the same effect on me. And though I wish I could sit here and talk to you more, Natalie has just called and is dragging me off to some party and time is ticking for me to get ready. Do you think we could pick up on this conversation a little later tonight?

When will you be home?

Late. Will you be up after midnight? Maybe even 1?

For you, anything.

My heart begins to pound, and now I wish I didn't have to go to Koisuru, but when I think about it, it's all good. Absence makes the heart grow fonder, right?

Okay, I'll meet you back here at 1 a.m.

I figure that way I can get into bed with my laptop and get comfortable. Hopefully talking until the wee hours of the morning.

Sounds good to me. It's a date.

Reading those words makes my heart grow three sizes and fills my chest so I can barely breathe.

The *requested* black dress hangs covered in plastic in my closet. Taking it off the clothes hanger, I have a choice to make— transfer out of my wheelchair and lie on the bed to change, or change sitting in my chair. Both are skills I learned seventeen years ago in rehab in what was traumatic fashion for a fourteen-year-old. In my hospital room one day, my occupational therapist sat on the bed as I, in only my underwear and bra, fresh out of the shower, sat opposite her in my wheelchair. Her job that day was to coach me in getting dressed sitting in a wheelchair. I had already learned to dress lying in bed, which is easier in my opinion, but she spent ten minutes lecturing me on how I wouldn't always have the luxury of dressing in bed. Therefore, it was her job to oversee the learning process of dressing from the chair. Personally, I found it unsettling that it was actually someone's job to watch other people get dressed and undressed. Dressed and undressed. But that's what she did until I could get a pair of jeans up my legs, slid under my thighs, tugged over my bum, crested up and over my backside, and buttoned in front. It's not as easy as it seems without the privilege of standing. Tonight, I choose to transfer to bed, slip the dress over my head and then lie down so I can wiggle it down the rest of my body. Then I roll over onto my side to get the zipper started up my back. Transferring into my chair, I zip the dress the rest of the way, then tug and pull so the right parts of the dress cover the right parts of my body. I push into the bathroom to the full-length mirror to have a look. Natalie was right. The dress has a square neckline with one-inch straps that crisscross my back and perfectly displays my sculpted biceps, shoulders, and back. There is no doubt I have been training hard lately. And not to be vain, but I love looking at the results. I wonder what Brian would think. I imagine him standing next to me in a tux. From the looks of his profile picture, I am certain he cleans up nicely.

I look at the clock, and it seems to be ticking in double time tonight, but perhaps it's because I'm half getting ready and half living in my dream world. I take a moment to breathe in my Brian fantasies, and then realize I need to get back at it.

As I sit at the pull-under counter of my bathroom, I think, from the belly button up, I look pretty damn hot! It's just going south that things really go south. I wonder, why is walking such a big deal anyway? I get places faster in my chair; I don't have to worry about "standing" in line, and, quite honestly, it's not all bad. And yes, my legs have atrophied and aren't a match in muscle or tone for my upper body, but all things considered, I don't look bad. I actually think I look pretty good. *I am good*, I think to myself. *I am pretty.* Right? So why when I think those words do I not quite believe them?

Natalie picks me up promptly at seven o'clock. Pulling into the driveway, she stops slightly in front of my garage door, puts the car in park, but leaves it running. She steps out and looks fabulous in a short red, strapless dress, and high heels. Suddenly any glamour I was beginning to see when I looked at myself in the mirror is gone. But as Natalie rounds the car, stops dead in her tracks, and says, "You look eff-ing HOT!" my confidence begins to come around again.

"See, I told you," she continues. "That dress is stellar on you. I can feel some action coming on tonight."

Leave it to Natalie. She has always known how to make me feel good about myself. Now, if I could only find the male version of her.

We get in the car, and as we're backing out, I ask where Seth is. "Oh, he's out of town tonight inking some big sports deal, so it's only us girls," she says. "As much as I love having him around, it's nice that it's you and me, Babe, 'cause we're definitely on a manhunt," she says and winks at me.

I don't say anything.

"What? You've given up already? Oh. No. Wait. You're falling for Brian85, aren't you?"

"Umm, yeah, sort of."

"Okay, so when is the first date?"

"Well, we're still sticking with the online thing for now."

"C'mon, Rainey. What are you waiting for? You don't want him to lose interest, do you? You have to meet. Men simply aren't that patient."

"I know. I know." Her questioning is causing me to feel the weight of an impending meeting, and the very thought makes me nervous. Right about the time we are getting in a groove, I'm already anticipating the downfall of our relationship. We haven't even met, and I'm planning our breakup? What is wrong with me? "I'm going to try to drag it out a little longer," I say, then add hopefully, "At least we started instant messaging. I actually have a chat date with him tonight when I get home."

"Oh, what has this world come to?" I tense up, ready for another lecture from Natalie, but all she says is, "Technology is such a crutch."

"Well, I'm further along than I was, say, two weeks ago. Wouldn't you agree?"

"Um, yes, and no. I guess I'll give you points for at least corresponding with a guy. Extra points if you try to pick one up tonight, though."

We get to the restaurant and pull up to valet. Nat turns off the ignition, and two valets come to the car to meet us.

One opens Natalie's door, and she is immediately up and out, heading to the back of the car to get my wheelchair. But as the other valet opens my door and expects me to stand up out of the car, I sit there. He looks at me questioningly. I tell him I use a wheelchair and I'm waiting for my friend to get it out of the back of the car. His head turns to the left as he eyes Natalie. But instead of walking back to help her, he looks back at me and says, "so you can't walk, huh? What happened to you?" Another wheelchair-ism I know by heart, but this one makes me fume. My mood, my tone, everything about me changes, and I feel that black cloud hanging in the air over this conversation. I look at him and say, "Nothing happened to me. This is who I am." Fortunately, at that moment, Natalie shows up with my chair and bumps the valet out of my way.

"What's wrong with you? What happened? Why can't you walk?" These are all questions that complete strangers believe they have the right to know or ask a person using a wheelchair. I find it inappropriate for a complete stranger to feel entitled to my personal information. Why an individual feels the boldness to ask me anything, yet to another person, practices simple etiquette. One would not ask the next person in line at McDonald's, "so, how do you have sex?" Or, "how do you go to the bathroom?" But I get those questions regularly, and from complete strangers.

When Natalie has my chair assembled and puts it in the crevice of the door, I transfer into it (with my new valet friend staring at me, mouth gaping open), straighten the skirt of my dress, and tuck into the draft behind Natalie's air of confidence as we enter the bar.

As we arrive, the restaurant is buzzing. People dressed to the nines standing everywhere. I look around, and all I can see are midsections. I remind myself to take deep breaths. This night will get better. But at the moment of our entrance, everyone looks down on me or worse yet, doesn't realize I exist behind Natalie's five-foot-ten-inch frame. She knows how much this gets me on edge, so she gets us quickly through the tall banquet tables at the entrance and finds us a regular height four-top table with a couple sitting at it. And then she does this thing. I don't know where she got it from, must be the movies, but she pulls it off famously. Maybe it's the want-to-be actor inside her.

"Ya know, y'all," she pulls the most perfect southern accent right out of her butt. "Ma friend here, she's in a wheelchair and all, and there's no place for a girl in a wheelchair around here, what with all these people walking around and all high bar tables. Ya know, all she can see is a bunch of crotches. Do you think maybe we could share your table?" And with that, they realize the audacity of saying no to someone they see as a poor woman in a wheelchair and immediately vacate their seats for us to have the table to ourselves.

"Works ever' time, don't it?" Natalie continues her accent and gives me a nudge.

"I will never know how you get away with that. You can make anyone do anything. It's sick!" I say.

"Ya know darlin', I guess it's just a God-given gift," she says back at me as she pirouettes and heads to get us some Saki and beer. I wish, just wish, I had half as much charm as she.

As I'm waiting, I pull my phone out of my handbag, which

I have neatly tucked in a sling under my chair, and check my messages. There's a text from my real southern friend, Jake. "Hey, darlin'! Meet me at the racetrack tomorrow?"

I text him back. "Sure thing. But it won't be before noon," I reply, thinking of my IM date with Brian later. It's going to be a late night.

As soon as I tuck my phone away, Natalie is back balancing a carafe of Saki, two beers, and a plate of sushi. I don't know in which of her past lives she was a waitress, but she does it flawlessly. As she sets it all down, two men immediately flock to our table and introduce themselves.

"What are you two lovely ladies doing here unescorted tonight?" says the one who introduces himself as Billy.

Natalie holds up her left hand that dons one of the biggest rocks I've seen up close and says, "Away on business, but meet my friend Rainey here." She points to me. Both guys reach their hands out to shake mine. Nat winks at me. "Have a seat," she says. And of course, being a directive from Natalie, they do what they are told like well-trained puppies.

All night, I work hard at making friendly conversation while stuffing sushi rolls into my mouth. I love sushi, but it's not the kind of thing to try and eat and talk at the same time. It's not like you can take a mini bite, chew, talk, and repeat. Once you put a piece of sushi in your mouth, you're committed—for a good fifteen to twenty seconds. It can seem like forever when someone has asked you a question as you open your mouth and place the sushi in, and then stares at you while waiting for you to chew and answer. I finally give up on the sushi. I talk to Dusty mostly. He's the quieter of the two, and at least he can take his eyes off Natalie. His friend, Billy, not so much. The diamond ring on her finger doesn't seem to bother him one bit. Natalie, meanwhile, pays only half of her attention to him, as she knows nearly everyone who walks by the table. I can't believe with her absence, that I have now lived in this city longer than she, but she knows at least ten times the number of people I do. I make a mental note that I should get out more.

At one point in the evening, I do get my moment in the spotlight when a sports reporter from The Post walks by and recognizes me.

"Rainey! How the heck are you? I haven't seen you since you won silver in Vail, was it?"

I nod my head and turn flush at the acknowledgment.

Dusty looks at me astonished, as if to say, "Why didn't you tell me you were actually someone?"

"How are things?" the reporter inquires.

"Great. I'm getting ready to gear up for the season. I'm hoping to go to the Games next year."

"Good luck. I'll be watching for you. We'll do another spotlight story on you when the racing gets underway. Take it light on the Saki tonight. You're in training," he winks and smiles as he turns and heads away from the table.

Dusty turns to me and seems a bit more interested after that, but he isn't my type, and as much as Natalie wants me to have a boyfriend, I'm not desperate.

Once Nat has finally had enough socializing and is nearly hoarse from talking to every person who's walked by, she finally looks at me and gives me the shrug, as if to say, I'm ready to go, but if you're into Dusty, we can stay. I give her the, let's hit the road glance, and moments later we are saying our goodbyes and heading home.

"That was a good night, don't you think," Nat says as we pull out of the restaurant. "Dusty seemed interested in you."

"Yeah, sure. Whatever." My mind is already on Brian and the conversation we are going to have after I get home.

"Wow. You really are stuck on this Brian, aren't you?"

How can she always read my mind? "I know it sounds crazy, after only a couple of weeks, but I like talking, well, writing to him. His messages are … insightful. Sensitive. He doesn't try to act all macho or self-important."

"When are you going to meet him?"

"As soon as I get the guts to do it. I'm working on it. I promise." We ride in silence the rest of the way home. My mind is already on my computer date.

———

When I get home, I give myself a long look in the mirror. Even after five hours of being out, I still look pretty good. I wish Brian could see me in this dress. I know in this modern age, I could easily take a picture and send it to him tonight or we could even Skype, but then I remember last week's trip to the hair salon where I began the journey back to my normal hair color. It's not quite back to the blonde it was before, but it's definitely not the chocolate brown by which he's come to know me.

I slip out of my dress and put on an XL t-shirt. I hate to disappoint him, but I don't sleep in sexy lingerie. I mean, does any woman do that when a man is not on the other side of the bed? It simply isn't comfortable. Or practical. It's either a tee or nothing. Come to think of it, most men would probably prefer nothing anyway.

I'm nervous. I don't know why. It's not like we're meeting in person, but I feel like he's going to ask questions I won't want to answer, and it seems harder to avoid answering when he's there in real time waiting for a reply.

I log onto MFEO and check to see if he's online. He answers immediately.

Are you home now?
Yeah, I just walked in the door.

I have often been called out on the fact that I still use the words walked and walking—like we walked here, or I just walked in the door, but it's habit. And besides, one can get the point. In a wheelchair, the more accurate comparison to walking is pushing, as in *I just pushed a mile to the store*, but it's just as easy to say walk. Misleading, maybe. But, it's not an unusual statement.

How was the night out?
My night out was fun. Had some sushi, talked to some folks.

Meet any cute guys?
No. By default, I did get stuck talking to a guy, but I definitely wasn't into him. By the time you're our age, you can size people up pretty quickly. And

he wasn't the one.

Well, that's good to hear. I guess that means I have made the cut?

So far. But don't mess up.

I'm trying to be on my best behavior, but sometimes it's hard only being able to sit back and wonder what you are thinking when you read my messages. How do I know you're not making gagging noises as you read through what I've written?

You know this because I write you back!

Okay, good point.

What did you do tonight?

I decided to pick up my nephew and take him to the movies. Casey's at that awkward age, about to get his license, but not quite there, so a night out consists of asking his dad to drive him and his buddies somewhere. It makes him crazy to have to do that, and I think being his uncle instead of his dad, he feels more like he can relax and have a guys' night out without his dad overseeing the whole thing. Plus, he's good at opening up to me and talking about what's on his mind. The funny thing is he wanted to talk about girls and dating. I hardly feel like an expert on the subject, so I don't know what light I could shed on his crush on some girl named Rachel.

Well, despite the fact that you are not currently hitched, I'd like to believe you still have more experience than a soon-to-be sixteen-year-old.

Good point. I gave him the best advice I could.

I smile at Brian's honesty.

Can I ask you something?
Sure. Shoot.
Do you sing in the shower?

Huh, I think to myself? *I'm braced for some deep, probing question and he asks about singing in the shower.*

Where did that come from?

Just wondering. Are you going to answer the question?

Doesn't everyone sing in the shower?

Why is it that when you don't want to answer a question, you always reply with another question?

Busted. He's picked up on my tactics. Yes, I sing in the shower. But that's because I live alone and I can. I always turn my music on in the morning when I'm getting ready for work.

What's your favorite shower song?

Hmmm ... that's a tough question. What do you sing in the shower?

Well, I think I'd have to list one of my all-time favorites as AC/DC, *Back in Black*. Now stop answering questions with more questions. What's your favorite?

Reading that, I can't believe that we're both AC/DC-in-the-shower-listeners. What are the odds?

> Okay ... it depends on my mood, but, not to be a copycat, just the other morning I started my day off with AC/DC too, *Shook Me All Night Long*. That's a good scream in the shower kind of song. Happy now?
>
> **I am, actually. And happy to know we have something in common. I suppose that means we could get along in the shower, if nothing else.**
>
> Works for me, I won't argue with that.

I think about us taking a shower together. In his mind, I know he's imagining a tall, thin, naked woman, plastered against the length of his body, and again I feel as if I'd be a disappointment to him. This conversation is getting a lot less fun. But he's none the wiser, so he keeps at it.

> **OK, what's your favorite song to listen to when you work out?**
>
> That's easy. I'm a Rocky fan. *Eye of the Tiger*. You?
>
> ***Lose Yourself*—Eminem.**
>
> OK, my turn. Best car tune?
>
> **Bugs Bunny.**
>
> Remember how you said you didn't like how you couldn't tell if I was making gagging noises? Let me end the suspense. I'm making them now.
>
> **OK, best car tune ... *I Love Rock n Roll*—Joan**

Jett.

Not bad, I'll go with that. *500 Miles*—The Pretenders.

What about best song to play at work?

I'm pretty much stuck with "the wheels on the bus go 'round and 'round ..." First graders, you know?

Right. I like to listen to a little jazz or something without words when I work, so I don't find myself singing along instead of putting words to paper.

I pause a second too long as I wait for another question to come to mind, which doesn't happen. Instead, he says,

Maybe we could make a whole playlist of our favorite songs. Our soundtrack. Then we will have something to think of each other until you're ready to meet.

I like that idea. It's sort of romantic, for a guy and all. OK, what is the one song that reminds you of high school?

Sweet Child of Mine—Guns N' Roses. **You?**

Oops! ... I did it Again – Britney Spears. Best happy song?

Well, *Happy*. Duh! Pharrell Williams.

I Gotta Feeling—Black Eyed Peas. What about the best breakup song?

We haven't even met yet, and you're already

talking about breaking up?

A girl can't be too prepared, I type. Then I sit back and think about it. Brian probably thinks I'm being funny. How can he know that's what I think about most? What happens if we meet and things don't go well? As hard as I try to push the thought to the back of my mind, it continually resurfaces.

> If you insist, but I prefer to think we're going to hit it off. How about *Here Without You*—3 Doors Down?
>
> I'm thinking a woman's version of angry. *You Outta Know*—Alanis Morissette.
>
> Yes, that is angry, isn't it? OK ... our theme song?

Oh boy. What do I answer to this one?

> Thinking of songs on the spur of the moment is hard. You've got me backed into a corner, so I am going to default to a song from a movie my mom used to call her guilty pleasure. One of the top pop culture love songs of her twenties—*The Time of My Life*, from *Dirty Dancing*.
>
> Cheesy, but I like it. I like that you like it ... for us.

All I can do is smile. I have no idea what to say in return, so I stumble and think for a second. And before I can type anything else:

> May?
> Yeah?

He suddenly changes direction on me. **How many other guys are you currently corresponding with?**

Funny thing is, yours was the first and only profile I responded to. I've gotten a few other messages from people who have responded to my profile, but all of those messages have ended up in the trash. I hate to be cliché, but you had me at hello. I liked what you wrote in your profile. It made an impression on me. How about you?

I've been online for the past few months. Talked to a few women. Had a couple of dates. But I like you. At least the part of you you've let me get to know. I hope we can meet soon. I know you didn't want to jump into anything but think about it. I don't want to rush you, but at the same time, my curiosity is getting the better of me.

You know what curiosity did to the cat don't you?

I do. And I'm willing to risk it.

We spend the better part of three hours online, back and forth, alternately talking and making our playlist, when finally, I decide it's time to say goodnight. Brian says he is tired too, so we promise we'll keep things status quo until I am comfortable with meeting.

Have a good Sunday, I type to him.

Considering it's 3:30 in the morning and the day

has technically begun, I have to say it's already looking promising.

My heart skips a beat. Goodnight, Brian.
Sleep with the angels, May Belle.

My heart feels so full tonight—like all of the holes have been plugged. The hurt is gone and in its place, is a feeling that good things await. I am cradled in love—or, like, anyway. For the first time in forever, I fall asleep with a smile on my face.

CHAPTER 8

I CAN'T STAND IT ANYMORE. EVEN THOUGH THE blinds in my room are closed, I can see the sun shining through the cracks, and I can't stay in bed any longer. I roll over and look at the clock, 11:30 in the morning. At first, I can only think about how exhausted I am, but then I start replaying in my mind my conversation with Brian last night. It was so nice to be able to talk, real time, about anything and everything.

I pick up my cell phone from the side of my bed and see two missed calls from my dad. Oh shit! It's Sunday, and he's been expecting me since ten o'clock for our weekend quality time breakfast. I hit his number on speed dial and apologize profusely for not being in contact earlier. I know this scares the crap out of my dad when he doesn't hear from me because his mind always goes to the worst-case scenario. I learned a long time ago always to remain in close contact with him and never be late with a phone call. After I calm him down and beg for forgiveness, I ask him if we can have our quality time over dinner instead, and he reluctantly agrees. I know he looks forward to our Sunday morning visits because he's lonely. I can recognize his yearning for more human contact than he gets from his coworkers, students, and occasional golf buddies, but I don't think he knows how to get back on track—it's been so long.

It's been the same for me, but now I have an idea. It'll have to wait until tonight, though. Right now, I have all this nervous energy flowing through my veins, and since it's only September, it's too early to hit the slopes to burn it off. There's only one thing to do … head to the racetrack. Besides, I already told Jake I'd be there. I suppose I should get up and stick to the plan.

I jump out of bed, figuratively speaking of course, and head for the shower. I turn on my music and blast "Back in Black," the first song of the Rainey-and-Brian playlist I downloaded last night, and transfer from my chair to the shower bench with a smile on my face. Even though I should have turned the water on to ice cold to wake me up out of my overtired stupor, I instead take a leisurely shower with the hottest water my body can stand. I need to relax my muscles and get myself in the zone, even though I will probably only do a couple of laps at the track and spend most of the day doing mechanical work on the car rather than driving.

I pack up my gear and head out to the garage. As I hit the button to open the electric door, I sit facing my two cars, each of which takes me to a different part of my life. Regardless of which car I get into, I am likely headed to I-70, the highway that crosses Colorado from east to west. If I get in the dark gray Subaru Outback, I am typically headed west to the mountains and my life as an elite skier and member of the USA Ski team. If I jump into the cherry red Audi RS 3 LMS, I'm likely headed east to Crestone Raceway, to enjoy my passion and hobby of racing cars. Today it's the car on the left, which will take me, hopefully speeding-ticket-free, to the track where I will drive it at speeds of 100 miles per hour.

Crestone, a road-racing course, is about forty-five minutes from my house, even though it feels like it's in the middle of farmland. Although it's still miles from the actual Kansas border, Eastern Colorado gives in to the flatness of western Kansas. People who don't live in Colorado assume we only have mountains, but we have plains too. This is where a new auto course was built a few years ago to attract attention to some of the smaller Colorado towns. They run a wide variety of races and different car classes, and occasionally host events with some of the big names in racing. During the downtime, however, it's ideal for the locals like me. They have a massive bank of garages where you can work on your car and a track with open training hours.

As I drive to the track, I think about my dad's racing career and how, between having a family and then ultimately the accident, he threw away his passion, as if somehow, he no longer deserved to do what made him the happiest.

When my parents were first married, and before Sunny was born, my dad slowly began to phase out of his professional racing career, but I had the opportunity on several occasions to watch him in action in a handful of the premier events, facing off with some of the biggest names in the sport. He was known for having many talents behind the wheel, as his experience spanned a variety of styles of racing, including autocross, dirt track racing, and even hill climbs. But his specialty was putting the pedal to the metal on an oval track. He was a stock car racer at heart, and I looked up to his talent and dedication. It was exciting for me to witness as a young kid and it made an impression on me. I wanted to follow in his footsteps. A couple of times, when my dad would travel to races, my mom and I traveled along, and I got to experience firsthand the remarkable spectacle of pro racing. It was a much different atmosphere than at our local Colorado track where I learned to drive.

In professional racing, for both driver and crew, there was an incredible amount of work involved in getting the win, but I will never forget the time I watched my dad hold the winner's trophy over his head. It was the 1987 NASCAR Winston Cup Championship, and my dad raced alongside the likes of Dale Earnhardt. I was six years old, and it was the last pro race he would do. The speed of the race was dizzying and the noise was deafening. Watching his mechanics jump from the pit wall and change four tires in under thirty seconds astounded me. Boy, those guys could move. Even more unbelievable is that by today's standards, that's slow. Today, pit crews can turn a set of tires in under twenty seconds.

When my dad retired, he moved over to SportsCar racing, which lends itself to the style of our local track. He kept his involvement and commitment much less intense than the professional racing he had done before. He was able to race alongside amateurs and those who raced for a hobby, allowing him to share his knowledge with those, mostly men, who wanted to follow in his footsteps, but maybe didn't have the skill or money backing their racing careers. It allowed my dad to actually be a husband and father, rather than a traveling driver who was on the road more than he was at home. It was during this more relaxed time in his racing career he taught me all I know about cars and going fast.

I learned quickly that road racing was what interested me the most. I would always kid my dad about his professional career and say, "Didn't going around in constant circles make you dizzy?" Even though I knew better, and saw it for the action and excitement, it still seemed to me that at some point it must get monotonous. But on the road courses, there are left turns and right turns, ups and downs. More like the nature of life itself, if you want to get philosophical about it.

Few days in my life have been as exciting as when I got my first car to race. It was a blue Corvette, automatic, and I drove it with traditional hand controls. But it was the presentation of the gift that made it even more special. For a while during my senior year in college, when I would see my dad on the weekends, he seemed more upbeat, like he had a little pep in his step. I thought maybe he was starting to make a turnaround, perhaps he'd found a woman to date, and I was so hopeful he was getting the nerve to move on and get back to living. I didn't know what had made the difference, but it didn't matter, I was happy for him. But on the twentieth of May, when we arrived home from my college graduation,

I realized what it was. Sitting in the driveway was a vintage blue Corvette with two parallel white stripes cresting it like a rainbow and topped with a prodigious red bow on the roof of the car. It was the car I had been helping him restore before the accident, and he finally completed it for my college graduation and birthday. So, while all of my friends were backpacking through Europe for their post-college reward, my dad put me in the trusty hands of a racing coach, and I was hitting speeds of 100 mph for the first time on my own.

When my dad first bought the car as a project car, I was twelve. We went to pick it up and brought it home on the trailer. Arriving home, I remember my mom coming out to the driveway shaking her head but smiling. "Thom," was all she said. But she knew it was his passion. It was as if he were bringing home his third child—almost as proud as when Sunny and I came into this world. *Almost.* He was beaming.

We got up bright and early the next day and headed to the local garage where my dad stored his current car and helped his buddies work on their cars. When we drove up in the Corvette, I could tell he was the envy of his group. He'd be riding this wave of pride for a long time. He announced, in front of all his friends (I have witnesses)—the car would be mine upon my college graduation. I couldn't believe it! At the time, I was fully immersed in my father's devotion to passing the skill of racing to the next generation and couldn't wait until I would follow in his footsteps. We spent hours at the go-kart track with Dad coaching intensely, while the other kids and parents were there for recreation. For my dad and me, this was a building block to my future auto sports career, and

I listened intently to every word, direction, or tip he'd give. When we weren't at the track, we'd be in the garage tinkering on the car. He wanted me to know the ins and outs of the machines I was operating. My path to racing was full throttle. Until the accident.

After Mom died, everything came to a screeching halt. The car went straight to storage with not another word. The days at the track were a thing of the past, and I couldn't even gather the courage to confront my dad about it. Ultimately, it was in a car that our lives had been shattered. And I was too young to realize, following my accident, that I would be able to drive again using my hands and hand controls. But he didn't allow me to get my driver's license until I had almost graduated high school. And I never saw the Corvette again. That was, until graduation.

I recognized the gift as an extraordinary sacrifice by my father. For him to be able to cast his demons aside to restore the car, I knew, on the one hand, how painful it must have been. On the other hand, there was a part of him that returned home during that time. Prior to mom entering his life, cars were his heart and soul. He grew up with them, turned to them for comfort—a cure-all for everything from boredom to stress to frustration. I know it was a bittersweet time working on that car, but my dad is loyal. He holds true to his promises and doesn't renege on commitments. It's his blessing and his curse and why, I presume, he has not moved on from losing my mom. His commitment runs too deep. And even if he loved working on the car to get it ready for me, I think he felt guilty for recovering his passion when my mom would never have the chance.

Once my dad fulfilled his promise of restoring and gifting the car, and it was now in my hands, he retreated into his funk and didn't want to talk about it. I knew it was a labor of love and tough for him to work on it and give it to me, but I had hoped for more. I wished it would reignite his desire to get involved in the racing community again. But it didn't. He got me set up at the track with a crew and coach, but aside from coming to a race here and there, he silently bowed out, and I didn't push it. I knew his reasons, right or wrong. If I wanted a racing career, I would have to take the initiative of being in charge of it.

That car is back in storage at the moment because there isn't room for three cars in my garage. I love to take it out occasionally because of the memories it brings back for me, but for racing, I have graduated to a more technologically advanced car with more sophisticated hand controls, which allow me to be competitive with the other racers. In the Corvette, I was always at a disadvantage because the car was an automatic and extremely slow off the line, in racing terms. Now, in my division, other hobbyist racers see me as a force to be reckoned with. I have the car, handling skills, confidence, and racing knowledge to beat many of the racers at my level. And, might I add, at our track, that's a bunch of guys.

I imagine Brian and wonder what he would think of a race car driving girlfriend. Would he appreciate this sport of equal parts danger and beauty? Would he watch my races in amazement as I watched my dad when I was a kid? Only time will tell.

After driving thirty miles outside of town on the highway, I take the exit that leads to the track. I drive down the two-lane road. If I had a passenger in my car who didn't know any better, he might think I was taking him on a corn harvesting adventure. Instead, as I crest a hill of the two-lane county road, my heart starts to race when I see the cars doing training laps. This is the place I call home. Well, my eastern home. Here, I don't have to worry about being defined by my chair. When I'm in the car, whether racing or training, my chair is nowhere near me. I am free of the perceptions of a wheelchair, and I become car racer. Period. I am on the same level as my competitors. The other racers know me, and they know my skill, so I never feel out of place. I don't feel less than. Here, I feel complete confidence in who I am and what I'm capable of. This is what hours in the car teaches you.

I see the sign for the track, and as I take a left and enter the half-mile drive to the Crestone Raceway entrance gates, I think to myself about the last guy who made my heart race and gave me a smile from ear to ear, like I have now when I think about Brian. This other man is the one I will see as soon as I get to the track and drive up to my pit stall. Jake Coulton.

A couple of years ago, when I became solidly enmeshed in the racing crowd at Crestone, a buzz began around our tight-knit community. Some hotshot had moved to town and was about to join our happy racing family. I remember the exact moment I met him. I was in the paddock talking to the track manager, Philip, when I looked up and saw this drop-dead gorgeous man walking toward us. My heart skipped so many beats I thought I'd fall out of my chair and pass out.

I lost my train of thought as I was telling Phil about how my car seemed to be handling a little loose. The words dribbled out of my mouth until I finally became speechless, and Phil turned his head to see what had gotten me all flustered.

"Oh Rainey, that's Jake. Jake Coulton." Phil gave me the quick 4-1-1 on this guy. High school star running back, played college ball. "Started in go-karts like you, and has been racing most his life, but started getting serious a couple of years ago when he made an impressive showing in the SportsCar Challenge," Phil said. "Helluva racer. Moved to Colorado for a job, but I suspect we'll see him racing full-time in the near future. You're looking at one of the up-and-comers in professional racing."

Whew. If I could have been standing, my knees would have been knocking. He had a bad boy look to him but in the most gorgeous way. *He could be a male model,* I thought as I stared at him walking confidently in our direction. His straight hair went every which way, but in that, so-messy-it-actually-looks-good style. It was brown with streaks of natural blonde highlights. His face was a pout, framed by a narrow and perfectly trimmed beard and mustache. He wore a white t-shirt and jeans. As he walked toward us, I had to work to keep the saliva in my mouth instead of drooling all over the place. I tried not to stare, but I couldn't stop. He was plain hot. As he walked, I watched him closely. Not only because I decided he was the best-looking guy I had seen in ages, but he walked with the most interesting gait. Sort of side-to-side like a bowlegged cowboy, instead of straight ahead.

As Phil stared at me staring at Jake, Phil said, "What you

don't know is that under those Levi's, Jake has a couple of the most high-tech mechanical legs you've ever seen."

"You mean prosthetics?"

"Yep," Philip spouted out. "Double-leg amputee. Wrapped himself around a tree on his motorcycle one cold rainy night a few years ago. I suppose you could say you and Jake have a few things in common. The racetrack saved your lives, not from your respective accidents, but from yourselves. Apparently, Jake found refuge at his home track and rehabbed his mind by going fast and loving it.

When Jake reached Philip and me, he stuck out his hand to Phil and introduced himself. "You must be the guy to see around here, I reckon?" he asked.

"Sure am. I'm Philip, the track manager. And this is Rainey. Don't let her chair fool you … she's schooled many a guy on this track."

"Yeah, well you must be good. I've already heard about you," he said with a sexy southern twang. Up close he was even more gorgeous, with dimples as deep as craters when he smiled.

"I've heard about you too. You're pretty much the shit … is the word on the street," I said, trying to play it cool. I held out my hand disguised in a handshake, but I really just wanted to hold his hand.

"Yeah," he said, cracking a half-smile. "Don't say it too loud. I'm my own secret weapon. Don't blow it."

I couldn't help but immediately start crushing on him. I gushed back.

We stood there and talked. As Jake told us his car was out

in his trailer and asked where he should put it, my eyes stayed on him, never straying an inch as we talked about cars and racing and his home track. And as soon as I was fully in love-at-first-sight-mode, up walks a tall drink of water. Flowing strawberry blonde hair, straight cut Levis on her model-thin legs, black tank top, and a flannel—that must have come from Jake's closet—on for warmth. She looked like a cross between the most dazzling woman you've ever seen and a NASCAR race fan. She came up and planted a big one on his cheek.

"Hey, baby," she said to him, and he grinned widely.

She was as bubbly as the day is long, and stuck her hand right out to me and, sounding as southern as Jake, said, "Hi, my name is Amber. Amber Coulton."

Aahhh, another good one taken. But as much as I wanted to hate Amber for her luck, she was nothing but sweetness with a cherry on top. *And what a great looking couple they make,* I thought.

The three of us became fast friends and spent a great deal of time together on the track and off. We bonded over the experiences that got us to where we were but also talked about the future, our goals, and more than once, my love life.

"Rainey, I don't get it," Jake would say. "How is it that a girl like you, who races cars and downhill skis, is tough as nails but cleans up real classy, does not have a boyfriend? I mean, if I were single, I'd love a girlfriend who knows the first thing about cars and tools and goin' fast."

Amber would grin and elbow him and say, "But you're not single darlin', so it's a moot point."

"The least we can do, though, is help Rainey find this

eligible bachelor," he replied.

I loved hanging out with Jake and Amber, and over the past few years, I've gotten to know them well. Jake is one year older than I am and Amber is a year younger than I, and they're both from the south. Amber, from Mississippi, crossed into Jake's home state and went to Auburn for college, while Jake played ball not too far from his neck of the woods at the University of Alabama. They should be rivals, but they seemed to have gotten that part worked out.

When Jake first graduated from college, he took a job in construction management. He was young and single and lived modestly. He liked his toys, and one of those was his prized possession, a Honda crotch rocket, which he used to drive back and forth to work instead of a car. And, although he was a good bike handler, he was a young male who liked to go fast. One day, the rain had started to come down as he headed home. He was taking it easy on the roads but was also trying to dodge the heavier part of the storm, which was imminently approaching. As he pushed the limits of what a bike can do in the rain, a car turned in front of him on a two-lane, winding road, and Jake lost control, spinning out. With only momentum behind him and a tree in front of him, Jake could see in a blink of an eye that things weren't going to end well, but there was nothing he could do to stop what happened next. The tree won, as his body tangled around it, breaking multiple bones and severing arteries. And, even though the driver of the car that turned into him never stopped or even looked back, another car was on the scene within seconds. As luck would have it, the driver was a doctor, accompanied by his wife. Knowing that Jake's life was at stake, the doctor didn't bother with an ambulance. He called the cops to report the incident, put tourniquets on Jake's legs, and sped him in the back of his Mercedes to the hospital as Jake continued to bleed. Jake's injuries were so severe that had the doctor not made such split-second decisions, Jake might not have survived. As it was, he had to have both legs amputated—one above the knee and one below. The accident left him angry and ashamed, and it took him years before he came out of his funk. But he credits the raceway, and then Amber, for his recovery. Now, he says, he doesn't give the incident and injury a second thought. "So what if putting my legs on is part of getting dressed in the morning? The alternative is, I could be dead. I got a second chance, and I intend to live it."

Amber still flinches when she hears him talk that way, because she knows auto racing can be every bit as dangerous as the motorcycle, but if it's what keeps him sane and passionate about being alive, she'll take it.

Of course, Amber's daddy loves it. Even though Jake has two strikes against him—the fact that he played for the Crimson Tide and doesn't race NASCAR, her father loves the rugged boy from the south who enjoys going head-to-head at speeds that would make most people's heads spin. Jake's good enough he will eventually make a living racing cars, but for now, he keeps construction jobs going on the side because he needs the benefits. Amber is about bursting out of her skin to get pregnant. She's already begun to orchestrate her exit out of her job as a paralegal. She hates it anyway. She had intended to go to law school, but after she met Jake and they moved to Colorado, she decided it wasn't her path. I'm not sure she knows what her path is, but she seems to be content to be the lovely bride of the sexy up-and-coming racer that is Jake Coulton.

Now, two years after Jake and Amber arrived, I consider them my next closest friends to Nat, and the ones I come to whenever I need advice, which happens to be today.

"Hey, Jake," I nod and wave as I push my chair up to the garages. He looks as great as ever, wearing a tight black t-shirt and jeans. Something I've learned about Jake is that he has two looks. Black t-shirt with faded out jeans or white t-shirt with faded out jeans. The white t-shirt is his dress-up outfit. But truth be told, he'd be drop-dead gorgeous if he wore a brown paper bag.

I pull right up next to his car, and he's fiddling with his brakes. Jake likes to work on his car as much as he likes driving it. Says he always needs something to keep his hands busy, and his car is as good a toy as any to be tinkering with.

"What's up wheelie girl?" Jake says to me. "Your brow is furrowed."

Jake is the only person who can get away with calling me wheelie girl, and he's probably the only person I can talk to about why I feel so stuck in my current situation. I explain to him how I got talked into this online dating mess and tell him all about Brian. I squeamishly admit my omissions about my true situation and throw in the part about my fears of what Brian will think of me if I let this get to the meeting phase.

"First of all, Abbott," Jake begins, "dating isn't easy or fun for pretty much anyone. It doesn't matter if you're able-bodied or not. I mean, I guess there is a time when you're young, and it's fun to meet a bunch of folks, sow your oats, and test your pickup lines. But when it comes to genuinely wanting to find the one, it gets much more complicated because it's not about a roll in the hay or someone to hang out with for a couple of months. There's letting someone see who you really are, inside and out. And when they don't like what they see, whether in the first minute they meet you or eight months of dating down the line, it hurts. It's personal, like you're not good enough. But at the same time, if you don't lay your cards on the table, you can't get to that spot where they know you the way they need to for a lifelong connection. It's kind of a catch-22 ... you're afraid to let them get to know you because you don't want to get hurt, but you'll never get the relationship you want if you don't give it your full effort.

"I had the same concerns when I met Amber. I was pretty fresh off my motorcycle accident and scared to death. I didn't even feel whole in my own body, and here I was trying to get her to feel like I had something to offer. There she was, tall and charming and, frankly, quite intimidating. I'd see her at the park in Birmingham where we were both living at the time, and I knew every day, like clockwork, what would happen next when she'd be out walking Lady, and I'd let Beau off his leash, because he'd walk over and start sniffin' that Cocker Spaniel of hers."

"Smart," I say. "Let the dog do your dirty work."

"Yeah, you got it. Eventually, Amber and I started talking and walking the dogs together. I don't know how I thought I was fooling her with my legs and all, but I always wore jeans or running pants and never broached the subject with her. Finally, one day when we were saying our goodbyes, she said, *'Jake Coulton, are you ever gonna ask me out? Cause if you're not, Lady and I are going to start walking elsewhere, and I sure as heck am going to start sleeping in later. I'm tired of waiting.'*

"She caught me off guard because I was still trying to decide what I was going to tell her about my legs, but I only had a moment to figure it out, or I was gonna lose her. I figured if I didn't ask her out, she'd think I was a pansy and walk away anyway. Guess I didn't have anything to lose. I looked her straight in the eyes, pulled up my pant legs and said, "I'd have asked you out a long time ago, but I was afraid you wouldn't go for a guy who has no legs."

"*'Jake Coulton, I am ashamed of you,'* she said. *'How shallow do you think I am that I would believe you are merely a pair of legs? Do you not realize that I schedule my day around walking Lady at 5:30 every morning, even when I'd rather be sleeping because I know I'll run into you? Do you not know how much I love to hear your goals about a career in construction management, or your secret wish of getting picked up by a race team so you can spend all your days driving around in circles? Do you realize I have listened ad nauseam about what happened on Monday Night Football when I don't even give a damn about that sport? And, for the record, I can see. I've watched you walk. Doesn't bother me because I look into your kind brown eyes, and I see a man who believes the best in people, who has stopped to share a few passes with a little boy who was kicking his soccer ball against the tree before you showed up, and I've seen the way you look directly into my eyes when I'm talking, like nothing else on earth matters in that moment. Why, oh why, do you think I'd give a flying hoot that you've got prosthetics for legs?'"*

I watch his expression as he recounts the story, voicing Amber's monologue in the most perfect womanly southern accent. I see his eyes water up, thinking about how she loved him no matter what. I am envious at how it all seemed to fall into place.

He continues. "Rainey, they don't call it falling in love for no reason. It's like being out of control but in a good way. You can't control how Brian is going to feel about you, and you shouldn't want to try. If it's right, you'll know it. And it will happen naturally. He won't see the chair, and you'll forget about it too. But you have to be willing to take the risk, or you'll never know what might have been."

I breathe a huge sigh. "Jake, I know you're right. This isn't the first day I've lived with myself. But what do I do about it? What if it's not the Jake and Amber kind of fairy tale?"

"Rainey, there are going to be people who don't want to date you because of the chair, and there will be others who don't want to date you because you're a blonde, because of your tough personality, or because you know more about tools than most men. And that's okay. But there will be someone who loves you because you're easy on the eyes and smart as a whip, and for a bucket of other reasons. He's out there. I know it. I promise."

That's what I love about Jake, and it makes me envious of Amber. She is married to such a kind and understanding man. *How is it that some girls get so lucky?*

I spend the rest of the afternoon pondering it and listening to the Brian soundtrack I made in the wee hours this morning while I tinker on my car to get it ready for a spin around the track.

CHAPTER 9

ON THE HIGHWAY BACK TO TOWN, AFTER AN exhilarating afternoon of training runs in my car, I am a happy camper. I'm not sure if it's the speed of the car and the record time I accomplished on my training lap, or if it was Jake's pep talk.

Maybe it's simply the suspense and excitement I have felt around Brian for the past three weeks. Regardless of the reasons, when I open the door of my dad's house, and he comes around the corner from the living room to greet me, an ear to ear grin has surfaced on my face.

"Rainey, you seem to be in an awfully good mood today. Want to share? I don't remember the last time I saw you grin like the Cheshire Cat. What gives?"

"Dad, I think I'm in love!"

"Rainey, that's wonderful news. Who's the charming fellow?"

"I don't know, exactly. I haven't actually met him."

"Hmmm. I think you're going to have to elaborate. Listen, I bought a couple of ready-made crusts and all the fixins, so you can create your own pizza. How about we multitask and cook and talk at the same time? It sounds like I'm in for an interesting story. He winks at me and nods his head toward the kitchen.

I follow him through the dining room and into the kitchen. As he opens the refrigerator he asks, "Is this that new style of dating you young people do these days, where you meet in those chat rooms or something?"

"Not in a chat room, Dad. It's online dating. You go to a dating site, set up your profile, talk about who you are, what you're looking for, and then you … well … go shopping. We met through this site, and we have only corresponded via email up until Saturday night. That's when we started talking in real time on the computer. It's called instant messaging, and you can type back and forth in a conversation."

"So, what happens next? Are you ever going to meet him?" Dad asks, somewhat confused as he neatly layers rounds of pepperoni on his pizza.

"Interesting you should ask because technically that's how dating works. You have to meet the person and go out. But I'm scared, Dad. I'm worried about what he's going to think of me," I say, surprised by my candor.

"What do you mean, Rainey? You're a joy to be around, thoughtful, and a good conversationalist; you have so many talents.

"I know, it seems like it wouldn't be that hard, but I feel consumed by this stupid wheelchair. Face it, Dad, I'm not your typical girl."

"But your individuality is what makes you so special. You're one of a kind. I know I'd much rather date a unique and wonderful woman like you, than a bumbling, babbling idiot whom I didn't find interesting or intriguing."

"Easy for you to say." I decide to make a smiley face with black olives on my pizza. "You're supposed to say stuff like that. You're my dad. It's not that easy with a regular guy."

"How do you know, Rainey? You've barely dated since Nate, and that was more than ten years ago. I know you women don't realize this, but guys grow up too. They mature—eventually—and most of them view women with a much wider lens than perhaps they did in high school or college. Before you write anyone off, make sure you're keeping your assumptions and judgements in check."

My heart feels heavy with the frankness of his dialogue, but regardless of my fears, I see the perfect opening to call my dad out on his own avoidance. "Okay, Dad. Then two can play this game. What about you? You haven't tried either. I know you consider Mom your one true love and soul mate, but do you think you could ever find a connection with another woman again?"

"Oh, Rainey. It's so complicated."

"How can you give me a pep talk about dating and how you'll never know if you don't try, yet when the tables are turned, you back off and act the same way? What's complicated about it?"

"One point for you, Missy, but it's different. I had the greatest love on earth. Your mom was the apple of my eye. I adored her. She was the cat's meow. The bee's knees. All those things. I had her more than fifteen years in the best relationship I could ever have imagined, and I can't fathom having that with anyone else."

"I know, Dad, I loved her too. And I saw the way you looked at her and acted around her. But I think there has got to be a woman out there who will once again make you feel the way Mom did."

"You might be right, Rainey. It's not like I haven't thought about it, but at my age, I don't know where to look. I don't go out. And when I'm with the guys, we're not running into women on the golf course. And I certainly haven't met anyone around the university who floats my boat."

"Dad, I'm going to tell you the same thing Natalie told me, 'MFEO dot com, baby.'"

"MFEO?"

"Made for Each Other," I say as if he is so last year for not being in the know.

"Do old people like me really get on there?

"Dad, you're not old, and yes, "grown ups" look for love online too. Haven't you ever thought of how nice it would be to have a date once in a while? Go to the movies, hold hands in front of the fireplace? Long walks on the beach?" I feel like I'm turning into a commercial for some lover's all-inclusive vacation resort.

"I guess, I've thought about it," Dad says, "but never seriously considered that there might be someone out there for me. Most of the women I know are married, and the ones who aren't, well, let's just say I know why. But your mom was perfect for me. I have such special memories of her. I'm not sure I'd know how to start over again."

"Oh, it's like riding a bike," I say as if I'm one to talk.

After dinner, I lead my dad into his office and boot up his computer. I'd seen him spend hours in front of his laptop and now he is looking at it as though it might bite. I grab the keyboard and the mouse and take the wheel.

"Okay, here's how we do it. Let's see what we can find."

I log him onto MFEO, and we start working on his profile, which I have to admit, is kind of weird. I mean, I want no part of *sexy, fifty-something engineering professor seeks hot mama for romantic nights and, heaven forbid, sex. TMI,* I think. But at the same time, I would love to see my dad with a woman who makes him happy. Who wakes up the romantic within him and makes him smile. It's been too long since I've seen my dad genuinely beaming. I think we both deserve to fall in love, and if neither one of us is going to have the guts to do it alone, we'll have to embark on this adventure together. No matter how weird it is. I trudge forward.

I look over at my dad, and he seems terrified as I introduce him to the website.

"C'mon, Dad, you have to do this. Let go. Think about it. What if Mom had survived the accident and you didn't. Would you want Mom being lonely for the rest of her life? Just going to work every day, coming home and sitting on the couch and watching TV, while eating frozen dinners?"

"Hey, are you saying my life is lonely and boring?"

"I'm asking you what you think? If she were in your shoes, wouldn't you want her doing things she loved and being with someone who could give her companionship, and affection and…" I stopped mid-sentence and looked at him. He looked slightly wounded, but at the same time, pensive.

"Mom would have wanted you to do this. She would want you to be happy. And if she's not here to make you happy, don't you owe it to yourself and to her to find someone who can be for you what she no longer can?"

"Okay, you win." He let out a heavy sigh.

"At least give it a try, and I'll never bother you with it again. Deal?"

"Deal."

"Now, let's see. We have to put together a profile for you. 'Handsome old man seeks …' I glance at this face, which has a look of amusement, telling me he is warming up to the idea.

"What do we say?" he asks.

"Well … what would mom say she liked about you? What was it that attracted her to you?" I use my famous answer a question with a question trick.

He looks at me with a stare, loaded with emotion. I can tell he is conflicted and unsure about what he is doing—sort of like my mom is watching down on him, waiting to see his next move. But I can see, I've also piqued his attention. *Will he or won't he?*

He slowly reaches over, takes the keyboard from my lap, and inhales. He doesn't exhale right away; he's actually, nervously holding his breath.

Hesitant But Willing to Give Love Another Try

Appropriate title, I think, *all things considered.* He types very slowly, and I watch as each carefully thought-out word appears on screen.

About me: *It's been over thirty-four years since I had my last date as an eligible bachelor. I was twenty-three when I proposed to the love of my life, sitting by a lake in Wisconsin over the Fourth of July. We were on vacation with her family, and I had requested her father's permission, before whisking her off on a "walk" that would end with asking her to stay with me until death did us part. Unfortunately, that time came much sooner than I ever imagined and now it's been seventeen years, and I've been fearful to give love another try. I admit I didn't know when it would be time to move on, or if it was okay to want to. But after all these years, I am opening myself up to the possibility that love doesn't have to come only once in a lifetime.*

What Are You Looking for in a Relationship?

This may sound overly idealistic or too sappy to be genuine, but it is truly how I feel. There are so few things in life that are truly ours. Money—it can slip through our hands—by greed, carelessness, or simply paying the tax bill. Time—how precious it is, but it too can be taken from us without consent. But our love, that is one of the few things we are born with that no one can take from us, and one thing we are free to give without condition or reservation. Love is unpredictable; that is what makes it exciting, fleeting, and worth it. If a woman chooses a man to love, there is nothing a man wouldn't do to experience such exhilaration. It makes him feel taller, stronger, smarter, with luck on his side. Everything is better, richer, and clearer when a man is loved by a woman.

This is the point where a man finds joy in what makes her happy, not in what rushed pleasures await him. To have a woman come from behind and drape her hair over him is magical, as it flows across his face. To kiss a woman's soft skin is incredible. To be holding hands and have her open her clasp, so his fingers interlace, this makes a man's heart flutter. Yet, he will hold perfectly still to maintain the moment, the rush. These are the small gestures; these make life worthwhile. To have her choose him above all others is worth everything. With a woman's love, all things are possible.

After all these years, I have finally admitted to myself how much of this I have missed and how I'm willing to put it all on the line to fall again for the one who makes me smile, makes my heart beat wildly, and who is prepared to love until the end.

As I read over my dad's shoulder, tears well up in my eyes. *No wonder I am a mess! What guy am I ever going to meet who can possibly match up to this?* Even his words, written so eloquently in this online profile, exude the raw emotion I saw him display so many times when he looked at my mom. My dad is rare, and I wonder if I have inherited this … is it a curse? …this feeling that goes so deeply, this feeling that, once it's been shattered, it seems impossible to put back together?

As my dad puts down the keyboard, he turns to me, and I can see there are tears in his eyes too. He has not written about the woman he is looking for; I can tell he has written about my mother.

He takes a deep sigh and returns to the present moment. To reality. To the fact that he has entered an online profile so that some woman on the other end of the computer might write him back.

I ponder our collective courage to step out of the darkness

which has enveloped our souls for so long. Being in this place I begin to understand our power to heal comes only from the willingness of our hearts to start to open, even a crack, and let hope stream in. At first, it's like turning on a light in the middle of the night—eyes squint, eyelids flutter in indecisiveness. Is it safe to open? Will it be painful or imposing? Will I gradually adjust to this new stimulus which might bring a new perspective? Should I give it the opportunity?

After I take a snapshot of him with my phone for his profile picture, we wrap up his personal descriptions and then get to work scanning the menu of love. We find him a couple of dreamy, wistful, and perhaps kindred souls and begin crafting messages to them.

"So, what's next?"

"We wait. We have to give them time to get on the computer and write you back."

"How long is that going to take?" he suddenly seems impatient, the door to his heart set on a timer while the fear grows that he may lose his nerve before the clock times out and the walls reemerge.

"Isn't it funny how we've gotten accustomed to living in a bottomless pit of dashed hope? Where it's more comfortable to look at the darkness and loss, instead of permitting ourselves to let go of the bad memories and tragedy? When I think about it, I know moving on is what Mom and Sunny would want for us, Dad. To know that in the light, love still exists for us. It's there and ready for us to grab it. But neither of us have had the courage to believe love is out there—whether you're looking for an encore or I'm beginning from square one."

CHAPTER 10

BY THE TIME I GET HOME, I'M BEAT. IT'S BEEN A
long weekend, and I think if I'm not in bed by eight o'clock,
I will never make it through Monday. Plus, I have to start
resting up. Next weekend I travel to Switzerland for some
of the final qualifying races before the Paralympics. Since I
traveled most of the summer skiing and have been training
hard in the gym, I feel confident about my abilities, even
though it's the beginning of October and the snow hasn't
even begun to fall in Colorado. I think my chances of making
the team are looking good, but now it's starting to get real.

Not so real, though, that I don't get on my computer and
send a message to Brian. I have always thought being in love
can either escalate your sports performance or it can tank it.
I guess it all depends on how things turn out. *Another reason to*

keep it low key for now, I think. As the autumn rain taps down on the roof, a slight breeze comes through the window and spits of water enter through the screen. I wonder how I got here—this man, I don't even know, yet I can't get him off my mind.

> Brian,
>
> How was your Sunday? Did you keep the momentum from the wee hours this morning or did you crash? I crashed and burned for sure—didn't wake up until 11:30, but I had a fun day even if it was an abbreviated version. And miraculously convinced my dad to sign up for MFEO. I'd like to say I inspired him to get back to dating since he hasn't dated at all since my mom died. I'm excited to see what happens. I would love to see him happy. I'm sure it would be difficult to see him with anyone but my mom, but I believe that if and while we are on this planet, we must make the best of what we've got, no matter what it is. It's not always going to be what we want or expect, but we have one chance and one chance only to live life, right? Roll with the punches, I always say.

The fact is, I rarely say that. I *think* I believe it. I wouldn't be where I am now, if I didn't believe it to some extent, but then again, with Brian, with dating, with the unknown, I think rolling with the punches is the thing I am least adept at. Oh well, it sounded like an upbeat statement to add. I want him to think I am lighthearted and before I can sign off, I leave him a question, the pleasure of which delights my curiosity.

I'm sorry for such a short message tonight, but it's time for me to sign off and hit the hay, but I have a question for you to ponder. What is something about you that no one else knows?

Sleep tight...

May Belle

We'll see what he says in the morning. In the meantime, I flip off the computer and head to bed. My eyes close and I'm immediately transported to dreamland.

When my alarm goes off, I struggle to stay with my dream, but the snippet of a tune that my phone keeps playing over and over again keeps me from being able to stay where I was. Ever since the accident, my dreams have perplexed me because even though in real life I have no use of my legs and I need my wheelchair to get around, in dreams, I am rarely in a wheelchair. When I do envision myself in a chair, I am able to get up, walk around, and even leave it behind. It's almost like a symbol for something, but it's not attached to me. It doesn't restrain me and doesn't hold me back. Many times, I even see myself skiing standing up, but then suddenly when it comes to race time, I can never start the race because I have a foot injury or leg injury that keeps me from going all the way and doing what I want to do. Still, there's that time, that hopeful moment when I am doing what I love and the wheelchair isn't even in the picture. I know it's my brain playing tricks on me, but I wonder what it's trying to tell me.

May:

I'm definitely getting the feeling that by the time we meet, you will know my weaknesses in and out. Your line of questioning is straight and to the point. You seem to have me wrapped around your finger because, again, I answer. Something no one knows about me is how much of a softie I am on the inside. I've always felt showing emotion would be to show weakness, so I never let on to nerves, anxiety, hurt, anger, or stress. I will bend over backwards to hold the even keel and be the outgoing and upbeat guy people know me as. But at home, alone, especially when I feel the need to gather or understand my emotions, I immerse myself into movies—dramas, love stories, movies that tug at your heartstrings. It's my opportunity to put down my guard, even shed a tear, which I haven't done in front of anyone since I was twelve years old and the dog died.

People see me as outgoing and extroverted, but that is my outside persona. Inside, I often can't wait to get home and process or revive, let off emotion or simply be. You said before that you liked the anonymity of an online relationship, and although I am anxious to meet you, I do agree, it's easier to let one's guard down by putting the words to paper. It's also eye-opening to see where my thoughts lead me when my fingers are put to the keyboard.

I'm only telling you this because guys do not dare

let other guys know their emotional side. But with you, I feel safe. Someday we will meet in person, and perhaps on that day I will feel naked, stripped down to my core, but my impression of you is that you too have much to bear and within that will be our connection.

Now that it's out there and can't be taken back, it's your turn, mystery woman.

Brian

Dear Brian:

Trying to make me confess, are you? Something about me that no one else knows is that I believe in signs. Whenever I am unsure of my next move to make, what's coming for me on the horizon or how my life should play out, I look for signs to believe in and direct me. I have become a master interpreter, so when I hear a certain song, see a name in print, read a passage in a book, I believe I can predict the future or, at the very least, trust that I have been given some supernatural intel to guide my course. I guess, in everything I do, I look for roadblocks or green lights. You might see this as superstition or faith—I simply look at it as life guiding me on my path and making sure I have everything I need to become who I am supposed to be. That doesn't mean, of course, that I am perfect in following the path. Sometimes I get sidetracked or ignore the signs. Sometimes they are hard to recognize. But when I pay attention and the stars align, amazing things happen.

I'll leave it at that for now, as I am receiving the sign from my drooping eyelids that it's time for bed. Another busy week awaits, and I must get some sleep.

Goodnight for now,

May

―――⌒―――

My week gets off to a roaring start and never slows down. There's work, training, and getting ready for my first international trip of the school year. This is where things get difficult but also when I appreciate my principal for supporting the life of an elite athlete. My team teacher, Lisa, is also a dream. No way could I have this lifestyle without her picking up the pieces every time I leave the U.S. And this year, it'll be a lot of trips outside the country as I work my way toward qualifying for the Games.

Unfortunately, this is when Brian takes a bit of a back seat as I fall behind on my daily messages. I still love reading what he writes, but I feel like I haven't had a moment to put together a thoughtful message to him to let him know what's really going on in my life. I know I'll blow my cover if I start talking about ski racing or what is happening in my day-to-day—and I'm still not ready for that.

By Thursday, there is a sense of hurt and confusion in his voice through his emails.

May:

The rain has turned to sleet today, and I imagine at any moment, the heavy, wet snowflakes will begin to fall. It has turned into a lazy day for me. The gloom of gray has put a damper on my zeal. It seems like your messages are getting fewer and further between. I don't know if the weather has got me seeing through a dark gloom, or if I am correct that things might have cooled down between us. Maybe this is a sign?

I don't want you to feel like you have to write every day, and I feel dumb even writing to ask, but I have barely heard from you, and when I have, your messages are short and shallow. Please tell me if things have changed. You are my favorite part of the day. I don't think I have ever found anything that puts a guaranteed smile on my face so quickly as your messages.

My days at work are numbered, and I'm beginning to feel lost. You keep me grounded, or at least give me something to look forward to. It's hard for me to admit all of this to you, but you have become part of me now. I miss hearing from you.

Brian

As I read this email on Friday night, it fills me both with satisfaction and regret. I am happy to know he likes me, at least as much as one can make that determination through computer messages, but I feel bad for having let my side of the conversation slide for several days and allowed everything else to take precedence over him this week. And tomorrow I leave for Switzerland. I figure I better write him tonight before he thinks I have fallen off the edge of the earth. But what do I say?

Brian:

I'm sorry I've been such a lousy pen pal! I've had so much going on this week. I didn't feel I had the time to sit down and write a message that was worthy of your reading time. It pains me to know your job is going downhill, but I know you will rebound. What is your heart telling you to explore next? Remember—look for the signs! And know, life is an adventure—it's not about getting it right, rather taking ownership of the precious moments you have on this earth and creating your own masterpiece. Easier said than done, right?

Sometimes I have fantasies about dropping everything I'm doing and starting all over. I know I like teaching, but sometimes I wonder if this is all there is to life. Working for the paycheck at a job that is good and doesn't pain me, but ... could I be happier? Could I have a different job that would make me ecstatic to wake up and get going every day? Is that passion something I should get from other places in my life? Sometimes I feel like people don't take enough risks. We sit back and settle for okay. We work to pay the bills, buy the things we need and want, but I think there is an adventurer in all of us. How many people actually follow that road and become the hero of their own stories? It's something I think we're afraid to do because intuitively we know the adventurer is also a rebel. And we're taught to follow the status quo, but there will always be part of us that wants to stand out, do something different. Instead, we allow ourselves to get tied down to the should— what we believe others want from us. And then we get pulled in by how much money we should be making and doing things the same way everyone else is doing them. It's almost like a constant state of being in high school and being afraid to go out and do what's in your heart without worrying about what anyone else thinks.

I have no idea where this sermon is coming from or where it's going. I think maybe I'm talking to myself because I remember clearly a time of trying to strive for what everyone else's version of what life should be. When I went back to high school after my accident, I was so afraid of being different. I mean, I already stuck out like a sore thumb in my wheelchair, but I tried so hard, even overcompensated, to appear *normal*. But if anyone were to have the power to unzip my outer layer to see the person inside, I was a frightened little girl—worried about how I looked to the outside world, tormented by inner demons who made fun of me every time I struggled to do the simplest things, opening doors, having to sit at the special table in class because I couldn't fit in the compact chair and desk sets, like my classmates did. The learning curve was so steep. The worst was trying to change quickly into my gym clothes, while the other girls speedily transformed, it took me nearly half the period to get my school clothes off and shorts and t-shirt on. The gym teacher told me I didn't have to do it, but *no*, I was going to be *normal*. Even as the process threatened to devour me, I was stubborn in my resolve to be a regular high school kid. And still, after all these years, I have healed, I think I have, but underneath the resolute and confident exterior of the athlete, the teacher, the friend—is a heart of skepticism and doubt. Am I the person I *should* be, to be loved? I think to myself about how Brian and I may be talking about two different things, jobs versus love, but in the end, it's insecurity that is our common enemy and the feeling of not measuring up—not to ourselves, but to the world. One that seems cruel and judgmental. But is it, or do our perceptions cloud our view, skew our awareness, and paralyze us with fear?

Brian, you are young and single and have the rest of your life ahead of you. What is the adventurer inside of you saying? I feel helpless on this side of the computer from you, but I hope at some point I can grasp your hand and embark on this journey with you. Uncertainty is easier with a friend along for the ride. Who knows, maybe soon we'll be walking side-by-side.

Sweet dreams, Brian.

May

I hit send and then reflect on my own insecurity. On the outside, I know I appear different. I mean, I am different … than the status quo, certainly. But on the inside, I am as human as anyone else. What if I'm getting caught up in the stories that I make up, instead of the stories that are true? Just because a person can walk, doesn't mean their path is clear, well-defined, or free of obstacles. We all have our moments of uncertainty, our doubts about our worthiness, and how we come across to others. Why can't I get myself to trust that although all lives have followed different paths, we have most certainly been sculpted by the human experience, and in that alone, we can find some semblance of common ground.

The thought weighs on my mind as I stare into the bathroom mirror brushing my teeth. As individuals, we're more alike than different. Aren't we?

CHAPTER 11

I HATE RUSHING, BUT I'VE OVERSLEPT THIS morning, and I have a long day ahead of me before I get on tonight's 7:00 p.m. flight. I'm glad I'll be flying overnight, as it is a long haul to get to Europe from Colorado. It could be worse; I've skied in New Zealand several times, a trip more than a day in the making. I frantically search through my closet for winter clothes, ski racing outfits, and do a million other things I could have done before now. But, as usual, I waited until the last minute. I can't help it. It's my nature.

My phone rings and I'm tempted to hit ignore, when I look at the screen and realize it's my dad calling, as he always does, to wish me good luck.

"Hi, Dad," I answer the phone.

"Are you ready to sock it to 'em?" he asks in an enthusiastic little league parent-to-child voice."

"Um, yes, as ready as I'm going to be," I say, trying to match his energy. "How are you?"

"Well, things have taken a new turn now that I've spent some time on MFEO. There are a few women I've been corresponding with. It's dating with a new twist, one I never imagined, but it makes me feel so much more alive than I have since the accident. It's a daunting thought to imagine connecting with a woman other than your mother, but at the same time, it seems, in a way—freeing. I've been shackled to memories and guilt and pain for so long, I'd forgotten what it was like to have a sensitive and open conversation with a woman. It's getting easier with each message I read or write."

I think about Brian and how he makes me feel. With every step further we get in our relationship, the more fearful I become. My dad, on the other hand, is so assured in his feelings and his statements. Almost to proclaim dating as being liberating and exciting. I wish I could absorb even one ounce of his optimism. I shake my head to get back into the conversation at hand.

"Dad, you sound like you're on cloud nine. I'm so happy you've been making friends online. Maybe that special someone is right around the corner! Promise me you won't run off and elope before I get back in the country though, okay?"

"Thank you, Rainey. Thank you, for opening my world. I guess I've missed a lot, closing myself off all these years. Please tell me you're ready to make this transition to a new life also.

Perhaps a date with Brian when you get back?"

"That's a lot to ask," I say. A chuckle escapes me at the thought of going on a double date with my dad. It's so weird to be in this situation together, yet something about it I find endearing. I cross my fingers and silently wish for a happy ending to our family story.

Suddenly, I'm interrupted from my fantasy vision as I eye my watch, noticing that the minutes have been busily ticking away. "I've got to go Dad. Nat is on her way over to hang out for a bit and take me to the airport. I better get back to packing."

"Have a good trip honey," he replies. "I can't wait to hear good news about your races when you return. And maybe, I'll have some good news of my own."

His hopefulness makes me smile. "I love you, Dad."

"I love you to the moon and back, sweetie." I can almost feel him beaming through the phone.

$$\smile\frown$$

Natalie shows up in the middle of my frantic preparations because we were supposed to go to lunch today and spend a little time together before heading to the airport, but I told her that if she wants to see me, she'll have to come to my house and watch me pack. When she enters my room, she plops down on my bed, and we start catching up on everything that has happened during the week. She got a new, prominent PR client at work and has been buried herself. Between both our schedules, we haven't had a chance to chat.

"How are things with Brian?" she asks first thing.

"Okay, I guess. He's a little worried because I haven't emailed him as much lately, but it's simply a lack of time, that's all."

"Are you sure you aren't getting cold feet? You know you can't hold him off much longer," she states as if I didn't already know this.

"You're right, but at the moment I have a huge competition to worry about, and I'm going to have to turn off the sap and turn on the speed. I really need to do well in Switzerland."

"I know you do, and for that reason, I'm going to let it lie. But think about it on your flight back home. Not that I'm pulling for Brian over you, but there will come a time when you're simply being unfair. He has the right to see you, to know the truth and, quite honestly, you both have the right to see if this relationship can go somewhere. Otherwise, you're wasting your time."

The word of Natalie has been spoken. I grab my bag and say, "Alrighty then, let's make an equipment stop in the garage and head for the airport."

In the car, Natalie, fortunately, lets up on me a bit and she starts telling me a story about how Seth came home the other night from his New York business trip with a little blue box from Tiffany's.

"I love it when he surprises me like that," she giggles. "He's so thoughtful and has such good taste too. It wasn't even a celebration or anything. He was thinking about me, he said."

I know she isn't trying to make me feel bad, but sometimes I think she says this stuff to remind me of what I am missing. I sit there wondering if Brian will be the one to make me feel giddy inside like that. *Seems so far out of reach,* I'm thinking, as we park the car. Natalie gets a cart to load my things and we head inside the airport. At the check-in counter, Natalie hugs me and says goodbye.

"Good luck, doll," she calls out as she walks away. "We'll be cheering you on from here and watching the results online. Try to email or call if you can. Love you!"

"Love you too," I answer, thinking how sad it is that there are only two living people who I truly, truly love.

As I settle in on the plane, I pull the hood of my sweatshirt up over my head and plug my earbuds into my ears. I don't want to talk to anyone, and I don't want anyone to talk to me. I need time to think. As I drift off, I imagine Brian and me walking hand-in-hand along a beach in Mexico. It is quiet between us, yet we are communicating on the most intimate level. We have one of those relationships where we can say so much without saying anything at all. I am completely in love and entirely at peace.

"Please put your tray table and seat into the upright and locked position," the loudspeaker seems deafening after such a peaceful dream. I can't believe I've already crossed over half of the U.S. and the Atlantic Ocean in no time. I have reached my destination.

By the time I land, it's early morning in Switzerland, and our National Team Coordinator has already been in Europe for a couple of days. He's there to meet me and four of my teammates at the airport. He has a full day of sightseeing planned for us, so that we can take it easy yet not fall asleep. He wants to ensure that we get accustomed to the time change as quickly as possible.

From the moment we hit the ground, it's go, go, go. I want to stop and write a message to Brian, but on a team trip like this, it's not my schedule, but the team's schedule. I drag along with my teammates as we fill the day with eating and visiting the local sites. Finally, around dinnertime, the athletes all decide to override the coaches. Before dinner, we hit a café for a hit of java and some Wi-Fi access. Each one of us is addicted to our electronic devices and wants to connect with social media, catch up on news or reunite with loved ones after our long journey. I pull out my tablet and stare at it for a moment, while I try to think of what to say. My feelings are tangled in my guilt, mixed signals and omissions. On one hand, I sense our hearts growing closer as we talk about our hopes and fears, or bare our souls much more quickly than we would upon meeting in person. On the flipside, I know my arm is held out against him, keeping him as far away from the real me as I can. It's not right; I know it's not. I'm conflicted. I love the feeling of being so close to someone that they are the first thing I think of in the morning and last thought permeating my mind before bed. But I am a fraud. Will he forgive me? I decide instead of trying to move the needle on his feelings for me or elevating our computer-generated romance, I will stick with a generic topic to keep my concerns at bay. I talk about the last day at work before I left on this trip, as if it had just happened.

Dear Brian:

I'm sorry I didn't get a message off to you earlier. How was your day?

Mine was the usual. In the mornings, I get my kiddos into the classroom and then get them settled down. I like to take a moment and breathe in the energy of my bright-eyed and eager pupils. The angel faces eager to get started on their day. Happy to be at school and not minding that they will spend the next seven hours in a classroom. I know at this age, it's the beginning of the end of that feeling. Soon enough, they'll despise school and become challenging for their teachers. But for me, it is a reward in itself that at this point they still want to hear what their teacher says. To learn from me. They soak it all up like a sponge. It's exciting and rewarding.

Today, my job made me think of you and what you were like at that age. Do you remember being in first or second grade? Can you recall your favorite color, snack, best friend?

Questions again. I hope these questions are not as intrusive on your manhood.

May

I add a winking, smiling Emoji, hit send, tap my screen over to a game of solitaire, letting my mind go numb.

Dear May:

As always, I love to hear from you. To see life from your perspective, so I will answer your questions first before I tell you about my day. I do vividly remember first grade. My teacher's name was Ms. Walker. I loved the color purple, or at least I pretended to because that was Amy Watkins' favorite color, and I sure had a crush on her! We'd sit next to each other in class, and I was certain I would marry her someday. Isn't it funny, how at such an early age, we even bother to think about these things?

My favorite snack? That's easy since it remains the same today. Pizza. I'll eat it for breakfast, lunch, or dinner ... and anything in between. Hot, cold, doesn't matter. My best friend? A guy named Billy, whose family moved away in third grade. We were inseparable for those years that he was my next-door neighbor, but come to think of it, I wonder whatever happened to him. Perhaps some cyberstalking is in order on Facebook today. Thanks for the prompt.

As for my day, I'll have you know that while I got *nothing* done at work yesterday, today I have been on fire, so thank goodness for productivity. I feel much better going home knowing I actually earned a few of the dollars that will end up on my paycheck.

I am taking a break, though, because I felt compelled to message you, simply because I can, and I want to tell you how you make me feel when I hear from you. I like the freedom of not being self-conscious in sharing what I am thinking or feeling—even if it's something as insignificant as what I have to tell you now.

Since we started talking (does messaging count as talking?) you have become my best and favorite inspiration when it comes to writing. I don't know what it is, but every time I read a message from you or write one in response, the thought of you leaves me with a million words swirling around in my head. Sometimes they are about you and sometimes they have nothing to do with you. Other times, they help me with something I am writing for work, but I love it because I know you have helped me tap into my emotions in a way no other person in my life does. And when I'm working on something, and it literally spills onto the paper and writes itself, I know it's true and straight from the heart. I don't know why it's you, but it is. It's been so long since I've felt this sense of contentment and vulnerability—which you've begun to bring out of me in the fiercest of ways. And what I like about it is that, for a guy who, like most others, is notorious for not showing his feelings, it makes me feel more alive when I hear from you. You are the only person with whom I allow myself to feel totally exposed (a feeling to which I have a strong aversion) and be okay with it. I feel comfortable with it and embrace it. I hope I am reading you right—that I can trust the feelings between us will grow because with you I imagine I can plummet off the edge of a cliff, figuratively speaking J of course, and still feel safe.

I hope you feel the same way about being able to open up to me, and I hope this feeling continues after we meet. To me, that's what makes this so exciting. You make me think, feel, and be happy. And ... I'm going to leave you with your next question. Tell me about your very first boyfriend.

Thinking about you—always.

Brian

When I read his message the following morning, I feel touched. Exhilarated. And more terrified than ever. He has admitted to me his sensitivities, but I won't let him see mine. Sitting in my hotel room, I decide to write a quick message to him before heading to the ski hill to train for the day. It's early for me, but I know Brian is likely fast asleep in bed. I decide to keep the message short and sweet. And right now, I don't have the time or energy to delve into my relationship with Gabe. My first "love." My first broken heart.

Brian:

Thank you for such a sweet, heartfelt message. I am happy that I can bring out such emotion in you. And I love the writer in you who is so good at expressing what he is thinking and feeling. It makes this relationship exciting and freeing. Now I fear the possibility of not having chemistry between us when we actually meet. Writing to each other is one thing, but what happens when we meet in person is quite a different thing. I want so desperately to see you, but I fear I won't meet your expectations. What if I fall short and all of this has been for nothing?

I love to hear from you too. You always brighten my day.

May

I hit send, throw my ski bag on my lap, and head to the lobby to meet the rest of my team. It's an intense day of training, and by the time I return to my room, all I want to do is sleep. My jetlag has hit me hard, and I'm definitely noticing the time difference. But as I open my email, I discover I'm not the only one feeling the change.

Dear May:

Are you OK? Do you have insomnia or something? I keep getting your emails at unusual times of the night. I'm not saying it's bad, but a little out of the ordinary for you. Your last message was time-stamped 1:00 a.m. Are you OK? Not sleeping? When I can't sleep at 1 a.m., it's a sure sign of stress or anxiety.

Wow. Perceptive. I keep forgetting he doesn't know I'm in Switzerland.

Why are you so worried about when we meet? I have seen your picture, and you are gorgeous. You are engaging in conversation, and we have so much in common. You distract me in the most satisfying way. Of course, we both have jitters, but that is to be expected since neither one of us has ever done anything like this before. It's exciting because there are so many possibilities.

Each day I look even more forward to the moment we will finally meet.

Brian

I like how Brian pays attention to the subtleties of my messages—from the timing to my thoughts and words—a cautious buzz fills my body, and a braveness washes over me. At this moment, I feel like I might just be bold enough to meet. I want to meet. But I wonder if this courage is me or is it the 5,000 miles that separate us?

The fourth morning of the trip, I am awakened from my slumber before the sun comes up. I look over at my teammate Heather, in the bed next to me and she is fast asleep. I only wish I would have had such a solid night of rest, but the truth is, I was tossing and turning most of the night with all of the pieces of my life rolling around and around in my brain—skiing, and the fact that this will be my last season before I retire; Brian and the fact that I haven't written in a couple of days, his trusting tenderhearted messages to a woman he has never met—with such a desire to connect and intentions so genuine. My job as a schoolteacher and the uncertainty of not knowing if the path I have chosen is one which will sustain and fulfill me when I settle back into full-time work after the ski season is over. The uncertainty of these life factors are not unlike the uncertainty of skiing.

I transfer out of bed as quietly as possible, so as to not wake Heather, and direct my chair the three feet from my bed to the window of our typical, cramped European hotel room. Gazing out the window, I see the snowfall ... only flurries but if it has been steady all night, the racing conditions won't be ideal. Skiing on snow that is packed to near icy conditions is optimal, though the best athletes are those who can adapt to any conditions. While the usual recreational skier does snow dances to coax a powder day, racers are the opposite. Fresh snow on the mountain foreshadows a course with potentially dangerous bumps and ruts, which deteriorates with each skier who takes his or her turn. And for the unfortunate skiers with the later start times, the course can become more difficult and dangerous with each athlete who has traveled the terrain.

Although I feel sound in my competition rankings and outlook for qualifying for the Games, I know every performance matters. So, in the silence of the early morning, I close my eyes and envision the elements of my race that will garner the best outcomes—carving clean turns, how I'll shift my weight in the bucket seat of my monoski and the intense focus I will have as I speed through the gates down the hill. Prior to my races, I'll have a chance to do a course inspection—viewing the course by sight, or in the case of the downhill and fastest event, by completing preliminary runs. My coach's input will be important as we talk about the lines I will take down the course. Skiing is a sport of agility and catlike reflexes, strategy, and guts. While I crave the adrenaline of the events, to me, the ultimate satisfaction is the sharpness of mind required, in order to keep up with the pace and technicalities of the race.

"Hey, speed demon," I am brought out of my thoughts by a good morning greeting from Heather. "Are you ready to kill it today?"

"Oh, yeah," I reply. You?"

"As soon as I get my cup of Joe and my eyes fully open. Let's get at it!"

CHAPTER 12

IT'S A LONG RETURN TRIP TO COLORADO AFTER a lengthy ten-day stay in Switzerland. The flights home can often be more excruciating than the race. It's when the anticipation and excitement are over, the suspense about the race has been answered, and you've either had a great race and medaled or you're going home with disappointment and regret. There's either the feeling of a full heart and you want to share the fun of the trip with everyone else or you want to go home and bury your head and not even talk about it. Time can drag along on the return flight with the knowledge that all of your questions about your preparation, potential, and possibly luck, have been answered. In my case, it's a somber flight home.

I return on a Saturday evening and know from the way my body feels that I will be wide-awake for hours. I tried to be disciplined on the flight and not take a nap, but I was exhausted from the racing and the ache of my body from the horrible crash I took in the super giant slalom. Sitting for hours on the airplane and not being able to get up or stretch has caused burning and throbbing in every muscle I can feel. The rest of me is deflated from the demoralization of doing so poorly in a race where I was the favorite to win. Even with my coach's reassurance that my performance hasn't hurt my standings on the team, I am disappointed by the technical errors I probably could have avoided. To escape, I slept the whole way back and now my body is on a totally different time cycle.

On the descent from just below 40,000 feet, I begin to wish that Brian and I had already met. Then, perhaps I could have called him when I got home, and I'd have a date for a drink or a movie. Something to do together to drown my sorrows and relax my battered body.

But that's not the case. *What should I do?* I text Natalie, but she and Seth are going to dinner and a show. Jake and Amber are likely out too. Even Jenny has a blind date tonight. I feel like I'm the odd one out, so even though my dad and I have our Sunday ritual, I decide to pay him a surprise visit on Saturday night. He is the only other single person I can turn to at the spur of the moment who won't have already made plans for the night.

CHAPTER 13

MY DAD IS SO PREDICTABLE. DINNER AT SIX, A DVD or TV show at seven. I decide I'll stop by and surprise him with some lo mein and a movie. But when I get to his house, I simultaneously ring the doorbell and unlock the door with my key as he comes around the corner whistling and tying a tie around his neck. *Wait. Who has swallowed my dad and left in his place this incredibly happy Dixie-whistling imposter?* My hands, full and at the ready to present tonight's entertainment for the singletons of the world, drop dead at my side—with the lo mein nearly slipping from my grasp.

"I thought I'd bring us dinner and a movie, but clearly you have other plans," I say.

"Oh Rainey, I'm so sorry. I wish I would have known. I'd have spared you the trip."

"Well," I respond, trying hard not to feel insult from injury. First a horrible ski trip, followed by a rejection from the one steady man in my life. "Where are you going?" I know it can't be a fancy work function. I'm always his date to those.

"Rainey, you're a genius!" he exclaims. "I actually have a date with a woman I met online two weeks ago. Sara. Sara Evans. She sounds like a dream."

Two. Weeks. Ago. Sounds like a dream? "What do you mean she sounds like a dream? You've talked to her?" The words spurt incredulously out of my mouth.

"Well, I know I'm way past my prime, but back when I was dating, that's how it worked. You talked on the phone, and eventually, you dropped the big question and asked her out. Although back in the day when I asked your mom out, I also had to clear it with her father."

The more he talks, the more my brain fills with a fog. *My dad. Has a date. With a woman he's known a mere two weeks. And he's so giddy. I feel like I'm talking to a schoolgirl.*

My eyes start to burn. I've been talking to Brian online, never even heard his voice, and it's been almost two months now. In the background of my thoughts, Dad is rattling off his plans ... fancy dinner at Le Chateau, an evening walk through the Botanic Gardens, and dessert at Clydes Café.

"How do you know you're going to like her enough to invest all that time and energy?"

"I don't. That's part of the suspense. The allure. I never in a million years thought I could meet someone as wonderful as your mother. But there are eight billion people on the earth. And as silly as it seems, meeting people online, talking again, and finding a new world out there has woken me up and made me see how much I have been missing—wonderful conversations, the first date jitters, meeting women I wouldn't have met had I not gotten online. I will never be able to replace your mother, but if I can find someone who shares my interests and is enjoyable to spend time with, perhaps together, we can reignite the warmth your mother used to bring to our lives," he says. "If I can get anywhere close to that, I have to give it a try. It's time for me to start living again."

"I know it will happen for you, Dad. But don't be hard on yourself for not trying until now. Maybe you weren't ready yet.

"You're right, Rainey. It's taken me a long time to get to this place, to be willing to open my heart to another woman. It's just that your mom truly was my kindred soul."

"I get it, Dad, but beware, to move on you have to be open to beginning with a blank slate. Remember, comparing two lovers is the kiss of death in any romance." In the back of my head, I'm wondering where this relationship advice came from. Must be one too many romance novels, devoured as I fantasize what my love life might be like in a perfect world.

"I promise, Rainey. But remember as long as we're sharing parables, made up as they may be, remember that to not risk sharing one's full heart means to never find true love. I have to be going. I don't want to be late for my first date. That would send a message that I'm not taking this seriously and she sounds like she's just my type. I don't want to miss my opportunity. I love you madly darling. Have a great night of movies, and I'll give you the scoop in the morning." He practically sung on his way out.

Did my dad just say he'd give me the *scoop* in the morning?

The next day, I head back to Dad's house for our Sunday morning ritual. I am exhausted, sore, jetlagged, and half-dreading what I'm going to hear about his date. Of course, I want him to have had a good time, but I also know I'll feel bad if it didn't go well, especially since I was the one to put him up to the whole thing. Yet, if it went well, I'll feel guilty for not being able to be as happy for him as I could be if I weren't so scared about meeting Brian. As I drive to his house, I'm thinking there's a ninety percent chance I'm going to feel like shit either way.

When I open the front door, the house is full of an aroma I have not smelled since before my mother died. When I was growing up, breakfast and dinner were family affairs. We always ate together. You had to have a really, really good reason for missing a meal. Most of the time, we had to arrange our dinners around Sunny's swim practices because there was no way my mom would let us eat without her. It was a time for bonding, checking in with each other and sharing everything about our day. It was Mom's way to ensure that we remained close to each other and on the same page as a family.

The smell of my mom's famous cinnamon rolls hits me as I push into the kitchen to see my dad cooking furiously. The rolls are in the oven, scrambled eggs and bacon on the stove, and a pitcher of orange juice is on the counter. This is a huge departure from our usual store-bought bagels and cream cheese or the simple cheese omelet without any fanfare that usually greets me for our Sunday breakfast.

"Um, hi Dad."

"Oh sorry, Rainey. I didn't hear you come in. I must have been lost in thought. How was your night last night? Did I miss a good movie? That lo mein smelled good. I hope you enjoyed it."

I hug my dad and ask, "Is there something you want to tell me?"

"What makes you think that?" he asks in return.

"Well, you haven't cooked this big of a spread in, oh, that's right … ever. And I'm wondering why today you've decided to dust off Mom's famous cinnamon roll recipe and make them for breakfast."

"Rainey, I just wanted to show my appreciation for you and your help. I had the most wonderful time last night. I feel like a new man."

In the back of my mind, I go directly to wondering if he got laid, but this is my dad we're talking about, so it's more like a rhetorical question. I absolutely do not want to know the answer.

He continues. "Sara was positively wonderful, and our time together was nothing like a first date. It was like we had known each other forever. We talked and talked for hours. I suppose it's easier to jump into a conversation after you have been writing back and forth for a couple of weeks. We got a lot of the cursory stuff out of the way over email and on the phone, so when we met, it was like we were old friends.

I didn't have to ask her what she does for a living; I could ask her how her week at work was. Or if her dog was doing well after surgery. We'd already shared all of the basics."

"So, what's she like?" I'm trying hard to be happy that his dating experience seemed so uncomplicated.

"She's fifty-two years old and works as a nurse administrator. She spent most of her career on the nursing floor, but now she does the behind-the-scenes work. She's compassionate and funny and quite pretty. She is also a widow. Her husband died suddenly, five years ago of a heart attack. Although she wasn't as young as I was when I lost your mother, she knows what it feels like to lose your spouse when you never thought it could come so soon. We talked about that a lot, and it was good to have someone who understands how hard it can be."

"When are you going to see her again?" I ask.

"Soon, hopefully, tomorrow. She said she can make time to come over to the university to have lunch with me. I thought I would take her to Mona's. What do you think?"

My dad and I love to go to Mona's when I meet him at work for lunch. It's a great Italian food restaurant. But I feel jealous. "Great idea, Dad. She'll love it."

The rest of the morning we talk about other things. My time in Switzerland, the upcoming race season, even my day at the track before I left on my trip. I usually try not to talk about car racing to my dad because it seems to be hard for him to hear about it, but I figure since he got to talk about his date all morning, what the heck, why not try to engage him in a conversation about cars and driving fast? This time I get a totally different reaction from him. He actually asks questions.

Wants to know about the car, my training laps, Jake. He asks when I think I'll go back. Even says something about getting back behind the wheel.

Wow. I'm blown away once again at seeing what love does to people. It appears (what would I know?) to be such a solid and complete emotion. It's flirting, and I love you's, honesty, and sacred moments. It's a link between souls where a fearlessness takes over, and you begin to believe anything is possible. At least, that's what I imagine. What I do know, for sure, is that love does weird things to people. Makes them see life through a whole new lens. The thought of it happening to me causes me to squirm in my chair. And I'm not even sure how to feel about it.

When I leave my dad's house, I feel utterly conflicted. He had the guts to go on a blind date without worrying about what's going to happen next. *Why can't I do that?*

I go to bed thinking about it. I have to get the guts to move forward with Brian. I have to be strong. No matter what happens. Sure, I might get rejected, but I'll never know if I don't give it a try. If I don't risk anything, I'll never get anything. I make up my mind. It's time to consider moving forward. *Consider.*

CHAPTER 14

MONDAY IS A STRUGGLE AT WORK. MY BODY IS still in Switzerland on the mountain, my mind is on relationships and meeting Brian, and my emotions are on a rollercoaster. I am not myself. The highlight of the day, though, is my sweet students and the welcome home poster they've made for me. It has a crayon drawing of me skiing down the mountain and across the top it says, "We missed you, Ms. Rainey." With all that is going on within me, it brings me to tears.

"Why are you crying?" asks Jillian, one of the sweetest little girls you could ever meet.

"Because I'm happy. You've all made my day. These are happy tears." Certainly, I know better. They are the tears of exhaustion and confusion, but these kids don't need to know that. It must be nice to be young and carefree. To not have adult worries.

After work, I do a few errands—there's not a bit of food in the house, and I need to stop by the tailor to pick up a skirt I had altered. When I get home, I cook dinner and decide to get in bed with the laptop to see if there's anything good on Netflix. Or maybe to see if there's anything new from Brian.

May:

How are you? I can only hope you've had a better day than I have. Why is it that all the shit has to hit the fan at the same time? I apologize in advance that I'm not going to ask for permission today, but I'm going to unload on you. I had such a crappy day I'm ready to get in bed and call it good. First of all, the magazine went belly up. I lost my job today. Now I'm officially a starving writer. Before I was merely a financially challenged writer. Maybe it's time to write the great American novel. Or lie on the couch and pout. I'm sure I'll be able to find something else, but I was doing what I loved.

Then my mom wanted me to drive halfway up the mountain to Evergreen for a family dinner, and on the way, my trusty Subaru finally hit the wall. I shouldn't be surprised. It's my fault ... should have taken it to the shop for its 100,000-mile service about 15,000 miles ago. But suddenly during the drive, I heard a turbulent whirring sound like something was spinning out of control inside what is typically a nicely humming engine. My car started sputtering and then stalled. Left me stranded on the side of the road until my brother came to pick me up. It's still there. I don't even want to go back and get it. I'm simply tired of this. I guess I don't pay enough attention to my car since I generally commute to work on my bicycle. It looks like I'll be riding my bike a lot more now since my car is dead.

May, I know you are enjoying being the mystery woman, and I do love our correspondence and especially our instant messaging, but I want to take things up a notch. I need to take things to the next level. Please help me to soothe over my bad day. Can we talk? I can't do suspense much longer. Please. 303.335.6890

Brian

I think about how, after two weeks, my dad has already gone out on a date, and after two months, the most courage I can gather has been to instant message. I immediately grab my cell phone and dial.

He answers the phone in a professional tone of voice, "Hi, this is Brian."

"It's your timing belt," I say, the first thing out of my mouth.

"Excuse me?" this sexy, male voice replies, confused.

"I said the reason your car broke down is that your timing belt is worn out. I can't be sure, of course, unless I diagnose it in person, but it's probably a pretty accurate guess. Probably a hundred bucks or so for the kit to fix it. Plus labor. Unless of course you did it yourself or had someone like me to do it for you."

"May?" he sounds dumbfounded.

"Yes?" I answer, mocking his questioning voice.

"You have me rendered speechless on two accounts. First, I didn't expect to hear your voice within thirty seconds of my message, and second, I most certainly wasn't expecting you to know the first thing about car mechanics."

"Yes, well, I haven't given away all my secrets yet. What would be the fun in meeting if all the cards were already laid out on the table?"

"Okay ... well, it's nice to hear from you ... finally," he says. I think he's still in shock and a little intimidated by my quick diagnosis of his automotive problem. There's a long pause, and now I'm getting a little nervous because he's not saying anything.

"Um, should I not have called? I mean, I thought that was the reason you gave me your phone number," I have to break the silence because it is breaking me into a sweat.

"It's not that. I'm having a slow time rebounding from the turnaround time from when I gave you my number to when the phone rang. It's been two months, and suddenly you want to talk in under a minute? I'm a little confused."

"I decided it was about time to reveal at least a little of myself. So, how are you?"

"I'm fine," he says, "except for my lack of a job and a supposed timing belt problem."

"Too bad it's not time to meet in person yet, or I'd come

over there and fix it for you. But I'm still not ready for that. One thing at a time."

"Where does that come from? This car knowledge and being so confident you're right?"

"My dad. I told you he drove race cars, but he's also an experienced mechanic. When I was a kid, he'd take me to the track and teach me the ins and outs of cars, so I could grow up to be part of his pit crew. It's what happens when you don't produce boys ... you do what you can with the girls. I've replaced brakes, rebuilt engines, and transmissions, remapped engine control units, you name it, and I've probably done it. At first, I thought I would grow up to be a car mechanic. But then when I was eight, my dad got me behind the wheel of my first go-kart. And from there, becoming a professional driver was my goal. But, sometimes life has other plans for us, so I only do it for fun now. Still, I loved learning the mechanics of the car and working with the tools. And, I still work on my cars to this day."

"Wow. Impressive," he says. "But there you go again, stealing my man card."

"Sorry, I didn't mean to. I was trying to be helpful."

"Thanks for that. And thanks for the call. You made my night."

We made a little more small talk and then got back on the subject of cars.

"So, you still race cars?" he asks.

"I do. When I can, that is. The local SCCA organization—the Sports Car Club of America—has races from the spring to the fall that happen at various tracks around Colorado.

There are all sorts of events and divisions depending on what kind of car you drive. Racing is embedded in my genes, I think, because my dad was so passionate about it. When I was twelve, I was the only girl hanging around the track, so between racers and mechanics, it was like having an extended family of brothers. Each one took me under their wing and taught me everything I know about cars. They believed it was important knowledge for a young girl to have, so I'd never be stranded on the road with a problem I couldn't fix myself. It was cool too because I was the envy at school. My dad taught me how to drive a stick shift when I was fourteen, and one day I got to go to school and brag to all the boys that I had driven eighty-miles-an-hour at the track. That's how I landed my ninth-grade boyfriend," I say and almost add, *Gabe, the one who dumped me because I became paralyzed*. I'm glad I caught myself in time, but the nervous energy of nearly blowing it made me start to perspire and my voice sounded uneven and shaky as it reverberated in my head.

Finally, I realize I am dominating the conversation and ask him about his job.

"Tell me about your job search. Do you have any prospects?" I ask.

"Yeah, I guess I have a few irons in the fire. None that have me overjoyed, but at least options for paying the bills. I have an interview on Wednesday, so we'll see how that goes," he says. "Fortunately, I got a nice severance package, so I'm going to use my freedom from the everyday grind to spend some time with Casey. We'll probably head to the rock climbing gym and get caught up on movies. I can help him with his English homework. He inherited my brother's knack for science, but when it comes to writing, well, let's say he'll probably follow in his father's footsteps as an engineer rather than a writer. It's funny, while I like hanging out with my friends, there's nothing like being with my nephew. It makes me wonder if I want to start a family even more than I thought," he adds.

"Are you ready to nest?" I ask sarcastically. "Usually it's the woman whose clock is ticking."

He laughs. "I think I like the thought of having my own family. Sometimes I feel lonely. And not because I don't have plenty of people around me. I think there just might be more to life."

I look at the clock and realize our conversation has lasted two hours. We've talked about jobs and kids, sports, and hobbies. He is so easy to talk to, and we seem to connect without any awkwardness. I never felt I had to hold back or put on a show for him. I simply told him what I was thinking, and I can tell he feels he can be open with me too. *If only it could stay this easy.*

I hear Brian yawn into the phone. "May, you could keep me engaged in our conversation all night, but my eyelids are getting heavy and, from the little I know about relationships, I believe it's bad form to fall asleep in the middle of your first phone date."

I beam at the thought of him considering this a date. "I think that would be correct. But, Brian," my mind warns me to keep it simple, uninvolved, but my heart feels full. Wide open. It gets the message to my mouth quicker than my brain can stop it. "I enjoyed talking to you tonight. You've become the thing I look forward to the most in my days. I know how much you want to meet, and I do too. But can you be patient with me just a little longer?"

"May, something inside of me tells me you're worth the wait. I don't know what it is, but I sense that navigating the complexity of who you are is much like navigating a labyrinth of secret emotions. Ones you don't reveal lightly. I can tell that a relationship with you is much more than a flyby. I like it. You're intense. Introspective. Enthralling."

"Wow. That's a lot of big, descriptive words in a row. What, do you have a dictionary in front of you?"

"I'm a writer, remember? It's my job to have a vast vocabulary of enigmatic, intricate, sophisticated words."

"Now I'm certain you're reading straight from the Thesaurus."

"It's been a pleasure talking to you, my mystery woman."

"The pleasure is all mine," I say. "Thank you, Brian."

"No. Thank you. Buenas noches, May. I look forward to our next communication."

"Now you're bilingual?" A giggle escapes, but then, "Goodnight, Brian." My voice feels extra soft. My words cradled in affection.

"Goodnight, May."

My hand goes slowly to the red, end button on my phone. It takes Herculean strength to put my fingerprint to it. I don't want the call to end. I pause. For a long moment, I stare at my phone, like Brian might materialize right out of it if I stare long enough. *I want this. No, not just this. Him. I want him, in my life.*

After I'm done basking in my conversation with Brian, I pick up the phone and call Natalie.

"I did it."

"Did what?"

"Called him."

"Well, it's about time! It's only been two months of your shenanigans! I'm surprised he waited this long to ask."

"How do you know he asked *me* to call *him*?"

"Because I know you were going to milk this as long as you could. You have to take the risk, Rainey. And yes, this relationship has gone on long enough that if he doesn't fall for you, you're going to get hurt. Love is like that. It's not perfect, and it certainly can cause pain. But if you don't risk the pain, you will never know the feeling of having that one person in your life who you can share everything with, who knows you better than anyone else and loves you unconditionally. I know you see your mom as that person. But she's gone. And eventually, you have to grow up and let a true romantic, loving relationship fill the space in your soul that has been hollow for the past seventeen years. There is this hole you have been carrying around in your heart that I can't fill and neither can your dad. It seems like it gets bigger and I fear one day it will begin eating away at you. Open yourself up. You might be surprised at what happens next."

CHAPTER 15

AS THE HOLIDAYS APPROACH, I CAN TELL BRIAN is getting anxious to meet. We both know that single life and the holidays don't match. But I have to hold him off a little while longer because I have a race coming up in Austria. It is the final tune-up and last chance to earn points to qualify for the Paralympic Games.

Before I leave, I receive a text message from him:

> I got a job! It's not exactly what I was hoping for, but a friend helped me land a position in the news organization where he works. I'm not dying to work there until I retire, but I'm employed!

I smile at the excitement and relief he must be feeling. I text him back and congratulate him. "I can't wait to hear more!" I tap into my phone.

I look forward to hearing about it. The simple pleasure of being the person he wants to share his most important news with makes me smile. Remembering our conversation from the other night makes me feel uncomfortable in the fact that I am hesitant to let him know exactly what is going on in my life in return. I want to let him in. I do. But I haven't let go of the reins. It has to be on my terms. I don't want him to stumble onto who I am, and if I start to talk about ski racing— my mind imagines that one thing will lead to another and the words will escape me without constraint, and then I'll blow it. This has to be perfect. But in trying to make it perfect, I know I'm only making it worse. I tell him a fib. Since I still am not ready to disclose to him my ski racing, I tell him I have to go out of town to visit relatives. I berate myself for it, but I promise. This. Is. The. Last. Time. Once I come home, I will find a way to repent. Better to ask forgiveness than screw everything up now? I rationalize, though I know I'm wrong. I say that I'll try to write as much as I can while I'm away, but we have a pretty packed schedule for the next week. We're going to New York City. I pick New York because I think that Natalie can help me figure out all of the fictitious things we'll do while there. Plus, New York is sort of like going to Austria. Well, not really at all, but I have a good imagination. I hope I can pull it off, even though the thought of being less than straightforward leaves me with a heavy heart.

When I return ten days later from my exhausting trip, it feels like I have been gone forever. I am thrilled when the pilot gets on the loudspeaker and announces that we have landed at Denver International Airport. I love skiing and racing, but the traveling part wears me down. I had great races, though, so I'm all smiles when I meet Natalie in the main concourse and unveil two gold medals.

"Rainey, you're on fire! Just wait until the Paralympics. You're going to crush it. I'm so proud of you."

"All thanks to many hours in the gym and the nice summer training trip I took to New Zealand. It really helped keep me sharp."

We arrive at the baggage claim and begin piling up my heavy load of luggage, which seems to have expanded over the course of my trip. Ski racing requires more equipment than I can handle on my own—monoski, multiple sets of skis for my different events, a massive duffle bag and my carry-on bag, off of which hangs my helmet. On this particular day, Natalie and I decide we are too tired to carry it ourselves, so we grab a porter and head for the parking garage.

As we drive, Natalie updates me on all of the gossip from while I was away. Apparently, Christine, our high school girlfriend, has officially moved in with the boyfriend she met only months ago. She also fills me in on our favorite TV show, and we concoct my supposed itinerary to New York, so I can be prepared for any questions from Brian about my trip to see the relatives.

After listening to all of that and feeling the hum of the

steady drive home on I-70, it's 8:00 p.m. in Denver and I have no idea what time zone it is in my head, so I start to drift off. Natalie turns on the radio, soft enough to let me doze, yet loud enough so she can hear what's being said. A song ends as I begin to drift off.

Then I hear it. At first, I think it's part of a dream and that I'm making it up. But it's unmistakable. The voice. That sexy drawl, inflection, and smoothness.

I pop straight up in my seat and exclaim, "O-M-G!"

I scare the crap out of Natalie, and she says, "Whoa, sister. What was that outburst? First, you're falling fast asleep, and then you're bouncing through the roof. And, on top of it, you sound like a high school kid."

"It's him."

Him, who?

"*Him.*"

"Okay. Let me start at the beginning, and I'll speak your language. W-T-F are you talking about?"

"The voice. That's him! That's Brian!"

"Brian? How do you know?"

"Remember? I talked to him on the phone before I left for Austria. He has a very distinct voice, to which you're now listening. A voice perfectly made for radio, as it turns out," I add. "It's him. I know it without a doubt."

"Well, I hope he doesn't have a face made for radio as well," Natalie giggles.

"He's a journalist and recently lost his job writing feature stories for the *Denver Vibe* when it folded. The only thing he's told me about his new job is that he likes it okay, works weird hours, doesn't have to dress up, and still gets to meet interesting people. I'd say that's this radio gig."

He introduces a local chef and interviews him about a new restaurant opening in town with Moroccan cuisine. As we listen to his voice, Natalie turns to me and says, "Yeah, I can imagine lying in bed and listening to this voice all night. Whew. I think you've scored. Even if he isn't all that cute."

"But he is cute! I've seen his picture," I say in defense.

"Well, you may have found the perfect package," Nat replies.

At the end of the story, he wraps it up by saying, "This is Denver Newsmakers, reported to you by Brian Matthews."

"Wow, you're good. That really is him, isn't it?" Nat says.

"I don't know his last name, but I know his first name … and I am certain of that voice."

Natalie looks at me suddenly while an impish grin creases her eyes.

"I tell ya what, Rainey. You happen to be sitting in the car with Denver's finest PR maven—or at least that's what I like to call myself—and you, miss double-gold medalist, have become Denver's latest Newsmaker. I am confident with a press release and a few hounding phone calls, I can have you on this show in the blink of an eye. Give me a couple hours in the morning, and you will be on your way to meeting Prince Charming."

"Wait! You can't do that."

"Why not? Your hair is thankfully almost back to normal. You'll go by Rainey—which, incidentally, is your name—and he's none the wiser. Men simply are not as perceptive as women. He will not recognize your voice, your new 'do, and certainly not your name. We're golden."

I have to hand it to her. That plan came together in the span of five seconds and is brilliant. I love my Nat!

When I get home, I immediately Google Brian. I see the stories he wrote for the magazine, his bio page on the radio station website, and some results for a couple of 10Ks in town. My imagination gets the best of me, and on my desk pad, I begin to write Rainey May Matthews. As I scribble the words, I say it over and over in my head: Rainey May Matthews, Rainey May Matthews. It has a nice ring to it.

Oh, that's so junior high, I think, and I quickly erase any evidence of the fictitious union.

CHAPTER 16

I CAN ALWAYS RELY ON NATALIE AND, SURE enough, she has me booked on Denver's Newsmakers within seventy-two hours of our trip home from the airport. She calls me the night before I am supposed to go on.

"Okay, as your press agent, it is my job to make sure you're prepared for the big interview," she says as if this were *People Magazine*. Before we get there, we need to make sure we have all your lies and truths straight."

"Lies? There has been no lying, only fibs," I say in protest of her accusations.

"Call them what you want, we simply cannot have him putting the puzzle pieces together. I said that men are not always perceptive, but they aren't stupid. Is there anything you have told him about May that definitely shouldn't be part of Rainey's world?" she asks.

"May already told him about car racing, so as far as sports go, Rainey only ski races. Hopefully, he doesn't ask about my family because I've already told him the story about Sunny and Mom. I'm sure he's done his research on me for the story, but I've Googled myself, and there aren't any telling details about the accident on any of my bios or newspaper reports. They all just say a car accident caused my injury. Mom and Sunny aren't mentioned. Fortunately, that all happened before the Internet became our go-to source. I think we're in the clear. Hopefully, our tracks are pretty well covered."

"Good. By the way, I put my middle name as the contact on the press release, instead of Natalie, so he won't make a connection on that either."

"All right, Grace, who is lying now?" Our scheming has reached an unsettling low. But I am steadfast in my desire to meet Brian before I *meet* Brian.

"It's not a lie; merely a fib. And I learned from the best," she murmurs in reply.

No wonder we're best friends. Through the good, the bad, and unfortunately, the ugly. I couldn't love her more.

When we arrive at the studio, we enter a large reception area. The woman at the desk takes one look at us and says, "You're here for Brian's show? Denver's Newsmakers?" It was the wheelchair. Dead giveaway.

"Yes, I reply. "I'm Rainey Abbott, and this is my agent, Grace Cooper."

"Very well then," she responds.

She gets on the phone and tells the person on the other line that Brian's ten o'clock is in the lobby.

Coming out from behind the glass wall surrounding the foyer is a young girl, probably twenty years old and likely the station's latest intern.

"Hi, I'm Cindy," she says with bubbly enthusiasm. She reminds me of a younger version of Natalie when the lights and action were merely a vision in her mind. Nat knew from an early age she wanted to rub elbows with the "it" crowd, which is exactly what she was doing in New York. Now, I feel bad that her star-studded dreams have fallen flat, and the biggest thing she has going today in her scaled-down life in D-town, aka Denver, is that she is now pretending to be the agent for a Paralympic skier.

Cindy walks us down the hall and into a room, which is not the studio but is connected to it by a door that is, at the present moment, slightly ajar. There is a window where you can see right into the booth, but both Brian and who I assume is his producer have their backs to us. With the door open a crack, I can hear that they are having a non-work related conversation between interviews. And the closer I listen, I realize they are talking about me. Not about me, *Rainey*, but me, *May*.

"How do you know she's not some chain-smoking elephant on the other side of the computer?" the blonde guy asks. I know that one isn't Brian because I scoured tons of pictures of him on the radio station's website a couple of days prior.

"I know," Brian says in defense. "She's pretty in her profile picture, she's active, athletic, and seems so genuine in all of our interactions. I don't know why she would lie."

"People lie on those dating sites all the time, Brian. A bunch of lonely thirty-something women who will never get married otherwise. Online is the stop of last resort. Besides, something is wrong with her. Why is she reluctant to get together and get on with things?" he asks.

"I think she's just afraid to get involved. Maybe she's been with too many guys like you," Brian says sarcastically, but then turns serious again. "I mean, you wouldn't get it. You go out, hookup with chicks, and never think twice about it. I'm tired of that scene. I want something real, something sincere."

"Sincere, huh?" Blondy chides Brian.

"What, do you need the definition?" he shoots back.

"Nah man, but we've been friends fifteen years, and I've never heard you talk like this. It makes me feel like someone stole my buddy and put some girly man in his place."

"Maybe that's what happens when you find someone who is truly worth your time. She's cool and doesn't seem like your typical girl. She's down to earth, realistic, doesn't talk about shopping and *Glamour* magazine. It's like she's been through things in her life that have forced her to grow up and given her a different perspective than most people have. I can't put my finger on it exactly, but I …"

"Oh, I get it," Blondy says. "You're falling in love."

The second I hear that I feel a delightful dizziness, and then a flood of panic flows through me. I want so desperately to hear the next words. I want his answer—an emphatic "Yes!" But instead, Blondy opens the door all the way and introduces himself as Ted, producer of Denver's Newsmakers.

"And you must be our next guest?" he says cheerfully. "Let's see. Rainey, is it? Welcome to Studio 26. Come on in and meet our reporter extraordinaire, Brian Matthews.

I can't believe that right in front of my eyes, is my man *Bri*, in the flesh. I lock eyes with him to see if there is any hint of familiarity. Not one bit, but he is warm and kind and holds out his hand to shake mine. While he leaves me breathless, I can tell he is analyzing my appearance, noticing above all else, the wheelchair. Seeing it instead of me. Typical.

He looks at his show rundown, which includes my bio and Natalie's press release. As he glances up at me, he says, "Looks like you're up." Brian points me into the studio and leads me to the microphone where I will be sitting and answering his questions. The chair, where the last guest sat, was in position in front of the mic. "Guess you won't be needing this, huh? Looks like you brought your own." Another wheelchair-ism, but I'm willing to forgive it, as he sheepishly looks me in the eye, and I melt a little inside. He strikes me as being on the edge of nervous and I can't tell if it's me or the chair. But he moves swiftly, getting me seated at my mic and going to the other side of the broadcast desk and standing at his microphone, next to the control panel, where he will turn the microphones on and adjust sound levels. Just before we are about to begin, he raises his eyebrows at me. "Ready to go live?"

"Yep." It's all I can say.

He waits until the current commercial is over and then turns his mic on and gives his introduction. "This is Brian Matthews, coming to you from 106.9 KXTY and today's

Colorado Newsmaker is Rainey Abbott." He turns to me. "So, Rainey, let's introduce you to our audience today. You're a Paralympic skier, and you've just won two gold medals in a World Cup event in Austria?" He looks directly in my eyes.

"Yes," I say, afraid to match his gaze.

I can see the gears turning in his head. "Paralympics. Now, is that the same as the Special Olympics?"

I shake my head no and explain. "The Paralympics are different from the Special Olympics. The Paralympics are for athletes with physical disabilities, and the Special Olympics are for athletes with cognitive disabilities. They are different in both scope and intensity. The Special Olympics gives athletes with intellectual differences the opportunity to participate in sports, stay physically fit, and experience the camaraderie and accomplishment that comes with participation. Whereas, the Paralympics are elite sport and are highly competitive, on the same level as Olympic competition."

"Oh, okay," he says.

I can tell he still isn't grasping the fact that I am 99.9 percent sure I can ski circles around him, fly by him like he is standing still—basically bury him in a ski race. And at that moment, I think *forget it. He's not my type.* But as we get into the conversation, it's easy to talk to him, and he seems genuinely interested in and intrigued by what I have to say.

"So, what do you do for a living, Rainey?"

"Aside from being an athlete, I also work part-time as a teaching assistant." I have to be careful, but I also have to be consistent with what is known about me.

"Your students must be proud to have a gold medalist for a teacher?"

"I think so, and I try to involve my students in what I'm doing because it gives them a sense of pride to be a part of my cheering section. More than that, though, it gives me some great teaching moments about working hard and not giving up to reach your goals and become successful."

As I talk, I can't stop fidgeting. I can tell I've been talking with my hands more than normal. I wonder if he's noticed. *Can he see how nervous I am?* I wonder if he can sense there is something else at play during this interview. *Does he recognize me, even with my blonde hair?*

He asks me briefly about my wheelchair and about the accident. I don't mention anything about my family and say my injury was due to a car accident a long time ago. After that, he is quickly on to skiing. He asks me about my favorite place to race. I tell him that I love the area of Queenstown, New Zealand and a resort called Cardrona.

As I tell him about my favorite resort, my mind takes me back to that trip. The last time I skied there, it was magical in every aspect. My race performances landed me atop the podium in two events, the team of athletes who qualified as the United States delegation jelled, and when we didn't have our game faces on, the trip was full of laughter, bonding, and practical jokes played on both fellow teammates and coaches. The best thing was hitting it off with one of the guys from the Australian National Team. His name was Oliver, and together one night, we snuck away from the Village, where all the athletes stayed, and went to the most romantic restaurant in all of Queenstown. It was a stone building that looked like it could have been the vacation cottage of a Hollywood star. On the inside was a smattering of fireplaces, with tables interlaced throughout. Each table seemed to be placed so that in the midst of all the other diners there was the feeling that each dining party had its own isolated space.

The lights were low, and Oliver and I ordered a bottle of wine. Our coaches wouldn't have appreciated that, both leaving the Village and drinking were against team rules, but we did it anyway. As we stared into each other's eyes, we ate the most succulent meat and seafood, and on several occasions, I stopped and closed my eyes and listened to Oliver's smooth Australian accent. It was one of the most romantic nights of my life. Not that I've had many to choose from. As I described the restaurant to Brian, minus the romantic details of the evening, he exclaimed, "I have been there! I know exactly where you're talking about."

Suddenly, our conversation diverged from interview to personal conversation. I couldn't grasp whether, like me, he had been there with a date, but he described it with the same longing for the flavors of the exquisite cuisine, soft lights, idyllic atmosphere, and fine wine. As we talked, the rest of the room, the microphones, even Ted and Natalie faded away, and we were locked in our own private conversation. It was like the peace of being underwater and sharing a moment before we both came up for air. I think it surprised each of us as we realized how we were momentarily swept away. When we finally came back to the sterility of the interview, I realized how at that moment we'd connected. There was something there.

Brian cleared his throat, as if to get himself back on track, rattled his rundown sheet, and got back to the business of asking questions. And before I knew it, time was up, and the interview was over. He concluded with his typical closing, "This is Denver Newsmakers, reported to you by Brian Matthews."

As he finished, his eyes seemed to look right into the center of my being, but his face showed a look of confusion. He seemed conflicted, but composed, and reached for my hand to shake it in appreciation. "It was very nice to meet you, Rainey. Best of luck in your endeavors," was all he said, and Natalie and I took our cue to exit the studio.

CHAPTER 17

AS SOON AS WE'RE IN THE CAR, I TURN TO Natalie and say, "Spill it. What do you think? Did you like him?"

"He seemed genuine, and it appeared as though you guys even shared an intimate moment there when you were talking about that quaint café in Queenstown. I don't know if I was imagining it, but he seemed to lean in a little bit more and was more focused on you rather than anything else going on in the room or the interview."

"So, you noticed it too? I thought it got a little cozy for a second. I think I started to break a sweat. What do I do now?"

"Definitely don't talk to him tonight while your voice is still fresh in his mind. Can you instant message? Find out how his day was? See if he brings up his interview?"

When I get home, I desperately want to talk to him right away, but I decide to play it cool, head to the gym, and talk to him when my heart settles down later that evening.

While I'm on the computer doing my lesson plans, an instant message pops up. My heart is pounding.

> **Good evening, Miss May Belle! How are you?**
> Had a good day today. Nothing special. Work. Workout. You know, the usual. How was your day?
> **Good. Interesting.**
> Interesting, huh? How so?
> **I interviewed this girl. Actually, she's a woman. Probably our age.**
> Oh really. What was so interesting about her?
> **For starters, she's a skier.**

This makes me smile. Because for once, someone says skier before "in a wheelchair."

> What's so interesting about that?
> **Well, she is also confined to a wheelchair.**

Smile erased.

> So how can she be confined to a wheelchair if she's a skier?
> **What do you mean?**
> If she's confined, that means she can't get out of the chair.

Oh c'mon, you know, that's the phrase you use to describe someone who uses a wheelchair.

Hmmm ... actually ... I don't think it is the phrase you use.

Oh?

Yeah, I've worked with kids who use wheelchairs and they are anything but confined.

Okay. Sorry for not being politically correct. Anyway ... she was interesting and nice, but somehow, I couldn't help but feel sorry for her. I think I would feel like my life was ruined if I had to be in a wheelchair.

Ruined. *He said ruined.* I'm not infuriated yet, but I can feel the simmering begin.

Was she cute?

Was she cute? Why do you ask?

I was making conversation. I mean, you think she's interesting and all. Would you consider dating a girl like that? One who uses a wheelchair?

Wow. You're confusing me a little bit here tonight, but um, as much as she was pretty (but I'm sure not prettier than you), and she was intelligent and nice to talk to, I don't know if I would date someone in a wheelchair. There'd be so much you couldn't do together.

I feel the tears begin to well up in my eyes. All I can do as I sit there is wish this conversation could be like a computer and I could reach up and touch the delete button, and it would be like it never happened.

What if you were married and the person you were married to got into an awful car accident and was paralyzed and had to use a wheelchair ... would you stay or would you go?

Oh, my. Have you suddenly become some big-hearted activist? Why so intense tonight? You seem overly concerned with people in wheelchairs.

I just wanted to hear about your day. You're the journalist who said you like to know about people. I'm interested in your point of view and how you look at the world around you. And, people with disabilities *are* a part of the world.

Well, if it were my wife, I'd like to think I would stay, but it's hard to imagine that situation. I'm only saying I think it would be hard to date someone like that.

Someone like that? Like what? Damaged goods?

I've finally had enough, so I tell Brian I need to grade papers and quickly exit our electronic conversation.

Instead, I immediately text Natalie and tell her I'm on my way over. I need to talk.

When I arrive on her doorstep, my eyes are red, puffy, and wet.

"Honey, what is wrong?" she asks with sincere concern.

I sit right there in front of her house and begin to ball my eyes out.

"At least come inside while you have your nervous breakdown," she says. Seth is in the study, so we can go talk in the living room." She leads me through the house, first stopping by the kitchen to pour two glasses of margarita on the rocks, premade, from a pitcher in the refrigerator.

"Now tell me, what happened? You had the most extraordinary day today. I would have thought you'd be surfing the waves of happiness right now."

"He's never going to like me!" I spit out between hyperventilating breaths. I fill her in on our IM conversation and his first impressions of me. "I can never go to meet him. I can't take it."

"Yes, Rainey, you *can* take it," she says as she begins on another of her lists: "A—You came into this knowing that it was 50/50, which it would be for anyone on the planet, chair or not, B—You are better and stronger than any situation he could hand to you and C—If he doesn't like you, take it like a crash n' burn on the slopes."

She launches into her pep talk. "Rainey, look at it this way. Think about the fact that you have put your heart and soul into all that skiing you do. And each day when you show up at practice, you never know if it's going to pay off in a win or if you're going to crash on your way down the mountain. But you do it anyway because you believe in it. You do it for the rush it gives you and the satisfaction that you gave it all you've got. Think about dating the same way. You will crash and burn sometimes. Maybe a lot of times. And every time you go down, you have a choice to make. Will you get back up and try it again, or will you let the mountain win? You're tougher than that. You don't give up. Look at all the things you've done in your life. You could have easily hung it up back in high school when you got injured. You could have called it good and put in the least amount of effort to get by. But that's not you. You're not a quitter. This is another test, and maybe Brian's words got you down, but you have the choice of whether you're going to get back up and try again, maybe with him, maybe with someone else. But have you ever considered that maybe Brian has never been exposed to someone with a disability? Sometimes people simply fear what they don't know. Remember how it was in the beginning, even for your family and closest friends? None of us knew what was going to be possible for you. Remember how you thought you'd never be able to do the normal stuff we were used to doing, but the next thing we knew, we were back to our old selves and our teenage antics? It was a learning curve even for us, and we were right in the thick of it. Give him the chance to see all that you are and what you're capable of. He knows you from the inside now, give him a chance to warm up to the rest of you. Don't throw in the towel yet. As much as you think you can read the future, let me be the one to break the bad news. You can't. If you could, you would have known Jenny wasn't going to take very kindly to her twenty-first birthday prank."

"Oh yeah, she was pretty mad, huh?"

"Yeah, but it was kind of funny," she said of the high jinks we pulled on the morning after Jenny's twenty-first birthday when she bit into one of our mayonnaise-filled donut creations. That, combined with her hangover, was pretty much a mood killer. She spent the rest of the day in the bathroom, hugging the toilet bowl and wouldn't speak to us for a week.

"It was pretty hilarious," Natalie said. "But in all seriousness, with Brian … leave yourself open to the possibility that he might surprise you. Okay?"

I looked down at my lap as if I had been reprimanded. "All right. I will."

There was a pause in our momentarily lighthearted and jovial conversation and then Natalie, who has been sitting calmly on the couch, curled in position with both legs bent up in front of her and her arms wrapped around, gets up, and starts to nervously pace the floor. I look at her in confusion as she gets up the nerve to tell me whatever thoughts she has been trying to organize in her head. I've never seen Natalie look like this before. She's always carried an air of complete confidence and control, but now is the first time in my life when I see her look insecure and afraid.

"Rainey, can I tell you something? And you have to promise not to hate me since I didn't tell you before?"

This must be serious, I think, because Natalie and I tell each other everything. "Nat, I really don't think there is anything you can tell me that would make me hate you."

"When I was working for the PR agency in New York, and Seth and I had been dating for seven months, I started having some, well, let's say "woman" problems. So, I went to see a doctor at the university med center, and after some exams and being sent to a world-renowned gynecologist (remember, we are in New York), I found out that I have what's called premature ovarian failure. When I asked the doctor what he meant by that and what it would do to me, he told me that I would most likely not be able to conceive. I had a five to ten percent chance of having children. He said, "*You can try, but don't count on it. When it comes time, you might want to consider adoption.*'" She looks down at her feet and continues with the story.

"Suddenly the room started spinning, and I nearly threw up. And there was a huge burst of pain that came from my insides, and my eyes were spilling over with tears. I couldn't believe his words. I wondered, *what, is wrong with me? Why are there millions of women in this world who are able to have children, and of the small percentage who can't, I am one of them!* And before I knew it, I had slid off the exam table and broken down in tears and sobs on the ground. The doctor looked at me in shock. I'm sure he'd seen it a hundred times, but I might have been the worst he'd witnessed, because he had a terrified look on his face and called for the nurse 'Stat.' What he didn't know was what had transpired three nights earlier."

She swirls her drink, and ice cubes clink against the sides of the glass.

"Seth had taken me to dinner at a romantic upscale New York restaurant, where I could tell he had put much time and thought into the night. I couldn't tell if he was going to propose to me or what, but I could tell it was something important. But that was the night we had *the* talk—the one that comes *before* the proposal, where you discuss what you're both looking for in life, love, and marriage. I was thrilled to find out how serious he was about our relationship. I had the jitters and couldn't sit still; I was so full of excitement. I was head over heels in love with him, and I had been waiting weeks for confirmation that he truly felt the same."

Focused on her body language, I began to see a Natalie I had never seen before. Insecure. Apprehensive.

"We had a great conversation that night. I wanted everything he wanted—a life in the city, working our way up in our careers, saving money, setting ourselves up for a lifetime of financial security so we could buy a house, maybe in Connecticut, so we could still commute to the city for work. We talked about how we both wanted to be active in volunteer work, stay in shape, and maintain a healthy social life. And then he asked me about children.

"'Of course!' I told him. 'I can't wait to have a family. Beautiful blonde babies,' I couldn't hold my excitement. They would undoubtedly take after my looks. Not that Seth isn't handsome, but who doesn't want their little girl to be created in their spitting image?

"Seth agreed, but he wanted the boys to have his athletic prowess and interest. 'I want to procreate a whole football team,' he said. 'We'll be like the Mannings with Peyton and Eli and Cooper.'"

I see Natalie's eyes begin to water as she recounts those few days. And I can't believe she had kept all this from me. If it weren't such a serious issue, I'd contemplate giving her a truckload of crap, but I can see how much this news destroyed Natalie's world.

"Imagine how I felt, having to go to Seth and tell him

that the woman he loves, and who he has confirmed is *the one* for him, can't have kids. Rainey, I was so upset and ashamed, I couldn't even tell you—the *one* person who knows *everything* about me. Anyway, not only did I blow you off those days after finding out, but also, I successfully avoided Seth for four days, and when I saw him I broke up with him. No explanation, no nothing. I simply told him we had to end it."

I can see the torment in Natalie in a way I've never seen her hurt before. I've always thought of her life as all rainbows and roses. Things always fall into place for her, and I don't ever remember her running up against any big obstacles in her life. But maybe I've been too focused on my own tragedy, how my life was set off course, to realize she could possibly have a problem. I don't know how I even missed this one. Natalie and I talked four or five times a week when she was at school. *How did I miss this? What kind of friend am I?*

"How did you get through it?" I ask her. "Obviously, you and Seth worked things out, and you're together now. What did you say to him? How did he react?"

"Well, it obviously caused a tailspin in our relationship. For us to be that close and then for me to drop off the face of the earth with no explanation was definitely not the way to handle it. I know that now. He made it explicitly clear to me," she turns and sort of half smiles. "He was mad, sad, and hurt. He called and texted and dropped by to try to see me, and I avoided all of it.

"Finally, one day he cornered me as I came off the subway and was walking back to my apartment. He stopped and stood like a brick wall in front of me. I could tell he had been crying, though he was trying his hardest to make it look like he wasn't. I could see the hurt in his eyes, and the only word out of his mouth was, 'Why?'

"I couldn't look him in the eye. I bowed my head to the pavement, and the flood of tears started, and I couldn't stop shaking. He put his arms around me and said, 'Whatever it is, we can get through this. If it's someone else you want to be with, I'll let you go. But if it's anything else, we will get through it together. I don't even care what it is, Nat. You're the love of my life. The only woman I want to be with. *Ever.*'

"We went back to my apartment, and I sat him down and told him straight out. 'I'm never having a football team. I'm not even having a singles tennis player. I can't give you what you want, Seth. The doctor said I can't have children.'

"I didn't look at him, but he put his arms around me and sat there and held me. He said, 'Natalie, what did I tell you when we were out on the sidewalk?'

"'That we could get through anything together?' I said.

"'I meant that. I know I told you the other night that I'm excited to have a family, that I'd love a whole football team, but sometimes life sends you in directions you didn't expect. You can get disappointed and discouraged. You can fight it. But you can also go with the flow. If there's one thing I've learned from all the sports I've done in my life, it's that you can't control the game or the conditions, and sometimes you can't even control how your body performs. That's where you and I are right now. Our lives are taking a turn, but I'd rather be with you however the twists and turns place themselves. I know for some people, this news would be a deal breaker.

And I understand that. I fully get someone wanting their own gaggle of biological kids and nothing else. But what *I* want is you. The rest is icing.'

"I couldn't believe he was so open and accepting, having come from a huge family himself and wanting his own kids, but the fact is, he weighed our relationship against those desires and I still won. Maybe it doesn't always end happily like that, but then again, if it doesn't, it means you're not with the right person. Because there are always going to be things that come up and threaten to tear two people apart. And I think when you find the right person, they will at least be willing to go up to bat and give it 100 percent. But you won't know unless you try."

Leaving Natalie's house, I am still in shock. I can't believe the news she unloaded on me and can't imagine the devastation she felt. Natalie led such a charmed life; I thought nothing could ever go wrong with her. But her news confirmed to me that you truly can't judge a book by its cover. Even if it's a book you've read over and over again. You never know when you might see something new or unexpected in the words you know by heart.

I'm still unsure about my situation with Brian, so I decide I need a sign. One that will tell me what to do next. Where to go to find this sign I don't know, but after pondering it for a while, I decide to call Dad. I haven't even talked to him since I returned home from the ski trip. My dad isn't a big phone guy, but he loves texting. *Makes conversations short and sweet*, he says. I've sent him a couple of texts … *made it home safely … can't wait to hear about your dating … love you, see you on Sunday.*

This is something that can't wait. I decide to call him and if things are going well with Sara, I will move forward and tell Brian I am ready to meet. If they haven't gone well ... I'll figure out my next step later.

When my dad answers the phone, he sounds elated. Maybe it's because of my gold medals or my interview on the radio, but the more we talk, I realize, it's something else.

"Rainey, I'm so glad you called! Sara and I were sitting here talking and wondering when we might see you. I hope you will be able to spare a little extra time on Sunday because Sara thought it would be nice for us to take you to the theater."

As that sentence rolls out of his mouth, my mind gets stuck. He makes it sound so normal that Sara would just be sitting there, in my house, as if it was an everyday occurrence, and I haven't even met her yet.

He continues, "*Wicked* is playing in town this weekend, and I know it's a show you have been dying to see, so we got matinee tickets and have made reservations for dinner at Gatlin's afterwards. Oh, and make sure to keep Thanksgiving free too. Sara will be joining our improvised family this year for the holidays. I'm so excited for you two to get a chance to get to know each other. I know you will get along fabulously!"

Wait, what? They are making plans to take me to the theater. How does she know I like the theater? "Dad, what is going on?" I yell at him and then realize how full of anger my voice is.

"Rainey, why the outburst? I thought you were in full support of me dating? Is there something that's bothering you that you're not telling me?"

My eyes fill with tears because I know it's wrong to yell

at my father. And I know it's because he is moving along so smoothly and easily in this dating game and I am stuck, stuck, stuck. I'm jealous of his happiness and his ease in going out on dates and not worrying about what some woman will think of him. I'm feeling left out. The two most important people in my world are happily involved with others who can't love them more and don't care about their flaws or imperfections. And I still can't get the guts up to even go on a date, even though I potentially could have the same thing too—if I would only gather the courage to go out on a limb and meet my potential Mr. Right.

I quietly apologize to my dad, tell him how happy I am for him, and confirm that I'll see him and Sara on Sunday. Then I get off the phone as quickly as possible before bursting into tears.

I spend the rest of the night lying in bed feeling sorry for myself. I can hear the beeping of Brian trying to send me instant messages, but I ignore them. I don't want to think about my own life for a while, so I pull the covers over my head and try to drown out my thoughts.

CHAPTER 18

WHEN I WAKE UP ON THANKSGIVING MORNING, I feel like my head is draped with pounds of wet towels. I am absolutely and completely dreading going to my father's house. That's generally so unlike me because I enjoy the holidays, even though it's a hard time to be single, I appreciate the feeling of having somewhat of a traditional family around. Even though I could never see my dad with Natalie's mom, in my head I've always liked to pretend that Natalie and Cecile are Sunny and my mom and we have a full family of four again. That's how we spent our holidays all through high school and college. Of course, until Seth came along. That was quite an adjustment to try and figure out how he fit into the family. The first few holidays with him intruding on our makeshift family unit were definitely something to get used to. But eventually, I learned to accept him. After all, I knew how Nat felt about him, and, of course, once it was solidified with the ring and the wedding, I figured it was either both of them or no Natalie. So, I've made the best of it. And it turns out, Seth is a super guy. He is such a smooth conversationalist; he seems to know at least a little bit about everything. He also has a playful sense of humor and can have a room of people in tears of laughter in no time. After a while, I started to plug him into the role of the quirky uncle who everyone loves to have at family gatherings, and made do with that, but today, I wonder, *where does Sara fit in?* Certainly, she is pleasant enough. We had a good day at the theater. No, a great day. In fact, I adored her. She is talkative and funny. An extrovert to my more reserved personality. She bridged the conversation between my father and I, making the atmosphere come alive. But we've never needed a bridge before. Why do we need one now? We don't, which is the thing. The thing that keeps niggling through my brain. She's moving into our twosome. Is she trying to weasel her way into our family? Or does it only feel that way because I'm not as ready as I thought I was to let go of my dad so he could start fresh? Is it just me? My mind goes to my mom. I imagine her in heaven, a soft glow around her face. Her delicate features are focused on my father and me, and the lives we've created since she's been gone. She is clad in all white—angelic. As she is looking down, I try to discern if she is smiling or if it's something else. Sadness? Despondence? Lonely? As the feeling of dread seems to grow in me, I whisper aloud, "Please Mom, help me be okay. With *me. My life.* With Dad moving forward."

I know it was my idea. I was the one who got my dad online. I was the one who suggested he start dating. But subconsciously I think it was one of those things you want for someone else, but when it actually happens, you realize you were doing it more as a gesture than a genuine action. I feel as though I am spiraling in an ugly pool of feelings of heartbreak, hurt, and frustration all rolled up in jealousy. Not long ago, my misery had company in the form of my dad who didn't seem any further along in his emotional processing of our family's tragedy than I was. Now, it's as though he's been able to flip a switch and let someone new into his heart. When I look for that switch, it always seems to be just beyond my grasp.

I'm glad my dad is happy, and I genuinely like Sara. Knowing they are together and seeing how happy they are, though, only encourages the demon of insecurity inside of me.

I get out of bed, shower, dress, and, on my way out the door, grab the pumpkin pie I made the day before.

When I open the door of my dad's house, the aromas of Thanksgiving food mixed with cinnamon and a feeling of comfort wash over me. *It is good to be home,* I think, as my dad and Sara come around the corner from the kitchen, through the dining room, to greet me. I'm the first one there. "Rainey," my dad says as he hugs me. "It's so good to see you!" He exudes an enthusiasm about the holidays that I haven't seen in years. In fact, his bear hug feels like it did when I was growing up. Only this time, he doesn't lift me up off the floor. After he releases me, Sara steps in and says, "May I give you a hug too? It's so nice to see you again." As she leans over to hug me, I can smell the faint scent of vanilla mixed with lavender, and her body heat warms me after traveling to Dad's house on one of the coldest Thanksgiving days in the record books. She is firm, but nurturing, in her grasp of me. I wonder if this is what it would feel like if I got to hug my mom in my adult years. She gives my hair a slight touch and compliments me on my recent haircut. I'm surprised she notices.

As we pass by the living room, there is a fire roaring, with a glow that brings light and a compassionate warmth to our house. When we get to the kitchen, my dad pours me a glass of my favorite red wine, and the conversation seems to flow as easily as the smooth alcohol traveling down my throat. Soon, the front door opens again, and the rest of the gang is there—Nat, Cecile, and Seth. We all gather in the kitchen, and there are wine glass toasts all around. Suddenly, I feel like I am right where I am supposed to be. Surrounded not necessarily with relatives bound to me by blood, but by love.

Later that night I return home, and Brian and I have a quick instant messaging conversation. Not much, a few holiday pleasantries, as we catch up on our day, but that's about it. I still haven't totally gotten over our post-interview conversation, nor have I given up. I'm somewhere in the middle and know that with one holiday come and gone, I can't possibly make it through another without either meeting Brian in person or having him get bored and walk away.

CHAPTER 19

THE DAYS BEGIN TO PASS QUICKLY. AT A TIME OF year when most people are hunkered down, hibernating, and waiting out the winter, my life is in full motion. I have been skiing way more than teaching, socializing, or even thinking about Brian. My days in the mountains are intense with workouts and tryouts and the anticipation of the Games in March.

When I finally get a weekend off, I relish the opportunity to be in my own bed, sleeping in and enjoying the laziness most people take for granted. I open my eyes, and the sun shines radiantly, though there are still flurries coming down off and on. Yesterday was a downright snowy December day, and it felt weird to be in town while there was probably some great skiing to be had in the hills. But, on this Saturday, when the ground is blanketed with white, I have absolutely nothing planned for the day and no idea where I'm going or what I will do. I'm in a funk, probably because once I get into the groove of hard training; it's hard to take a day off. I feel like I'm losing my fitness and my edge, although realistically I know they don't simply disappear overnight. I also haven't had any great conversations with Brian, although we're still writing daily.

I roll out of bed, head to the shower, and get ready for the day. While I'm rinsing my hair, I come up with a plan. I'll head to the showroom where I know Jake will be working on his car, getting ready to put it on a trailer to head to South Carolina for next week's race.

With winter fully set in, it seems like forever since I've spent quality time with Jake as sounding board, confidant, fellow speed demon. Ever since I found out he was happily married and I would never be Mrs. Jake, he's turned into a pick-me-up, taking his role seriously. He always tries to make me feel better in moments like this when all I want to do is sit around and sulk.

As I push my chair across the linoleum floor of the showroom where we all keep our cars indoors during the winter, I spy Jake under the hood tinkering. I roll up to him in silence and manage a very slight "Hey." I'm so quiet, partly because I don't want to scare the crap out of him and partly because I don't have the energy to be any more exuberant.

"Hey, Rainey, how ya doing?" Jake turns his head to look at me while still ducked under the hood.

I don't say anything, only look at him with pathetic puppy dog eyes until he catches on that things in my world aren't quite right. He stops what he's doing, wipes off his hands with the nearest cloth, and comes over to me, getting down on one knee, so he is at my level. For a moment, I envision this gesture as the tender scene of a marriage proposal, but I know better. Jake is being polite. Getting down on my level to talk rather than standing tall and talking down to me. This is one thing I love about him. He thinks about these etiquette details, and I appreciate it.

"Jake, am I doomed to live my life alone? Why can't I get myself to call Brian, ask him out to lunch, and meet him in person? Why am I so scared?"

"We both know you're in serious *like* with Brian. You have to be willing to let go. Let yourself feel and take a chance. Even if it doesn't work out, it's giving it a shot that counts. He might not be the one for you. That is a definite possibility, and there is a chance you'll lose him, but that's part of life. You can lose anything, on any day. You know that. You can lose your ability to walk, lose your family, or lose this relationship you have been building online. But that doesn't mean you should live holding your breath, waiting for the worst. Why not go into this with hope instead of dread?"

"Because I want to be realistic."

He stops talking long enough to stand up and retrieve his soda from the roof of the car and then returns to his position in front of me. I begin to get uncomfortable since I know what's coming. It's me. I know it's me, getting in my own way.

"Rainey, you know what I believe? If you always go into situations expecting the worst, often that's what you'll get. I know you've learned this a million times as a skier and as a driver. When you're on the ski hill or the track, and you feel outclassed and believe you'll never win, you won't. You don't stand a chance. You have to have some amount of confidence and faith that things will work out the way they are supposed to. And it might not be with Brian. He's the first guy you've dated … if I can use that term … though you haven't actually even met him yet. Maybe it'll be the next guy who is the right one. Or the one after that. You realize that Amber is not the first woman I've dated, right? Don't tell her that," he says as he winks at me.

Amber, Jake, and I are all keenly aware that Jake is a hot commodity, and that he's had women throw themselves at him over the course of his thirty-three years.

Then he launches into the lecture that I know I need.

"Love is difficult. It can be fun, but it can also be exhausting. It's hard work, but ultimately, it's rewarding. That's why it's such a huge emotion. It has to be able to encompass all those things. It's not all sap and romance like in the movies. Even your parents probably had those spiritless relationship moments of 'Uh, you again?' But there's something about knowing you have that bond, and you're united by a common feeling that belongs only to the two of you. To get there, you have to be willing to stick your neck out. And that's where you're getting hung up. You realize this isn't all about the chair or your mom and Sunny, don't you? It's really about your unwillingness to open your mind. To be out of control and take the plunge. You're staying in your protective little shell."

Jake has me figured out, and as he looks directly into my eyes, I feel my body shrink into itself. I cross my arms and brace myself to take the rest of what he has to deliver.

"Rainey, it's okay to feel scared, but the only one who can take the leap of faith is you," he continues. "Being in love is like driving your car. You have to trust your machine, your mechanics, your tires. But more than that, you have to trust yourself. Think about how scary it was the first time you raced in a field of other cars. Did you ever get that lump in your throat when you were hitting a turn in a race, and there were cars on all sides of you, and you prayed that you would get through unscathed? You were totally out of your comfort zone, right? I don't know about you, but I love that feeling when your skin prickles and the little hairs on your arms stand at attention because it makes me feel alive. Yeah, sometimes I feel like I'm gonna crap my pants, but when it's over, and you've crossed the finish line, you know you're a better racer because you had courage. And the more times you crossed that line, the more comfortable you got. Now it feels like home. You get on the track, and as soon as the flag waves and the race starts, you settle in and know exactly what you're doing."

He is right. There was a time when racing scared me out of my mind. But the more I did it, the more comfortable and confident I got. I learned my car inside and out. Got to know its quirks and when something wasn't dialed in quite right. I wanted to learn to race so badly that I kept on pushing through all the scary stuff. I always thought—*keep my eye on the goal*.

"Approach falling in love with the same confidence and faith," he continues. "Picture yourself with everything working like clockwork. But instead of being on the racetrack, picture yourself on a Sunday afternoon drive. Don't rush to the finish line. Breathe it in and really feel it. Experience it for the butterflies it gives you. Even feel it for the lump you get in your throat when you disagree. Let yourself feel emotion because then you know you're alive. You are living, Rainey. If you don't, you're just as guilty as what you assume about all the men out there. You are confined. Not to your chair, like people might say, but to your thoughts. That somehow different is bad. You have so much to offer because of your situation. Turn it around. You are the prize and it's their loss if they can't see it. Not yours."

"Jake, I know. But I'm terrified. I want so badly to find someone who sees me as a person, not a chair or a tragedy. How do I get over this?"

I am so caught up in my woe-is-me drama that I don't realize someone else has walked into our area in the showroom and is standing within earshot listening in.

From behind me, in the corner, piping up in a demure female southern voice, she matter-of-factly answers my question. "Just jump." I can see the big loving smile on Jake's face as we turn around to see Amber behind us, having heard our entire conversation.

CHAPTER 20

WHEN I GET HOME, I KNOW WHAT I HAVE TO DO. It's time. And if I don't take the opportunity, someone else will, and I'll lose out on a prize of a man. It won't be long before Brian gives up and finds someone else. I don't think I can take another pep talk and, to be honest, the suspense is killing me. If he doesn't like me, it is time to find out. Amber was right. It's time to take flight, make the leap, and trust that, wherever I land, I will handle with the grace of a skier, the finesse of a race car driver and just enough pure me to make the trip worthwhile. But I won't know anything until I do something about it. I turn on the computer and go to my messages. Remembering that I didn't get on my computer in my funk yesterday, I see that I have not one but two messages from Brian in my inbox.

Hi, Ms. May Belle:

I don't know what's going through your mind, but I can tell you for sure that you are the only thing going through mine. I feel like it's been so long since we had a good heart-to-heart talk. I am missing you like crazy and wish my mystery woman on the other side of this computer would pipe up and tell me what's new in her life.

Can you believe Christmas is only two weeks away? I was wondering how you might feel if a present happened to fall on your doorstep, courtesy of one gentleman who is, at this moment, jumping out of his skin to meet the lovely spirit who has now become his dream woman. It has to be time, doesn't it? Please promise me, we can spend time together during the holidays. I would love to sit on a park bench with you and watch the snow fall on a moonlit evening, or sit by a fireplace at a romantic restaurant, drinking bottles of wine until we close the place down. Or how about an active date, visiting one of the outdoor skating rinks and we could do a few figure eights?

Let me know your preference, and I will plan a night you will never forget.

I look forward to hearing from you. And can't wait until I'm looking directly into those clear green eyes of yours.

Love,

Brian

Wow, I think. That's the first time he's ever signed a message "love." The thought makes my insides stir, and I begin to imagine us on one of his proposed dates. Well, except the skating one. But then I open his second message and whatever elation I felt after his first message disappears.

May:

I can't take it any longer. I'm at a loss for words. I've written, IM'd, laid out my best date ideas, and still nothing. I desperately want to meet you, but maybe it's not meant to be. Is it time for us to move on? I can't date a computer any longer.

Brian

I panic after I read the second message. I didn't mean to blow him off. This truly is an instance of, *"It's not you, it's me."* But now, I know he's slipping through my grasp. I held out too long. Made him work too hard. I am going to lose him, and I'll never know the feeling of truly getting to know the in-the-flesh person. I realize I must do something, and fast.

Brian:

I am so sorry. My intention was never to string you along. I do want to meet. I am scared. I am afraid of what might or might not happen. But I will never know if we never meet, will I? Ready or not, I'm ready to take the plunge. Though maybe not ice-skating....

May

I don't know what else to say besides that, so I take a deep breath and hit send. Then, with shaking hands, I dial Natalie's phone number. "Emergency," I say. "What are you doing right now? How does a pitcher of margaritas sound?"

"Oh my. We haven't had a pitcher of margaritas night for quite some time. This must be big. Let me go ask Seth if he minds if I come out to the rescue."

"No, we need Seth with us. This must be group counseling, and we definitely need a male's perspective. I need help. Coaching. I sent Brian an email and told him we should meet."

There is an audible gulp on the other line. "You finally did it? Rainey, I'm so proud of you! How do you feel?"

"Did my request for a pitcher of margaritas not convey my feelings? Can we go? Now?"

"Yes, ma'am. We'll meet you at the Rio, pronto!"

"Thanks, Nat."

When I arrive at the Rio, I don't waste any time. Head straight to a four-top table and order a pitcher of Margaritas. I immediately start drinking after they are served, so when Nat and Seth walk up, I must look like a lush.

"Wasting no time tonight, are ya?" Seth says, beaming at me.

"Nope," I reply.

"Okay, spill the beans," Nat says.

"I asked him out," I say. "Happy now?"

"You asked Brian out?" Nat asks as if there could be someone else in question.

"No, Justin Timberlake. Who do you think I'm talking about?"

"What did he say?" she asks.

"I don't know. I was too chicken to stick around. That's when I called you and split from the house. What do I do?"

"Well. A——" Natalie says as she starts her list, "You know he's going to say yes. B——you're going pick a neutral spot to meet, don't commit to a whole day of activity or anything. And, C——you're not going to chicken out. It's really straightforward, actually."

By the time Natalie has gotten through the first three letters of the alphabet, I am already through my first drink.

"Slow down there, sailor," Seth says.

"I'm just. So. Nervous. What if he doesn't like me?"

"We've gone over this a million times, Rainey. The only way to find out is to go." I can tell Natalie is becoming tired of my neurotic behavior.

"Okay," I put my head down. The rest of the night I sit, shoulders slumped, sipping my margarita through a straw, and wondering what I have gotten myself into.

After two hours of drinking, gossiping, and worrying about boys, with Seth only able to get a word in every once in a while, he has to drive two drunk, babbling women home. What a good guy he is to put up with us at times like this. That's one thing I can say for Seth. He's always been the designated driver when Nat and I need to have margarita nights. Which has been on many occasions.

As they drop me off in front of my house, Natalie has one bit of advice for me. "Remember Rainey, drunk texting, emailing, and IMing, or any other form of communication for that matter, with a possible future boyfriend is never a good idea."

I give her a big nod and thumbs-up as I transfer out of the car. I push up to the front door, and as I turn the key and let myself in, I turn and wave goodbye to them both. And then I do exactly what I was warned about not sixty seconds earlier. I head point-blank to the computer. I have to know Brian's response. I open his message:

> May! I thought you would never ask! I hate to act like a kid on Christmas, but I don't think I can wait. When can we meet? How about lunch tomorrow?

Tomorrow? The word is still swimming in my head when an instant message pops up.

> Hey, May. I saw you online and thought I would say hello. How's your night been? Do anything fun? I took Casey to dinner and paintball tonight and had a great time, but it didn't compare to what was waiting for me when I returned home. I'm so glad you're ready to meet.

Oh no, I have to form a sentence now. I'm not sure I can do it. Why didn't I listen to Natalie's advice and go straight to bed? The only words I can get out in my drunken state are:

> What time and where?
> I'm playing ball in the morning with the guys. How about a late lunch? One o'clock at Bittersweet?
> Okay. See you then. I've got to go lie down. I'm exhausted. Can't wait to see you.

I don't know if it is nerves or the margaritas, but the minute I hit the send button, I hightail it to the bathroom and throw up.

CHAPTER 21

WHEN I AWAKEN THE NEXT MORNING, IT IS actually very close to afternoon. I lie in bed, head aching, gut rotting, and feeling very much like shit. *At least I get to spend the day in bed if I want to. No ski practice, no ... OMG! I have a date! In less than two hours!* On top of that, my car is downtown at the Rio. I have nothing set out to wear, and I have so little energy, I can barely drag myself to the shower. I panic. *I should cancel. I can't cancel. He'll think I chickened out.* My mind flashes back to last night, and I think, *why didn't I listen to Natalie when she said drunk communications were not a good idea?*

Okay, one thing at a time, I coach myself. I roll my body over and scoot to the edge of the bed so I can transfer into my wheelchair. I feel woozy, but I have to keep moving. It's 11:30 and I have to be at Bittersweet at 1:00. *I can get ready in an hour, and I'll have to take the Audi.* I never drive that car anywhere except to the racetrack and back, but desperate times call for desperate measures. Although I think it might seem pretentious for me to pull up in that car, I don't have a choice. I also have to be extra careful not to drive with racer brain because that baby goes from zero to sixty in under a block. *If I'm not careful, I'll end up in jail.*

I hurriedly get dressed. I don't have to worry that my outfit will look contrived and over-thought-out because there is no chance of that in my effort to rush. I grab my newest pair of jeans and combine them with a casual maroon-and-white-striped sweater that I recently bought. I look in the mirror. No, the sweater isn't right. I try another and another. *Okay,* I think to myself. *Pick one! You don't have time for this.* I settle on a sweater that actually belongs to Natalie, but for some reason I haven't yet returned it, add in some black boots, and voila! I'm ready. There isn't much time to do anything special with my hair, but I don't want to go with the sporty ponytail I wore to the radio station. *Hair is always sexier worn down,* I think, so I pull out the curling iron and attempt to do some swirling and fluffing and pray I have pulled it off. As I look in the mirror and do my hair, I can see my hands shaking, and wonder how I am going to feel on the other side of this date. *Will I arrive home elated or deflated?* I try not to think about it.

When I get in the car I pray it will start because it's been a couple of weeks since I took the time to turn the key and get the engine revved up. When the skis come out for the season, the race cars get neglected, but I'm thankful when it starts fine. I look at the time on the dashboard, and it's 12:35. I think I can get there within five minutes of our designated meeting time, and even though being late is one of my biggest pet peeves, this is the best I can do for today. I quickly text Natalie and tell her to wish me luck. I tell her my nerves are under control. It's a lie.

I race to the restaurant, which my speed-limit-abiding-father would not approve of, and I do a little slide out as I turn into the parking lot for effect. It gives me a kick of confidence as I exercise my car handling skills. When I'm in the car or on the slopes, I'm in my element. And when it comes to "go time," I'm there. Even if I feel nervous on the start line, once the gun goes off or the start flag waves, there's a switch in my brain that turns, and I know exactly what I need to do. I wish I had that switch for the game of dating, but I don't, so I have to use the car as my reinforcement.

I enter the parking lot and look for an available accessible space. I pull my chair out—first the body of the chair and then the wheels. I assemble it next to me in the parking lot, transfer out of the car, settle myself in, and start pushing into the restaurant. I wonder if Brian is here yet and if he can see me from the restaurant window.

My anxiety has turned to horror as I envision how this meeting will go. There is no denying it, this time, it's the real thing—no computers, no messaging, no texts. Face-to-face time. This is going to happen. On the sly, I look down at my phone, pull up the camera, and change it to selfie mode so I can take one last look at myself. I love how a smartphone can also act as a mirror at a time like this. It's such a stealth way to gauge your appearance, and it looks so natural. Like you're checking your email one last time. First impression jitters soar through my body.

I wonder what will happen when we lock eyes on each other once I find him in the restaurant. *Will he show that wide smile with perfect teeth I saw at the radio station? Will he hug me? Kiss me on the cheek? Run the other way?*

Once I enter the restaurant, everything goes so quickly and none of it the way I've imagined. I don't even get a second from the time I enter the restaurant to the instant I make eye contact with Brian. For a moment there, I freeze, and so does he. I can tell the wheels in his brain are spinning, and suddenly he gives me a big smile, walks up to me, and says, "Rainey, right?"

"Um, yes," I say, as if I'm not at all sure that's my name.

"Funny I should run into you here today. I'm actually meeting up with someone on a blind date. This woman … we've been emailing for months. She's really something. I'm dying to meet her. I mean, weird to say, but I think she's the one for me."

"Um. Yeah. About that. Can I tell you something?"

"Sure, but will you tell me first—do I look okay? For a first date, and all? I didn't want to seem vain but…. Do you think the sweater is too much?" He asks this about his eggplant colored, ribbed turtleneck sweater. He comes in somewhere between trying-too-hard and *metro*. Though, he's easy on the eyes, so I wasn't going to be one to judge.

"Are you meeting someone here also?" Brian asks sincerely. "Oh wait, you said you wanted to tell me something."

"Yes," I answer very slowly, trying to pick my words

carefully because I have a feeling once the truth is out there, we'll both be shaken. "The thing is, I *am* here to meet someone … and that someone is you."

"What do you mean, exactly?" he asks, matching my slow pace of conversation.

"My full name is actually Rainey May, so you see, sometimes I go by May … to avoid all the wisecracks."

He looks at me blankly.

"What I'm trying to say is that you're here to meet me. I am May. Rainey May Abbott, to be precise. You know me as May. May Belle. Mystery woman."

His face turns as white as freshly bleached hotel sheets. "Wait a minute. You're the long-haired brunette, car mechanic, AC/DC-in-the-shower-singer?"

"Yes, that would be me."

"I don't get it. Why didn't you tell me?"

"Tell you what?" I ask defensively, just to force the words out of him.

"That … that," he stutters. "You were on my radio show, and you knew who I was. You baited me into a conversation about dating a woman in a wheelchair. You lied to me."

"Brian, I never meant to deceive you. But I was afraid. Afraid you would see me as undatable. That you would lose interest or never become interested at all. If I would have said in my profile that I was a paraplegic and used a wheelchair, you wouldn't have given me a second glance. If you did, it would only have been to feel sorry for me. You said so yourself. You didn't know if you could date someone in a wheelchair. But I wanted to give you a chance to get to know me first. It was the only way I could think to get you to see me and not my chair. But now I can tell that my chair is all you see. I knew it. It's easy to talk to an online ghost and imagine the closeness and feelings, but it's totally different in person. I'm not at all who you thought I was and, frankly, you're probably not the guy I thought you were either. I'm sorry for wasting months of your life and thinking that you could actually fall for a girl like me. Forget it!" I rotate the wheels on my chair to spin around in place, but not so quickly that I don't get a final glance of his furrowed brow and the puzzled look on his face.

Maybe I've moved too quickly. What is going through his head? Is he petrified? Hurt? I *overreacted*, I already know. But I've made my move and am facing the door, so I can't turn around without looking even more like a fool. At this moment, I loathe my insecurity. I'm ashamed. I move hurriedly through the exit and push to the car as quickly as I can to hop into the consoling, happy place of my Audi and squeal the tires out of the parking lot.

I head directly to the highway. I need to drive fast, so I pull the radar detector out of the glove box, find Pink's angry rendition of "So What." As her boisterous lyrics begin, I crank the volume and I'm suddenly envious of her to-hell-with-it attitude. I don't need him. I'm a strong independent woman. I can be my own person. But as I try on my suit of rebellion to match that of Pink, all I feel is hollow.

I drive all the way out to the track, and although I know it is trespassing to be there when the track manager isn't around, I have skills and I'm not afraid to use them. Thanks to the guys I grew up with, and our sometimes late-night shenanigans at the track when I was in high school and college, I know how to pick the lock on the main gate at the track. It's not the first time I have come here when the track was officially closed and burned off steam by driving to my heart's content at 100 mph. Probably not the safest thing to do when your eyes are so full of tears you can barely see, and your safety gear isn't on, but I know my way around the track, and I'm where I belong.

I knew it! I knew it wouldn't work. I was screwed either way. Either I wouldn't get a chance to know Brian because he'd skip over the wheelchair girl profile or I'd spring it on him, and it clearly wouldn't work. I thought that if he got a chance to know me and like me, I would have an opportunity. But no.

After several laps, I stop. Right in the middle of the track. I don't pull over or follow any of the other safety rules one must follow when there are other cars around. The truth is, I am alone. In every sense of the word. On the track and in my life. Once the sobbing starts, it's uncontrollable. I don't try to stop it.

CHAPTER 22

I MUST HAVE CRIED MYSELF TO SLEEP FROM exhaustion, hangover, and rejection because the next thing I know, I'm looking up and the sun is setting. Although it has been a relatively warm and sunny Denver day, as I lose sunlight, any heat that was in the air also dissipates. I am shivering in the car, my head hurts, and my heart feels like it has been shattered into a million tiny pieces. I start the car again and drive to the big chain link gates that fence me in my secret world and out of the larger one. They seem to confine me, and now I know for certain that my wheelchair confines me too. I've never thought that before. It hasn't stopped me from doing what I wanted to do, but now it has kept me from someone who I thought could possibly love and accept me the way I am. How could I have been so wrong?

I drive home following the speed limit, maybe even slightly slower because I have no idea what comes next. I don't want to call Natalie and get a lecture about how I went about this in all the wrong ways, and I don't want to call my dad and hear about his latest date with Sara. I know Jake and Amber are on their way to South Carolina, and all I want to do is disappear.

When I get home, I fly through the house gathering sweaters, jackets, hats, and gloves and shoving them into my oversized USA duffle bag, and decide to retreat to the mountains for a while. Normally, I do a lot of commuting from Denver to the ski hill for training, but for now, I decide that a change of scenery would do me good, and I should make a getaway to the mountains and shift my full attention to what really matters—skiing. How could I let a relationship distract me from the task at hand? I was supposed to be training, not trying to fall in love.

I call Jenny and ask her for an emergency favor. "I got a little drunk last night, and my car is still downtown. Do you think you could give me a ride to go pick it up?"

"Tied one on, did ya?" she asks.

"I guess you could say that," I reply in a monotone.

"Is there something wrong, Rainey?"

"Not really, I need to get my car to take care of a few things this evening, and I shouldn't have gotten so drunk last night. I feel like crap, and I could use your help."

"No worries. I'm happy to. I've got nothing going on today and nothin' but time. You know the life of a single girl," she adds.

"Boy, do I!" I leave the details out. You'd think I would feel comforted to know that I'm not the only single girl around, but the way I look at it, Jenny can take the world by the horns, if she wants to. No one is looking at her like she's different, or worse, defective.

Fifteen minutes later, she shows up, and we are on our way. She tells me about her Saturday night. Turns out she hit the bars too with a couple of her friends from work. "What is it with the lack of men these days? Are all of the good ones really gone? I can't seem to meet anyone of quality."

Sitting next to her, I think to myself how I found him and blew it. I don't know, maybe I never had a chance.

The car ride is becoming torture because I don't want to hear about Jenny's problems while I am busy stewing in mine. I merely want to get in my car and head to the safety of the mountains. She drops me off, and I thank her profusely for saving me in my time of crisis. She has no idea. I hop into my car and drive home. I quickly pack the Subaru, text Nat and Dad to tell them I am headed to the hills for a couple of days, and then I'm off.

As I drive, my phone rings off the hook. First Natalie, then Brian, then Natalie, then Brian, then Dad. I ignore all of them. Partly because I don't want to talk and partly because I can't drive with my hand controls and talk on the phone at the same time.

Driving west on the highway, the further out of town I get, the more my nerves begin to relax. As I reach Berthoud Pass, the snow begins to swirl out of the sky. It looks like little diamonds from above, and they sparkle and drift gracefully as they land silently on my car. I try to play over and over in my mind where I went wrong today. *Did I read Brian correctly? Did he actually make a face of surprise and disappointment, or did I overreact? I'm sure I had it right. He already said it would be hard to date someone in a wheelchair. I knew I didn't have a chance. But at least now I know. I know that he definitely isn't the one for me.*

An hour-and-a-half after I screech out of Denver, I land in Winter Park. The place where I am supposed to be. Where I will wake up tomorrow morning to fresh snow, a fresh day, and a fresh mission. No longer will I obsess over my lack of a love life. Instead, I am going to obsess over the mountain— over learning its every bump and turn, and concentrating on how my ski reacts to the changes in terrain and conditions. I will focus on what I am doing as an athlete because right now, that's what I have. When I reach the finish line of my races, I won't ski into the arms of the one who has pledged his undying love to me, but I will still have the support of my teammates, Dad, and Natalie. *I'll be all right.*

As I enter the ski town of Winter Park, I can hear the crunch and squeal of tires rolling over the uneven, icy surface of snow. I pay attention to the sidewalks to see if I see anyone I know. After spending so much time in this town, I have a lot of friends who are locals, but the streets at this time of night are quiet. There is a dusting of snow, and a gentle breeze picking up snowflakes and blowing them across my path.

I follow the main street as I pass restaurants, ski shops, and a grocery store and finally reach my right-hand turn that leads to the team ski house. The U.S. Ski Team rents a house just a few miles from the ski hill and any athletes are welcome to live there during the season. It's sort of a free-for-all at the house.

A rotating slumber party—people coming and going, you never know what room you'll get or if you'll end up on the floor. But it's a home away from home, and my teammates are like family.

I unload my car, head into the house, say hi to everyone, and make myself at home. It takes all of thirty minutes to unpack and sprawl out on a bed. Most of what happens in the team house is a lot of resting. After skiing hard all day, people want to eat big meals and veg. I grab my laptop and turn it on to surf the Internet. I find some great shoes and a blouse I think I might order ... *but for what? The date I'll never have? Maybe I can look at the latest concert schedule in Denver ... so I could go with whom? Oh, the date I'll never have?* Everything I look at makes me feel sorry for myself. Then I check my messages and find one from Brian.

I am surprised he still wants to talk after how I acted at the restaurant. I half want to talk to him, and the other half of me is terrified he is going to tell me what an irrational bitch I was. I probably deserve any bad things he wants to say to me.

Dear Rainey May:

I'm not sure what to call you or what to say. I guess today didn't turn out the way either of us hoped. I am so sorry I wasn't more understanding or friendly. But I don't believe you were being fair to me. I thought we were developing a relationship based on trust where we could tell each other anything and everything. But you took everything out of context. I was looking for a woman, 5'8" with chestnut-colored curly hair. Someone who rides bikes, likes to ski, and races cars. Someone who says things in her messages like, "I just walked in the door." You left out a very big detail, and I felt betrayed. And to be honest, hurt. I know my reaction was wrong, but when you describe yourself as a car racer, the first thing that comes to most people's minds is not a woman who uses a wheelchair. I know now, after interviewing you and meeting you in person today, that I have often underestimated people with disabilities, and I thank you for opening my eyes to a new world. You have taught me a valuable lesson about not taking things for face value and not making assumptions. But you deceived me by coming on my radio show and not revealing your identity. You misled me with the photo you posted online.

It wasn't that I didn't want to see or talk to you, but you caught me off guard. And remember, you're the one who ran out on me. If you'd have given me one minute to unscramble my brain, that would've been helpful. Getting your name straight was confusing, to begin with. But now I think I understand. You would have run out on anyone, and you can't blame *that* on a wheelchair. I have been nothing but honest and open with you. But you were right on in your very first message. You don't know how to open up. It scares you, and that's something that only you can come to terms with.

I want to try again. And if you change your mind, I'll be here waiting.

Brian

As I read the email, I can imagine the sincerity in his words, but we are already too far down the wrong path. *Aren't we?* He may be right. What is wrong with me? I made a fool of myself. *How did I get so insecure? And why couldn't I give him an opportunity to grasp what I'd just dropped on him?*

I know I shouldn't have left the way I did, but I can't help but remember the things he said when we messaged after my interview at the radio station. *I don't know if I could date a woman in a wheelchair. There would be so many things you couldn't do together.* The words still sting as I stare at the computer and recall our conversation. Part of me had to have had a glimmer of hope to show up, but now I feel like I failed.

Dear Brian:

What can I say except I apologize. I'm sorry to have misled you and dragged your emotions along with it. You're right on many accounts, but I was scared to trust you completely, especially after my interview. It's been seventeen years since my accident, and you have to understand that my feelings of distrust didn't come out of nowhere. I know now that I am not your dream woman any longer. I could see the look on your face, and there's no going back from that. Remember when you asked about my first boyfriend? I never answered your question. And, it seems silly to be talking about someone who I thought I knew and truly loved—in my fourteen-year-old mind—but when the accident happened, he wasted no time rushing out of my life. Seared in my brain is the look he gave me the one and only time he came to see me at the hospital. It was like I had turned into an alien with six legs and bug eyes. It felt like a stare of judgement, repulsion. I wasn't the bubbly carefree teenager I once was. He no longer saw me for who I was. For the girl he flirted with in the hallway, walked to her locker every day after third period. It hurt, and I wasn't old enough to understand. It was his immaturity and insecurity that made him run. And intuitively I get that now, but I also have a lifetime of experience that has shown me that having a disability is viewed as a disadvantage. Nobody envies me or wants to trade places with me. And even if I know my life is good, even great, I can't make others see from my vantage point. And every time someone on the street or in the mall or at the airport comes up to me and only says, "what's wrong with you?" After a while, it becomes part of you and your own brain tells you that *whatever did happen was bad, wrong, or unfortunate. It says not worthy.* I want things to be different, but I'm tired of people thinking I'm broken or that I need to be fixed. I don't want that for you. To have to defend yourself for what other people see as settling for a woman with a disability. Or for your friends, to give you, or us, a puzzled stare, as if to say, *how did that matchup happen?*

I'm sorry it had to end this way. I wouldn't trade

a word of our correspondence or the feelings I experienced with you, but I know I have lost your trust. Right now, I think the best thing to do is let you move on and find that woman who will truly make your heart sing.

Sincerely,

Rainey

After I hit send, I shut my laptop and head into the common room where half of my teammates are watching *American Idol*, and the other half are involved in a serious game of poker using Fruit Loops for betting chips. I pull up in front of the TV, where one of the contestants is singing "Hard to Say I'm Sorry" by Chicago. As I listen to the lyrics, I think of all that has passed between us—the words, emotions, and a feeling that he was supposed to be someone special in my life. The thought of letting go makes my heart feel as though it's caving in on itself, but at the same time, I think it must be the right thing to do. *I* have *to let him go. I can't go back. Not after the look on his face. Not after I made a fool of myself, running out of the restaurant like I did.* Some things are better left behind. I have other things to concentrate on. I shouldn't be wasting my time with dating and emotions and all of that anyway.

For the next week, I ski like my life depends on it. Even my coaches recognize it, but they don't know what to say because I'm skiing well. I always do when I have frustrations to air. The mountain becomes my punching bag. I know they know something's different, but they're not going to complain. I'm skiing like a bat out of hell, and that's where they want me going into the Games. This couldn't have happened at a better time because I need to be out of town to concentrate on skiing and my race preparation.

———

I plan to stay at the mountain house for the rest of December, but I'll go home for Christmas Eve and Christmas. Brian gives me my space, but the night I get back in town to spend the holiday with my improvised family unit, I receive a message:

Dear Rainey:

Now that we have everything in the clear, can we start over again? I realize there is so much more to you, and I want to know all of you. Your last message gave me an insight into your world, I never would have thought of. Gabe, the stares, the pity that is projected upon you. But I get it now. You've opened my eyes and made me see how extraordinarily strong you are. Every day you deal with this unconscious bias, and yet you shine. You don't let it stop you, and I want to be with someone so tenacious.

I want to go back—with an open mind and an open heart, if you will give me another chance to find a place in your life. I have so loved getting to know the real you (or so I believe) and the sense that you were genuinely opening up to me. I want to be a person you trust with your thoughts and feelings because we truly have a connection unlike any other I've ever experienced. I want to know when you're happy, sad, lonely and scared. I want to be the person you want to tell things to, even though you resist any closeness or personal risk. I am comfortable writing to you and sharing. And I want to feel like somewhere inside you, the things you said to me and the friendship we were developing was authentic and true, and that you were sharing sincere and candid feelings with me. I like how I can be vulnerable with you like I can with no other. Can't you meet me halfway? I want to open up to you. I can't say that about anyone else. I want you to know me, and I want to know you too.

I'm having a hard time sleeping tonight. I guess I'm so used to reading your messages before I go to bed. It's hard knowing that I've hurt you and done the very thing you feared. I get why you wanted to stay anonymous for so long and why you stuck up so much for "Rainey" the day I interviewed her. Maybe I already got my second chance that day. You overlooked my opinions and unkind comments. I realize it's my fault too. Can we meet and talk over coffee?

Brian

I read his message and appreciate his attempts to patch things up. The truth is, I miss him. But it doesn't make going back to the unblemished honesty we shared online any easier. I need more time to think.

The tradition in our house is to have crab legs for Christmas dinner. Dad and Sara are in charge of the seafood and dessert, and Nat and I have to put together a few side dishes, so we head to the store on Christmas Eve.

"So, have you heard from Brian?" she asks as we make our way through Whole Foods.

"Meh." I grunt. "He emailed me yesterday morning."

"And?"

"And nothing. I've got nothing for him."

"If he's sending you more messages, it means there's still a chance to resurrect your relationship. I can't believe you're not taking it." Then she pulls out the tough love. "This is on you, Rainey. You're the one snuffing this out. Not Brian."

"Maybe, but there's not time for it now. The Games are around the corner, and I need to concentrate on racing."

"No, this is what's called avoidance. If he's extending an olive branch, don't turn the other way."

Christmas fell on a Saturday, and we had Sara, Natalie, Seth, and Cecile over for dinner and presents. There was eggnog and merriment all around, but for me, it was merely acting. I didn't feel merry or bright.

That night I receive another email message. This one, short and sweet—a Christmas wish and he leaves it at that. I can't believe he is still thinking about me, so to be nice, I write him back and wish him a Merry Christmas too, but it still isn't the same. I don't feel like I can go back to the way it was before our lunch date.

The next day he is still on my mind, though. Before he was around, I didn't cry at the drop of a hat while hanging out at home on a random Sunday afternoon. My heart didn't feel as if a giant piece of lead were pulling it down into my stomach. And I certainly didn't feel lonely to my core. Yes, I'm still afraid to let him back in. To accept his apology and pretend to erase that look on his face that is etched in indelible ink on my mind. It was my first taste of heartbreak all over again. I wonder if I'm being unfair. I wonder what he's doing right now. I wonder if I'm in love with someone who could actually love me back.

I lie on my bed with my trusty Rufus. He lies spooning up against me, as I wrap my arm around him and he drapes his chin over my forearm. *For both of us*, I think, *this is bliss*. Love. And when he sees me, he doesn't look at my wheels or my chair. In fact, he likes my chair. It means there's always a lap to sit in. And he's sweet, loyal, and likes to cuddle—who needs a boyfriend anyway? I don't even care that Nat says I'm a cat lady in training and if I don't get a boyfriend soon, I'll adopt three more kittens. Maybe I will. Sue me.

CHAPTER 23

THE FIRST WEEKS OF THE NEW YEAR FLY BY quickly, and before I know it, the Paralympic team is being chosen. It's based on a cumulative points system of the last few months of skiing. I have worked my hardest and am ecstatic to learn that I've made the team. Everything I have worked for has come down to this, and I am more prepared than ever when I board the airplane to head to the Games, wearing my red, white, and blue USA jacket.

Fortunately, Dad, Nat, and Sara were able to secure the tickets and lodging so they can come and watch me race. By the time the Games roll around, I am getting used to seeing my dad with Sara, and I am happy for him. Sometimes, I see the glimpse of innocence my mom must have seen when he was a young suitor looking for love in his late teens and early twenties. I can see again my dad falling into his old ways, where romance ruled, and he gushed that familiar loving spirit. It is only a matter of time until Sara will officially become my stepmom. The thought is starting to grow on me.

It's a bittersweet moment when I step into the start gate for my final race of the Games. Before making my run for this year's team, I had decided it would be my last year of competition. At some point, boyfriend or not, it would be time to move on with my life, whatever the next stage might be. For right now, however, I'm concentrating on the race in front of me. I have already won one gold medal but won't mind capping my career with a sweep of my events, so I put on my game face, and when the starting tone goes off, I careen down the hill with my eyes focused and mind sharp. When I cross the finish line, the crowd goes absolutely crazy. At the front in the family section is a huge group of parents, siblings, and friends of the U.S. racers, and they welcome me with a cheer louder than I have ever heard in my life. I look around at the timing board and realize that I did a run time that will be nearly impossible for any of the remaining competitors to best. I have all but locked up the gold. I go to the fences and get hugs and kisses from my supporters, but for one time in my life, I wish I had a partner, the man of my dreams, the person who has stood behind me every step of the way, there to congratulate me. Unfortunately, that person doesn't exist in my life. I haven't received that kind of hug, kiss, and praise since Nate. With all that is going on around me, and though I am as happy as I have ever been after a race, part of me feels empty. If only Brian were here to see this.

CHAPTER 24

ARRIVING BACK HOME, I AM SURPRISED BY ALL of the exciting opportunities that my wins at the Games afford me. First, there is a parade downtown on a chilly, but sunny, spring day at the end of March for all the Colorado athletes who participated in the Olympics and Paralympics. Friends from all parts of my world are scattered throughout the crowd. On several occasions, I can hear them chanting my name. Then, there are upcoming television, newspaper, and magazine interviews. I've even been invited to throw out the first pitch at an upcoming baseball game. It is a crazy time, full of excitement that fills me with a true sense of accomplishment. All of the hours I spent in the gym and on the slopes paid off in grand style.

At the end of the parade, there is a party at one of the

restaurants downtown, and the establishment has rolled out a red carpet outside for the athletes to walk down as they come from the sidewalk and enter the building. And inside? It's a roaring good time with fans surrounding the local members of our nation's delegation. Natalie and Seth come and meet me, as does Christine and her boyfriend, officially introduced to me as Kevin, and, of course, Dad and Sara, Jake, and Amber. And while I am hanging out enjoying the festivities, I feel a tap on my shoulder from behind. Just the touch of the fingertip causes a rush of excitement through my veins, and I hope beyond hope that it is Brian. As I swivel around my chair to see who it is, I am stumped. I stare into the eyes of a handsome man, who seems to be my age, but can't quite place who he is or my faint recognition of his face.

He puts his hand out to shake mine and says, "Ben. Ben Schumacher from high school. Does that ring a bell?"

"Oh yes! Absolutely! We had Calculus together, didn't we?"

"Yes, you do remember."

How could I forget? I used to make googly eyes at him all during class. If he was a good-looking teenager, he's certainly grown up to be a stunning specimen of a man in his thirties. I turn my head an inch to make sure that Natalie is seeing this conversation going down. *Me. Talking to a man. A dapper man. An eligible man?*

"How have you been?" he asks. "From the looks of things, pretty darn good. Congratulations on the hardware."

"Thanks. It truly was an honor to get another shot at the Paralympic Games … and this parade was over the top. I couldn't have asked for more."

"What else have you been up to?"

"Well, I'm going to go back to full-time teaching at Joseph Elementary now that skiing is done, and other than that, just livin' the dream," I try as hard as I can to seem easy and carefree.

"Listen, I know you probably have a lot of people to talk to this afternoon, but would you be interested in meeting for a drink this week?"

"Um, sure. That would be great!"

"Let me put your number in my phone, and I'll give you a ring tomorrow."

We exchange numbers and that becomes the seeds of possibility for a new romance in my life.

CHAPTER 25

AS THINGS START TO CALM DOWN, I SETTLE into ski retirement. It's weird not getting up at early hours or dragging myself after work to the gym to train. I stop going, going, going all the time.

I go back to work and reach my three-week mark of dating Ben. I had hoped he'd be as interesting as he is good looking, but that has turned out not to be the case. It is most definitely nice to have someone to go to the movies with and have his arm around me, though, and it's pleasurable to have someone to kiss goodnight. Because the spark isn't burning so bright, I keep it very low key and slow moving. I know I am not ready to jump into something full speed ahead, no matter who the guy is. After how things ended with Brian, I haven't felt like I can. Brian continues to be with me in the back of my mind. Ben's presence, though nice, can't seem to keep my memories of Brian at bay.

To make matters worse, tonight Brian intrudes on my date with Ben and pretty much sinks the nail in Ben's coffin. Ben and I are on our way back to my house after a pleasant date—dinner and a trip to the theater. There are some things I can't fault Ben for, and one of those things is his love of the theater. He said he grew up with his parents taking him to shows and because of it he learned to appreciate plays and musicals and has kept theater as part of his routine. We've already seen a couple of shows together during our first few weeks of dating. On our way home after tonight's performance, Ben turns on the radio, already set at 106.9 KXTY, the station Brian works for. At night, the station uses a lone DJ on the air, playing a mix of music from the eighties to current tunes. It's a Friday night, and shortly after Ben turns on the station and a few songs have played, *he* comes on. *He*, as in Brian. I visibly jump in the car and Ben asks me what is wrong.

"Oh, it's nothing. Probably a shiver." *What on earth is Brian doing DJ-ing a music show?*

As in response to my thought, I hear Brian say, "This next song goes out to an old friend. She has recently accomplished a mind-blowing goal, and while she's probably not listening to my show tonight, I have an oldie, a special blast from the past, that I want to play for her." He is silent for a moment, and the song gradually increases in volume. It's "The Time of My Life" from *Dirty Dancing*. It was, for all intents and purposes, *our song*. Tears well up in my eyes, and I turn to look out the window so Ben can't see.

CHAPTER 26

SITTING AT MY DESK WORKING ON LESSON plans for the week and having some quiet time, the phone rings. I pick it up as I notice it's Natalie on the line. "Hey, superstar skier," she begins the conversation. We are all still basking in the glow of my recent medal-winning performances.

"Hi, Nat. What's going on?"

"I'm calling because I need your help."

"Oh, how can I be of service?" I ask, my curiosity piqued.

"Well, I'm working on promoting this celebrity ski challenge; it's a benefit for The Children's Hospital, and I was hoping you'd participate. The event is next weekend. The hospital has put together two teams of people who have collected sponsorships and donations for every ski run they complete. But the big draw to get support and make it a fun day is that we are including a media and celebrity challenge. We'll put local celebrities on the two teams to join in the event and compete. We have television news reporters and anchors, professional athletes, politicians, even Denver's best chef. And, I was thinking, we should also have a gold medal-winning Paralympian on the team."

"Hmmm ..." I answer. "That sounds like fun."

"It'll give you a chance to show off your skill, have some fun, and do something good for the community."

"Okay, count me in! It sounds like a blast and now that my skiing career is over, maybe a little *lighthearted* competition *will* be fun."

"Oh, Rainey, you don't even know what the words lighthearted competition mean. You're an all or nothing girl."

"You're right ... and whatever team I'm on ... we're gonna kick some ass! Plus, who knows? I might meet someone famous or cute! I can't wait."

"Thank you, friend," Nat replies. "You won't regret this one. It's going to be a great day."

On the day of the celebrity ski races, Natalie picks me up in Seth's four-wheel drive SUV. After last night's dumping of snow, we decide that's the best vehicle to take, plus she has a car full of supplies she needs, plus my monoski, and everyday chair. She has to be there early, but I don't mind having to get up and get going. That's a pretty normal race day for me, plus it gives us some quality time in the car driving up the mountain. We talk about everything from her latest outfit that she got at Saks to a dream she had last night about being pregnant, to my week at work. I think it's odd that she doesn't bring up my love life, but maybe she thought she'd give the topic a rest. I know she isn't thrilled about the fact that I have been spending more and more time with Ben. She thinks I'm settling, which is why I know she's holding her tongue. But I call Ben *comfortable*. The known versus the unknown. Somehow it seems easier to be with someone who knew me before the accident and witnessed the transition. I don't know why, it's like maybe there is acceptance with history. If I'm honest with myself, I know I am not with him because I'm crazy about him, but he seems to like me … and it's a nice feeling. I think I'll stay with safe—at least for a little while. That going out on a limb didn't do me any favors.

I'm glad Natalie asked me to ski in the event today because in another two weeks the ski resorts will be closed for the winter. So, for me, today is like the icing on the cake. The cherry on top. The denouement of my novel.

We arrive at the ski resort, and I help Natalie carry in her boxes of clipboards, credentials, office supplies, and who knows what else. Ms. PR Princess—and now event planner— has many tools of her trade. As I consider that I'm mostly familiar with crayons and wide-lined recycled pulp paper, I chuckle a bit. We definitely have different worlds in our professions.

"Rainey, you have no idea how much I appreciate your help and support with this," she says as she piles another box on top of the one already on my lap.

"Yes, there's nothing like having a human dolly for a

friend," I kid her. We both know the wheelchair has been useful more than once as a method for carrying way more than we could handle between the two of us.

As we arrive in the room, only four other women have beat us there, and they are hurriedly setting up tables and chairs, pulling out tablecloths, and getting the registration areas ready for the soon-to-be onslaught of weekend warriors who are going to ski for dollars.

I'm excited to be able to have a low-pressure day on the slopes for once, even though I know, just as Natalie already noted, that my competitiveness will kick in once we get started. It's like I don't have an in between when it comes to contests. I love the challenge, and I love to win. It's the simple truth.

As I push myself around trying to lend a hand wherever I can, Natalie comes up and hands me a large manila envelope with my race number, safety pins, and a badge to wear around my neck that not only designates which team I am on, but has a space at the bottom where an official will punch it each time I start a run. This will help keep track of how many runs I've done for my team. I look down at it, and my name is printed in a sophisticated calligraphy font on a blue piece of laminated card stock. We will be competing against the red team, she tells me, and I begin to wonder about the competition.

I let Natalie run around and do her job, while I scoot off to one side of the room to begin the process of sorting, organizing, and layering my ski outfit. As I rummage into my old ski bag, sorting through thermal socks and single gloves, I can't help but let my mind take me back to my last day on my monoski, the day I retired. It's funny how our senses play tricks on us.

The smell of my gear brought back memories like an old song does, the kind where you close your eyes as you remember something special. Winning double gold in my last Paralympic competition was the zenith of my ski-racing career.

I begin thinking about how funny it is that the worst tragedy one can imagine could lead to a life that has been extraordinary. To count, I've visited fifteen countries for racing and training, made a close group of friends with my teammates, represented my country, and earned the shiny metallic hardware to prove it. *Hardly a bad thing*, I consider.

I wonder for a moment what my life would have been like had I not had the accident. *Of course, I'd have Mom and Sunny—a big point in the plus column—but would I have found a passion for skiing? Would I have excelled in another area? Would I have learned to value the days of my life because I never knew when it would be my last?* My thoughts remind me of an old movie I once watched on late-night TV, called *Sliding Doors*. It starred Gwyneth Paltrow and took place in London. Gwyneth plays a woman named Helen who has been laid off from her PR job. As she rushes to catch the Tube, the doors close just in front of her face, and she misses the train. From there the movie turns into two parallel plot lines—one that follows Helen, had she made that particular train, and the other that follows what happens had she missed the train. The movie follows how that simple situation set off a chain reaction of other events and affected the course of her life. A small difference such as making the train versus not making the train changed everything, and the film takes her on two opposite life paths. It makes me wish I could see my very own sliding doors—the one in which the accident didn't happen and the one in which it did. Who is to say one is better than the other?

Suddenly my thoughts are interrupted, and I feel a tap on my shoulder. As I look up from my bag and spin my chair around to see who is behind me, my breath escapes like a runaway balloon. Standing in front of me is Brian85.

"Hi, Rainey," he says.

"Brian," is all I can get out.

Looking around frantically to see if Natalie is near and can save me, I notice her checking with the volunteers at the registration table. I will her to turn around, see me, and walk over to save me, but the next thing I know, she and her clipboard are walking further and further away.

"Looks like we're teammates," he says and flashes me his blue badge.

Oh, shit.

"Yes, it does look like that," I say at a complete loss for words.

"How have you been?" he talks to me as if I didn't storm out and basically never talk to him again after the last time we met.

"Fine," I say, thinking it best to stick to one-word answers. Yet, I look at him and melt. I can feel the blood pulsating through my veins. He leans over to give me a hug, and, instead of pulling away like I intended, his scent pulls me in closer. He smells like a combination of fresh soap and something I don't recognize. I think maybe it's him, his signature scent, and my body starts to shake. His smile opens wide, and he goes back in time to the picture on MFEO when I fell in love with his perfect white teeth and piercing blue eyes. I can tell in this first moment that all bets are off. Anything might happen today.

"Rainey, I know you weren't expecting to see me here, but I was hoping maybe we could spend some time together today and talk. I've missed hearing from you, and thought we could catch up or something."

"Sure. Great. It looks like we can start heading to the chairlift in about ten minutes. Maybe you could help me grab my ski, and we can go over together?" I say, impressed a whole sentence and thought came out of my brain.

As I sit next to him on the chairlift, I experience an unusual sensation I've never had before. It isn't about the skiing. I'm not nervous about that. Even though the people I talked to in the lodge were talking about their pre-race jitters, for me, this is child's play. I am full of confidence, having raced for so many years—and with the stakes so much higher. It feels like electricity flowing through my body. My breath is shallow, and my hands feel warm and clammy in my gloves. I feel Brian's arm move and rub against mine, as he readjusts on his section of wooden chairlift seat. As I become aware of him, the closeness of our proximity, I realize the feeling I am experiencing is intense attraction. And maybe … maybe I'm falling for him all over again.

Brian looks over at me. "Are you okay?"

"Yeah, I'm fine, why?" I ask defensively.

"You're quiet, and you look a little pale."

He puts his gloved hand on top of mine and says, "Relax. I know this wasn't what you expected to happen today. I'm sorry if you feel Natalie and I ambushed you. I wanted another chance. To see you in person. To talk. I've missed our long, late-night chats, and I've realized that even though we got off on the wrong foot, that doesn't erase the months we shared so much with each other. I realize now that we had something incredible and special and I want it back. A day without you in it feels empty."

As I half-listen to what he is saying, I'm stewing in my mind that Natalie knew about this plan and set me up. I don't know what to say. So, I don't say anything at all, and we ride in silence the rest of the way.

When we get to the top of the lift, we both ski off, but somehow go in different directions. I need to get out of whatever force field is surrounding me and get my breath back before it's my turn to head down the hill.

We don't have a specific order we have to go in. As a team, we just need to ski the most vertical feet in six hours to win. I have no idea what our competition will be like on the other team, but I aim to win.

I watch the first racers go off and then decide to ski over to get myself in line. I strategically place myself a few people behind Brian. I need some space from him at the moment. One racer off, two, Brian, another, and another, and then it's my turn. I know this is a charity race, but all of a sudden, competitor mode kicks in. I can't help it. It's part of me. My tally tag is hanging around my neck, and I stretch the cord over to the starter, so he can punch my card and I can be off. Once I hit the slopes, I'm home. I clear my head of Brian and do what I have done so many times before. What I do best. I focus on the run in front of me and jam down the hill.

Pure adrenaline and exhilaration courses through my body. I love the feeling of the air biting at my face, the swoosh under my body, and the unadulterated freedom of being out of my chair and knowing I am an equal with all my able-bodied teammates. Actually, I know I am better than most of them. Much better.

As I hit the bottom of the run and cross the finish line, Natalie is there cheering like she has been for every race I have done, except for the ones in college when she was in New York. Standing next to her with a huge smile on his face is Brian. The announcer calls out my time. The fastest so far in the early runs.

"Holy crap, Rainey May! You nailed that!" Brian says and gives me a big hug.

My heart skips a beat. *This is it!* I thought. The feeling I have waited for—for so long. For years, I've watched my friends and teammates have their significant others at the bottom of the mountain waiting to hug them after a great run, and now I finally get to experience it for myself! Even though he isn't my boyfriend, it feels good to hear the enthusiasm in his voice. For the first time since our relationship started, I feel like I have nothing to hide. Like I have put it all out there on the line and, not only that, but I can tell he is impressed.

I look over at him and say, "Well, what are you waiting for? Let's get back up there and start it all again. We have a race to win!"

I can feel the change within myself, and I sense that he can see it too. He flashes me a toothy grin and gives me a little push along the flat to get back to the chairlift.

This time as we head up the hill, the conversation flows. We are back to our lively selves, reminiscent of our phone conversations when we were full of stories and laughter and comfortable pauses. I tell him I heard his radio show and thank him for playing our song.

"I couldn't get you out of my mind, Rainey," he says. "And after you got back from the Games, I swear I saw pictures of you everywhere."

I smile and bask in the glow of his kindness. "What are you doing working a late Friday night DJ shift anyway?"

"At first I did it to help out one of the other guys, who needed time off from his shift, but I realized how much I enjoyed it, so the program manager let me have my own show. It's a good creative outlet for me. In that late-night slot, I get full control of what I talk about and the music I play. There's something empowering about being able to talk anonymously and uninhibited. Sort of like with online dating," he says and gives me a wink.

This time, as we exit the chair, we head in the same direction, and I line up in front of Brian.

I suppose we could have taken the time to get to know some of our other teammates, but we spend the majority of the day together in our own world. Each time we ride the chairlift, the conversations grow in both word count and depth.

Please don't let this end, I think, as we talk all the way up the chairlift. But what good is it to try to hold on to a moment? You can't. I always wished I could have gotten one more kiss or one more hug from my mom. But what good would it have done? She's still gone, and it still would have been further in the past. Instead of worrying about the past, I give myself permission to get lost in Brian's presence and to soak up every bit of his attention.

There is something about us being together that I can't explain. It goes further than what we have in common. It is all the words that pass between us when nothing is being said. It is the pull of wanting to be closer and closer to his body until we become one being. It is the look in his eyes that says, "I want to empty my soul into you," knowing my eyes match his stare. I have not felt this before. I start to get so comfortable that it begins to make me uncomfortable. Under my jacket, I feel my insides start to quiver. I draw away.

"What's wrong, Rainey?"

My move seemed so slight that I hadn't imagined he would notice. "Nothing is wrong," I answer. "I'm getting tired. Anxious to get off this last run. We've gone hard today."

"Need I remind you that you're a Paralympic gold medalist and you're probably in the best shape of your life right now? I know you've had much harder days on the mountain than this. What aren't you telling me?"

As we sit there, I realize there is more happening than a crush coming on or a relationship being formed. As I look into those eyes, I see something different than I ever have before. I don't know what to call it at first, but it reaches way into me, to the core of my being, and fits snug up against me like when two matching puzzle pieces come together. This is no ordinary connection. There is definitely something between us that I can't define. Any heaviness I came into this day with has lifted, and my worry about Brian is turned to joy. For this time together with Brian, I am riveted by a divine attachment, and the rest of my world fades away. He puts his arm around me, pulls me close and tenderly kisses my forehead. We lean in a beat longer than necessary, and when we reassume our positions, we say nothing. As we unload, we head to the starting gate for one last run. I let Brian get in front, so I can compose myself and regain my concentration.

At the bottom, Brian is there to meet me. "I think we've done all we can do here today. The allotted race time is almost tapped. Ready to call it a day?"

I look at him and simply nod. I want to sit still in place to hold on to this perfect moment, but it's getting chilly, so we head inside and directly for the hot chocolate.

Although the race was for charity, I am still anxious to hear how the blue team annihilated the red team, and confirm that Brian and I were a big part of that success. Brian is seated in a chair next to me as the group of skiers gather for the closing presentation. The announcer thanks the sponsors, donors, participants, and then announces the grand total of dollars raised. The crowd erupts into applause. It was a successful day for the charity. Now, last, but not least he says—"The winner of the team competition is…" And just as I look over to give Brian a huge congratulatory smile because I know the blue team certainly ended on top—out of the corner of my eye, I see someone walk up and put her hands on Brian's shoulders and then slide them down his chest, until her head bends over. With hair cascading down, her lips touch his cheek in a soft caress. It takes Brian off guard as much as it does me, and in shock and disbelief, he exclaims, "Shelly, what are you doing here?"

"I thought it would be great to surprise you and watch you race. I got off work early and was able to see your last run down the mountain," she says, oblivious that Brian and I are clearly hanging out together. Obviously, she thinks nothing of it.

The announcer's voice fades back onto my radar as he finishes his sentence "…the blue team!

"I have to go up with my team to get our award," Brian says as he shakes Shelly off his shoulders.

I push the wheels on my chair as hard as I can and try to go to the opposite end of the podium from where Brian is headed. Not so quick though, he changes direction, and as the fifteen of us stand on and, in my case, next to the four-inch podium, he whispers, "Rainey, please let me talk to you about this. It's not serious. I like *you*. I want to be with *you* and to go back to the way we were."

I sit there and try to fight off the tears. I've just had one of the best days of my life, with a guy I've come to absolutely adore in the last six hours, and to whom I've become physically attracted, and now this. After we all have medals hung around our necks, I head straightaway to the restroom. Natalie must have seen me because the door hasn't even shut before she is by my side.

"Why did you do this to me, Natalie?" I scream at her for the first time in my life.

"Rainey, honestly, I wouldn't have done this if I didn't think he was truly genuine in his feelings for you. *He* approached me. *He* asked to see you again, and *he* asked me for help. And this event was the perfect solution. When I suggested it to him, he thanked me over and over again. He really wanted to come and spend the day with you. And I watched you two together for an entire day. You were glowing like I've never seen before and his eyes were only on you. He's probably in a relationship that's as lukewarm as yours is with Ben because *he* initiated seeing you today. Don't you see that this as an open invitation? He wants to be with you, regardless of what the situation looks like from the outside."

I hear what she is saying but can't get myself to believe it. "I can't go back out there. I'm staying right here until he leaves. I don't want to see his face, and I definitely don't want to talk to him."

Natalie nods and says she'll come and get me when the coast is clear.

CHAPTER 27

I CRY THE WHOLE WAY HOME, AND I CAN TELL
that Natalie is beside herself for rubbing salt in an already
gaping wound.

"Rainey, I'm so sorry. But believe me, I know Brian isn't
over you. I watched you two all day, and, even as a bystander,
I could feel the excitement and intimate tension between you
two. I also got a chance to say a couple of words to him as he
left. He pulled me aside to get Shelly out of earshot. He asked
me to apologize to you. He said yes, they are dating, but it's
not serious. He said today was better than he could have ever
imagined. He misses you."

"But why didn't he say anything about her?" I ask.

"Did you tell him about Ben?" Natalie challenges.

"No, but ..."

"But what?"

"It's not like he's the man of my dreams. He's just, I don't know. I like spending time with him, but if I'm honest," I stop to think. "He's probably just a rebound," I add softly.

"And don't you think Brian may be doing the same thing? Are you the only one allowed to date other people? Maybe he doesn't see a future with Shelly any more than you see a future with Ben. Are you willing to consider that?"

"Maybe, but I didn't ask to be part of this day. I didn't come to spend time with him. I entered this race because you asked a favor of me. I didn't know what I was getting myself into. He knew. He had time to think and to plan. He should have told me."

"Well, before you go off the deep end, before you email him, or don't email him for that matter, think about it. Consider how he felt after your secret recon at the radio station. Watch what you say, and make sure it's truly the message you want to get across to him. You have a second chance. Be careful, is all I'm saying."

I take her words into consideration, but I am mad, and I'm not sure what I will do.

When I get home, I yank off my clothes and transfer into the shower. Since our lunch date went awry, I've added another song to the Brian playlist. It's my cry-myself-a-river song. I pick it now to listen to—"When You're Gone" by Avril Lavigne.

As the melody takes me to a pensive place, I find it miraculous that in our short months of contact Brian has become home to me. I think of him when I listen to our songs, when I want someone to talk to, when the simple act of arms wrapped around me for reassurance is all it would take for my problems to go away. Without him, part of me is missing. My soul aches for him, but I don't have the right. He's not mine. I know now he belongs to Shelly. And just the very thought leaves my heart reeling in agony.

I boost the volume to try and drown out my thoughts, get in the shower and turn the water to extra hot, hold the shower hose on me, and wish it could wash me right off this earth.

When I get out of the shower, I can hear my phone ringing. I look at the display. Brian. I don't want to talk and hit decline. He calls again and then sends me a text. *"Please Rainey, can we talk?"*

I go into the kitchen and put on a pot of water. I have almost nothing in the house, except my staple of spaghetti and a jar of sauce.

I finally decide to go to bed. It's been a long day, physically and emotionally exhausting, and I need a rest. I get in bed and do nothing but toss and turn for two hours. I keep thinking of Brian, his warm smile, how it felt when his lips rested on my forehead, how he seemed really interested in everything I had to say today. I loved it. I loved being with him. But I'm still so conflicted in my mind. If only he would have said one little thing about having a girlfriend.

Unable to sleep, I get out of bed, cross the room to get my laptop, and then get right back in the prone position, on top of my covers this time. I log on to MFEO to see if he is online and, sure enough, he is. I decide to skip the niceties of a salutation and go right into my soapbox lecture.

What was that about? You're perfect, sweet, we have a great day, and then you forget to tell me you have a girlfriend?

You're right. I have been dating someone. And I didn't tell you up front. But tell me this ... aren't you seeing someone too?

You broke my heart into a million little pieces and punctuated it with an exclamation point. What else was I supposed to do but trudge forward and move on?

Rainey, I never lied to you. In your words, it was simply an act of omission. I didn't know that Shelly was going to show up today, and I didn't tell you about her because it's not serious. We met, she was nice, we started seeing each other. But it doesn't mean I had forgotten about you, or the things we talked about and the time we shared, but I couldn't just wait around for something that didn't seem likely to happen. But today—I finally got to meet the real you. And I was cherishing the moments. I was having such a great time; I didn't want to ruin it.

Do you see how I might have been caught by surprise at the restaurant when we first met? Technically, you didn't do or say anything wrong either, but when you go through the drive-thru, order a burger, and end up sinking your teeth into a chicken patty, it catches you unprepared. It doesn't have to be a bad thing. You still got lunch, but it wasn't what you expected, and you have to take a minute to adjust. I stumbled for one second, and you split.

I had an unbelievable day today. I loved being with you. I already had it in my mind after less than an hour with you that I wanted to call things off with Shelly. But I didn't get the chance. I had no idea she'd show up to the race today. We've barely been out, and she's much more into me than I am into her … in case you didn't notice. But was I supposed to sit around waiting for you? In case Nat hasn't told you the full story, I ran into her at a media party, and we cooked up the scheme so I could spend time with you today. But I did have a right to move on with my life, just as you did.

If he knew that, why didn't he say anything? He has a point, and I know the right thing to do is to forgive him, but I need time.

You're right, Brian, I am seeing someone. But you hurt me today. I didn't arrive at this place of trust in you or us overnight, and now I need time to think. I feel like I've been bombarded from all sides. I need some space.

Rainey, what you don't know is that I have completely and totally fallen for you. I only wish you loved yourself in a way that matched my feelings for you. I don't think you can truly love someone unless you love yourself, and I get the feeling you haven't had that before. I wish we could have gotten there together. If that's not meant to happen, then it will always be a regret for me. I feel like we're a good match, but it doesn't matter unless you're willing to let yourself fall. Because if you trusted me, you'd know I'd be there to catch you.

I don't have anything else to say. He is right. I knew it was only a matter of time before our new beginning became the beginning of the end. I shut my laptop and go to bed.

CHAPTER 28

I AWAKE TO THE SOUNDS OF CRASHING thunder and the heavy drops of rain against my bedroom window. It's my thirty-third birthday and from what I have been told, this day is an awful lot like the one that gave me my name, Rainey May. As I lie in bed, I think about my mom and dad rushing to the hospital, rain jackets held over their heads because they didn't have time to put them on before they needed to rush to the car, jump in, or, in my mom's case, gingerly slide in. At full-term, she was ready to burst at any minute.

I imagine the ride to the hospital—one filled with anticipation, fear, and the unknown. I wonder how my mom felt being wheeled down the hallway. Was she in a wheelchair or on a gurney? All I know is that I came quickly and there wasn't much time to get anxious about the transition from being with child—to being *with* child, like right there in the flesh, in your arms. Must have been a bewildering transition.

I think about this, contemplating two major life changes currently going on in my immediate circle and how neither one of them is directly part of my reality. Last night, Natalie told me that she and Seth have experienced a miracle. Though the doctors had given her less than a fifteen percent chance success rate in the baby-making department, it's actually happening. She had been feeling a little off lately, so fearing the worst, she visited the doctor yesterday morning and learned that the "off" feeling was the beginning of a pregnancy. Even though she and Seth are being guarded with the news, they are cautiously optimistic that all will work out for the best.

The other event is that in one short week, I will have a stepmother. My father and Sara have had a whirlwind courtship, but it seems that they are over-the-moon happy. I haven't seen my dad act like this in so long. Regardless of my feelings for Sara, and let's just say that they aren't negative at all—I've finally come to terms with my envy at the seemingly effortless success of their union—I am happy for both of them. It's like my dad has become a whole new person. He and Sara go out for dinners, on vacations, out with friends, and he's even gone back to the track to do some racing. He's been working hard at remodeling our house to make way for Sara and has gently packed away the reminders of my mother, making space for something new. It's bittersweet for me, but I understand that at some point he has to move on, and this has been a long time coming. I am old enough now to understand that Dad, too, is human, and he needs and wants an intimate and romantic relationship. It's a weird feeling, I think, to have a new mom when you're thirty-three years old. Especially when you can barely remember the days with your actual mom, and those memories I hold on to with white-knuckled fists. Our lives, well some of our lives, are moving along. With my dad's marriage and Natalie's soon-to-be bundle of joy, I can feel change in the air. I wish I could have had half the luck that he and Natalie have had in the past couple of months.

I haven't talked to Brian since things fizzled out mid-April after the celebrity ski-a-thon. I guess I thought it was better for us to go our separate ways. I don't know if the timing or situation would ever have been right for us. In the meantime, I continue to date Ben, who we all know doesn't make me crazy, but he's someone to pass the time with, he cares about me, and I suppose I'm still in frog-kissing mode. One day I will move on, I think. *I hope.* And I guess that day should be sooner rather than later because I know he likes me a lot more than I like him and that could eventually become a problem. But, for today, I don't want to think about that. Today is a very important day. It is a Saturday, and one week from tomorrow my father and Sara will be married—and I have waited until the very last minute to purchase my dress. Fortunately for me, Natalie is once again dropping by to save the day. Our mission: to find a stunning outfit.

When she pulls up, I hurriedly grab my keys, purse, and a bottle of water—shopping can be an endurance event with Nat—and run out the door. As I transfer into the car, Nat takes my chair to the back and yells, "So what kind of dress do you have in mind, Rainey?"

"Oh, I don't know. Sara wanted me to find something in blue. She's going to have some blue hydrangeas in her bouquet and will be wearing a blue dress too. I guess she sort of wants me to feel like the Maid of Honor, though I really don't care much about that."

"Is Ben coming with you to the wedding?"

"Yes, I don't want to be the only person without a date, you know. There are going to be exactly twenty-four people at this wedding, and I don't want to be the one to ruin the perfect balance and even number."

"You should have asked Brian to come along."

"I haven't talked to Brian in over a month. Natalie, you have to let that go. It's a thing of the past. It never would have worked. I'm not the woman for him."

"I happen to think you are, but you're too stubborn to go back to him and apologize and work things out. I wish you would just admit your hasty judgments and give him a call."

I have no reply to that. Maybe it is all about pride, but I simply don't feel like going back through the drama. Besides, I don't know what his status is with Shelly, and I'm having a hard time figuring out how to break the news to Ben that he isn't the man of my dreams. Too many complications. Better to let sleeping dogs lie.

My week at work is hectic because of all the end-of-school rituals—track and field day, a trip to the Denver Zoo, and kids losing concentration, knowing that in two weeks they will be free for the summer. I don't have time to even think about the wedding, but before I know it, the weekend has arrived. Saturday night comes quickly and I host the pre-wedding cocktail party in honor of Dad and Sara. We've invited more than fifty friends, which is too many to squeeze into my house, so we've decorated the back patio, put up a tent, planted some flowers and done a variety of other backyard enhancements. Almost all of the guests actually show up to congratulate the happy couple and the evening couldn't have been a bigger success.

Dad and Sara decided to hold the reception before the wedding rather than after, so that Sunday can be a day for close family only, with the wedding at two in the afternoon, followed by a small garden party for the cake cutting and a fancy dinner at a restaurant called The Dove. My dad is going all out, treating the family to a pricey dinner that includes six courses of pure culinary delight, with a handful of waiters at our beck and call. Dad even included my grandparents— Mom's mom and dad—and Mom's only sister and her husband. We've seen them every once in a while, but over the years, the contact has waned. We talk on the phone, but our yearly trips to California have died off as have their trips to Colorado.

After everyone leaves my house following the party, I nearly fall into bed from exhaustion. I'm deep in sleep when my phone snaps me out of my dreams. I reach over to the nightstand and grab my cell phone. I feel a fleeting sense of annoyance to see Brian's name light up on the screen and wonder if this is one of those drunken *can we talk* kind of phone calls. But as I lay there contemplating exactly why he might be calling and watch the phone continue to light up, I don't think Brian is the type to do that. Especially after so long. He's more mature than that. If he wanted to reconnect, he would have done it at an appropriate time of day and thoroughly sober. And this thought leads me from annoyance to panic. It makes me remember back to the time when Natalie's mom was in the middle of some relentless chemo treatments and had to continually be rushed to the hospital for shortness of breath, rapid pulse, or some other complication. Her mom had a live-in nurse who took care of her, and Natalie told me she frequently had trouble sleeping because she was worried that one of those late-night calls would be *the* call. The one that would change her life. The one that said her mom was gone.

All of these thoughts flood my mind as if I'm riding on a river pass of class-four rapids, and I abruptly answer on the last ring before it goes to voicemail. Since it's rare that anything good comes out of a three a.m. phone call, I brace myself for who knows what and answer hesitantly. I am still drowsy, and a little out of it, and I know my voice projects that state of exhaustion when I speak a sleepy "Hello?"

There is a long pause on the other end. Then finally, "Rainey?"

I can hear the tremor in his voice.

"Brian? Are you okay?"

"I need to talk," is all he says. But his voice doesn't sound right. I can hear the shock in his words.

"Okay, I can talk. What's going on?"

"I need to see you."

"Okay, when?"

"Now?"

"Like, *right* now?"

"Yes, I wouldn't ask if it weren't important."

"Where do you want to meet," I ask as I look down at my body covered only in an extra-large t-shirt."

"Um. At your house?"

That's an *intriguing* thought. He's never been to my house before. But I say *okay* and give him the address.

I hurriedly get out of bed and go to the drawer to grab some pajamas that I think are cute and more presentable and wiggle into them in my wheelchair. Then I go into the bathroom and brush my hair and teeth. I don't want it to seem like I've gone to any extreme lengths to get ready for him, but I also don't want to look like I just rolled out of bed. Someplace in the middle. I put my hair up in a ponytail.

It takes only twenty-five minutes, and Brian is ringing my doorbell. I push from the bedroom to the door and open it to find my enchanting and adorable Brian standing in a heap on the porch. His clothes are wrinkled, his eyes bloodshot. Considering that I thought Brian was one of the most handsome guys I've ever seen, he looks like shit. I invite him in, all the while studying his mannerisms and wondering exactly what could have happened that was so bad.

"Would you like something to drink? Tea?"

"Do you have anything stronger?"

"Um, sure. Would you like some beer or tequila?"

Even though I'm not a regular hard alcohol drinker, I remember a night when Natalie, Seth, a few other friends, and I decided to play Monopoly as a drinking game, and whenever someone bought a new house, we'd celebrate the purchase with a shot of tequila. That game didn't last long.

"Yes," was Brian's reply.

"Yes, beer or yes, tequila?"

"Yes."

Alrighty then, I'll get both. "Be right back."

I return with a bottle of beer and a shot glass of tequila and Brian immediately downs the shot and looks at me.

"Brian," I say softly as I grab his hand. "What's the matter?"

He looks back at me and can barely speak. "It's Casey."

Oh no. "What's happened to Casey?" I ask, expecting the worst.

"He was rock climbing with some friends," Brian replies in fragments, in a voice I can barely hear. "It was a freak accident … a slip and fall … and with the distance between him and his last piece of safety gear … he fell thirty feet to the ground."

"Oh my God, Brian!" I exclaim as my emotions go on high alert. I'm afraid to ask if he survived, so I sit there and look into Brian's eyes, trying to brace myself to hear the rest.

"Rainey, he's paralyzed. From the chest down," Brian can hardly utter the words.

I look at him, and, in that moment, I see my father in his eyes. The way my dad looked at me when I was lying in the hospital bed, and he had no idea what to think. Uncertain of my future and mourning our losses, my dad sat and stared at me for hours. As I look at Brian, I remember those initial terrifying days in the hospital and the dark unknown of the jungle I had to navigate to get out from the void I was in, to end up where I am now. At the time it was incomprehensible, but in those few seconds as I focus on Brian, I realize how much I have accomplished since that time so long ago when we thought I was doomed to a tragic and desolate existence. My thoughts momentarily go off track as a movie montage of my life plays in my mind. I see the hurdles I've overcome—the anger and resentment I felt toward my wheelchair and everyone who didn't need to rely on one. The belief that my injury had robbed me of my dreams, and stolen my identity. The constant perception of being less. But then the theme of the film changes. I see myself crossing the stage at my high school and University graduations. The gold medals hanging in my bedroom, a family—as hodge-podge as it is—who loves me. And I see how I have lifted young children and made them believe in themselves, and how as I stare at this man in pieces in front of me, I feel a tenderness that makes me realize how much I love who I've become.

I keep my gaze on Brian and wait for more details. Casey broke several vertebrae in his mid-back, his leg, several ribs, his arm, and has a punctured lung. The accident happened thirty-six hours ago. Casey went through surgery and is now stable and in fair condition. Things were touch and go in the beginning, and Brian spent all of last night with his family at the hospital because they weren't sure Casey would make it through surgery and the night. As he recounts the details, Brian's eyes water, and he starts to shake. "Rainey, I'm the one who taught Casey to rock climb. I was the one who started him in the sport in the first place."

"Brian, you can't blame yourself. Accidents happen. I know you taught him the best possible safety, but sometimes, things go wrong and with no explanation or fault. You can't punish yourself for spending time with Casey and wanting to expose him to a different world. The two of you have spent countless hours bonding and enjoying climbing together."

"But now, he'll never do it again," Brian says, his voice trembling.

I look at him and shake my head. "That sounds like the old Brian talking. What did you learn when we skied together?"

"That you can kick my ass on the slopes?" He looks at me and a faint smile spreads across his face.

"Yeah. I *can* kick your ass on the slopes … and I don't need to be standing up to do it. Casey will be the same way with rock climbing. It will take time, Brian. Lots of time. And love, and patience. But, he will heal, and he'll get back out there. And if it's not rock climbing, it'll be something else. But I promise you, his life is not over. And there will be hundreds of things you two will still enjoy together. Some you haven't even thought of yet."

Brian seems to relax a little as we talk, and he sips his beer, but I can tell it is going to take a long while to convince him that things will be all right. Much longer than the amount of time we have right now. I suddenly feel my eyelids straining to stay open.

"You need to get some sleep," I say to him. "Why don't you stay here tonight?" I am surprised at the boldness of my statement.

He looks at me quizzically and asks, "Are you sure?"

"Yes, I'm sure. Brian, this relationship has been far from normal from the very beginning. Why should we try and change that now? C'mon, let's both get some sleep."

I grab his nearly empty beer bottle and the shot glass, take them to the kitchen, and start turning out the lights. He begins to follow me, and as we pass the couch, he asks, "Don't you want me to sleep here?"

"Why would I want you to sleep on the couch? Do you think that I thought you came here to be alone? You called me to be with someone for support. Am I right?"

"Are you sure? We've barely …" and his voice trails off.

"We've barely what? No, we haven't been on a proper date, haven't held hands or even kissed yet, but we have bared our souls to each other. You know everything there is to know about what I think and feel. The things that have happened to me in my life. The things that have made me who I am. All that trumps logistics. We know who we each are and you came to me at a really tough time in your life. You could have gone to Shelly tonight for consoling, right? But you didn't. You could have stayed with your family or one of your friends. But you didn't do that either. You called me. At three in the morning. That means something. Doesn't it? Or was this merely a poor attempt at a booty call?" I turn and look at him and another smile creeps across his face. He stops and stares at me.

"What?"

"I want to kiss you."

"Okay. You can kiss me."

"No, I want to really kiss you."

I guide his hand and pull him toward me. I direct his body so that he can straddle my legs and the chair and sit directly on my lap.

"Am I hurting you?" he asks, as if he's afraid he might break me.

"No, silly, remember, I can't feel my legs. Of course, all 170 pounds of you can't sit on my lap all night without potentially cutting off my circulation and probably doing some damage, but it's okay. It's really nice that we can look into each other's eyes."

Brian puts his hand on my cheek and caresses it with his thumb. His touch makes my insides turn electric. I think about the intensity of the pulse that ran through my body when he kissed me on the forehead on the ski lift, and multiply it by a hundred. Maybe a thousand. He leans in, and I feel his warm breath as his lips finally meet mine. At first, it's a gentle kiss and then his mouth opens slightly and meets mine with a passion that makes me squirm with delight. As I feel his tongue reach between my lips to touch mine, I lose all sense of anything else in the world that is or could possibly be happening around me. Instantly I know that I have finally found *him*. And I know it is love.

As he pulls away from my mouth, he looks me in the eye, and I see sadness on his face.

"What's wrong?"

"Casey is having the worst time of his life, and I'm about to get in bed with my dream woman."

"I know, it doesn't seem fair, but for tonight, let it be a much-needed diversion. Don't feel guilty. Appreciate this moment, preserve this feeling. Bottle it up and keep it. We've waited a long time for this."

We make our way down the hall, enter my room, and I push to my side of the bed, park my chair, and transfer into bed, first lifting my butt and swiveling it onto the bed, then lifting one leg at a time. Brian watches the entire time.

"Are you okay with this?" I ask him.

He looks at me. "You're breathtaking—your looks, your presence, the way you make me feel...."

I look back at him, hanging on every word.

"I can't believe it's taken us so long to get to this point— to get beyond our insecurities, assumptions. All of it now is irrelevant. The only thing I can think of now is how desperately I want to make love to you."

His words cause a small gasp to escape from my being, but I cover my anxiety like I often do. With sarcasm. "Well, you can't do much standing next to the bed. You're gonna have to strip down or lie down or something, but standing there is not going to give you much action."

I watch as he pulls his shirt over his head, displaying his six-pack abs, and think I'm going to pass out. Then the shorts and the navy blue boxer briefs with the light blue trim. All fall to the ground. My heart is beating like never before, as I stare at him, in the flesh, with nothing left to hide. He slides under the covers and over to my side of the bed. Before I know it, we are whisking my pajama shirt off, and he gracefully helps me disrobe my lower half. The whole time we kiss and touch—and not once do I feel self-conscious. Until now, I have only been with two men, and for a brief moment I feel too inexperienced to be with this incredible man, but he immediately makes me feel no less than completely desirable. Perfect, really. We take it slow, talking, kissing, caressing. I bathe in the intensity of the emotion that passes between us, as he cradles me with a combination of affection and longing. I feel secure and loved. And as the exhaustion of our physical bodies reach the same level of depletion as our emotional selves, after this night of crisis and concern, ecstasy and rapture, Brian moves from on top of me, to beside me, and holds me in his arms until we both fall into a deep sleep.

CHAPTER 29

WHEN MY ALARM GOES OFF IN THE MORNING, my eyes immediately pop open. There is something noticeably different about how I feel. I find myself transported back to a time when I was young and carefree when the weight on my shoulders felt immensely lighter. I think for a minute, and then I look to my right, remembering how Brain and I fell asleep in each other's arms after the most passionate night I have ever experienced in my life. But as my eyes adjust to the dimness of my room, I realize he isn't there. I call out his name, but no answer. The knot begins to grow in my throat, and my eyes begin to water, but I think, "*No, he wouldn't do that to me. No, no, no.*" I have to talk my brain into believing that it's not as it seems. I take a deep breath and get out of my bed to go into the bathroom. *Whether Brian is a prince or a villain, it doesn't matter because today is Dad's wedding and the show must go on.*

I switch on the bathroom light and see a piece of scratch paper from my desk that was placed on the counter. It is a note from Brian. *Never have I met a woman so intriguing, stunning, and kind as you. I can't believe it has taken this long for us to finally see all that we are together. Thank you so much for last night. I desperately needed you on so many levels, and I appreciate you welcoming me with open arms, even at three in the morning. I'm sorry to have left you without saying goodbye, but you were fast asleep, and I know you have a big day ahead of you. Plus, I wanted to get back to the hospital. Please call me when you get up, so I can tell you good morning and hear the voice of the woman I adore.*

He adores me? My breaths are shallow as I read that and my heart feels like it is going to explode. I feel like I need to call Dad or Nat, but then I decide that, for now, I want to keep this to myself. Hold it tight and savor it for a while.

There is a smile plastered on my face that I couldn't remove with an SOS pad and I know I've got to get ready for the wedding. I reach for my phone, navigate directly to the Rainey and Brian song list, and hit play. First the strum of an electric guitar and music that I can't help but bop my head to, and finally AC/DC *Black in Black* is full volume in my bathroom. I transfer into the shower and hurry through my morning routine. Hair washed, dried, curled, and make-up applied all in record time. And with quite stunning results, I must admit. I pull out the navy-blue two-piece dress that Natalie and I picked out at the mall last weekend. After wriggling my body into it, I look in the mirror. I feel like I am glowing. Not because of the dress, but because I can't believe the utter happiness that has descended upon my life.

Before I leave the house, I call Brian.

"Hello?" he says sweetly. "Is this my dream woman?"

"I'm not sure, but I certainly hope so," I reply.

"How are you this morning, sunshine?"

"To be honest, I feel light and airy, like a big weight has been lifted off my chest. I only wish you felt the same, but I know you've got some serious stuff happening in your life that didn't go away overnight."

"You're right, but you certainly made me feel better, in a lot of ways. Thank you for that," he adds.

"How are things at the hospital?"

"Holding steady for now. I sent my parents home to take a shower and get some rest, and my brothers will likely take the next break. I'll be here for the day."

"I wish there was something I could do for you," I say genuinely.

"Actually, Rainey, there is. Do you think you could come by the hospital and meet Casey and the rest of my family? I think it would do them good to meet you."

"Do they even know about me?"

"Yes, they know a lot of the bits and pieces, but I've never given them the whole puzzle."

"So, they don't know about the chair?"

"No," he sounds self-conscious. "I never told them. I would have, but things kept falling apart between us, and I never got that far."

"It's okay, Brian. Baby steps. But we'll sure surprise the heck out of them today, won't we?"

"Yeah," he says, sounding relieved at my lighthearted response to the situation.

"Well, I have the wedding at two, but I can come over during cake and cocktails, which will happen from the time the wedding is over until we head to dinner at six. How does that sound?"

"Perfect. Give me a call when you're on your way over."

"Will do."

"And Rainey," he adds quickly, as I'm about to say goodbye and hang up. "Thank you for being so kind and supportive."

"Any time. And Brian?"

"Yes?"

"I like you."

"I like you too, Rainey."

When I hang up, I hold my phone up to my chest and hug it as if to thank it for presenting me with the remarkable man on the other end of the line.

When I arrive at the Botanic Gardens, I am escorted to a white tent and seated in the middle of a small courtyard in the back where Dad and Sara's ceremony will take place. I see the members of my extended family, and through the science of deduction, realize that anyone I don't know must somehow be related to Sara. There are only two rows of six chairs each on both sides. Doesn't take a lot to seat twenty-four guests, so it looks like a mini-wedding. As I sit there and take in the sight of exquisite flower arrangements, the candles up front, and the bows that adorn the edges of the tent, I can't control my nervous jitters. I am elated for my father and happy that even though Ben will be my date this afternoon, by tonight I will be back in Brian's arms and all will be right in my world.

I felt bad when I made the call to Ben this morning, but I couldn't tell him what had happened over text, and I didn't want to un-invite him to the wedding the morning of. So, I called him and said, "Umm, Ben ... something has come up, and I'll have to miss my dad's wedding party and dinner today. Mind if we take separate cars and call it a day once the ceremony is over? I'll tell you all about it at the wedding."

I expect him to show up at any minute, but prior to that, I want to get word to my dad about all that's transpired in the last twelve hours and get his blessing to miss part of his special day.

———

Natalie arrives shortly after me, along with Seth and her mom, and heads straight over to me. "Stunning, as always, Miss Rainey May," she says and gives me a big hug. "How are you doing on this magnificent sunny day?"

"Nat, I can't even tell you how great I feel, and so I won't. At least not yet. I have to find my dad, and if you see Ben, tell him I'll be right back and don't say one other thing to him. I have to tell him first."

"Tell him what first?"

"About last night. But without all the details."

"Wait, what happened last night?"

"I told you, I'll tell you in a bit. For now, hold down the fort."

I take off to find my dad inside where the foyer, bathrooms, and staging area are located for the bride and groom. When I eye him, he is full of smiles and gives me his signature bear hug. "Hi, Daddy," I say. I haven't called him Daddy since my mom died, but I think that was because I thought my daddy had died in that accident too. But here he is, fully alive and back in my life. The man with a sparkle in his eyes, a wide grin across his face, and an air of confidence that's been removed for seventeen years.

"How's my pumpkin?" Also, something I haven't heard in years. Is this a sign that we are going to have a happy ending after all?

"Dad, I need to take care of something for a couple of hours after the wedding and before dinner."

I can tell he's picked up the seriousness in my tone, and he replies, "Of course, Rainey. Is there something wrong?"

Right there on his wedding day, I drop the whole story on him. Casey's accident, Brian's late-night visit, needing to break up with Ben after the ceremony and wanting to visit with Brian's family. My plate is suddenly overflowing.

"Wow, that sure is a lot for one day, isn't it? But I'm glad that you can be of support to Brian and his family. Maybe you can share with them all the wisdom you have gained over the past seventeen years. If you can help another kid get through what you had to deal with, and even make it a little bit easier for him, I want you to be able to do that."

"Okay. I promise I'll make it to the restaurant for dinner."

"I know you will, Pumpkin. And please, bring Brian. We have an extra seat if Ben won't be there, and I know we'd all like to meet this secret man of yours. The one who seems to have given you a little extra pink in your cheeks today. You look radiant, sweetheart."

"Thanks, Dad. I'm going to find my seat. Congratulations on opening your heart to someone new. I know Mom is looking down on you right now with both tears and a huge smile. She wants you to be happy and live your life. And, I believe she would absolutely adore Sara."

"But do you?" my dad asks with sincere concern.

"I do, Dad. I think she's perfect."

I can tell my answer means a lot to him. He kisses me on the cheek and says, "I will see you again after I am a happily married man. I love you."

"I love you too, Daddy."

By the time I get back out to the tent, Ben has arrived and is seated beside Natalie and her family, with an open spot next to him where he has already removed the chair and made enough room for me to park my own chair. When I pull up next to him, Natalie leans forward and looks down the aisle at me, like she is going to explode if she doesn't hear about last night. It's fun to keep her temporarily in the dark, but I begin to tell Ben the abbreviated story of the on-again-off-again nature of my relationship with Brian and ultimately conclude with Casey and how Brian needs me at the hospital for the day. I can tell that Ben is hurt. I know he truly likes me, but he puts his hand on my leg and says, "Rainey, I understand. As much as I have enjoyed hanging out with you the past couple of months, I always knew you were looking for more. Or, at the very least, something different. Honestly, I have been expecting this, but I guess I didn't expect it today. Breaking up at a wedding is, well, not an ideal scenario."

I grasp his hand and hold it for the duration of the ceremony.

When the wedding ceremony is over, I say a wistful goodbye to Ben and hustle to give kisses and congratulations to the bride and groom, and then hurry to my car to get to the hospital.

As I am getting into the car, I hear the words, "Not so fast, little missy. You're not leaving until you tell me what's going on." Again, I give Natalie the short story, but add in a few of the intimate details. As I shut the car door and back out of the parking lot, she stares at me, smiling and shaking her head.

I finally get to the hospital at 3:30 p.m., after calling Brian ahead of my arrival, so he can come down from the third floor and meet me at the entrance. When the elevator door opens, and he locks eyes with me, I can see his jaw visibly drop.

He walks over to where I'm sitting—next to one of the tan, tweed couches of the lobby waiting room—and for a moment, simply stares. Then the words finally come out of his mouth. "You look stunning!" He sits down next to me on one of the waiting room chairs, and turns to face me, grabbing and holding my hands tight. Again, he just stares.

"Okay, look this is getting embarrassing," I say, feeling anxious under the microscope of his gaze.

He still doesn't say anything, only shakes his head and smiles.

"Yes, women in wheelchairs can dress up, put on makeup, and actually clean up quite nicely. What of it?"

"If I were to tell you right now that I have to kiss you or my body will explode, would you let me or would you roll through the tiny pieces of my remains?" he asks as he circles my chair. He stops to take extra notice of my back, which is one hundred percent exposed. The top of the two-piece dress is a halter, and all that shows is my back and the tie around the nape of my neck. What little strip of material that crosses my lower back is completely hidden by the back of my wheelchair, so I look nearly naked from behind. In front, the halter cuts in deeply from my shoulders, so it doesn't cover much either, except for the pertinent parts. All in all, I have to agree with his sentiment. I look pretty damn sexy.

Again, he straddles my lap, puts his hands under my hair and on my neck, and gently pulls me toward him. He puts his lips to mine, tongue in mouth. It's the first kiss in my life that literally makes me see stars. As he pulls away, I say with a smile, and a bit breathless, "Actually, I think I'm the one who is going to explode in a million tiny little pieces."

He looks at me with a tender glance, but I can tell he is still hurting inside. No matter how good things are between us, Casey is still foremost on his mind. "Are you ready to go up to see the patient?"

I give him a sympathetic nod, sigh, and answer, "Let's get up there." We head toward the elevator. I push my chair with one hand as he holds my other and guides me alongside him.

There is no way either of us can let go.

We reach Casey's room, and the door is closed. Brian knocks softly and from inside we hear a faint "Come in." Brian leads the way, and I stay a distance back, but as he opens the door I can see around his waist through a gap between him and the doorframe. His whole family is gathered around Casey's bed as if it's a vigil for the dead. His family members greet him in unison as he walks through the doorway. I stay back and watch.

Casey pipes up, "Hey, Uncle Brian, you've returned."

"Of course I did," Brian says as he walks the few steps from the door to the side of the bed. "I had to go downstairs to get someone I want you to meet." Brian scans the room filled with family members and says, "Actually, there's someone I want you all to meet." All eyes immediately turn to me, and I can feel my cheeks flush. Brian walks the three steps back over to the door to welcome me in. He grabs my hand and says to his family, "I want you all to meet my new girlfriend, Rainey Abbott."

Did he say girlfriend? I can't help but beam, even though I can tell I am staring into a room of confused faces.

He continues, "You might know her as May."

Only Casey is brave enough to speak, and he says what they are all obviously thinking. "May, as in from MFEO? The skier and race car driver?"

"Of all the things I told you about her, Casey, that's what you remember?"

"Well, yeah. You said she was nice and stuff, but she races cars! That's rad, especially for a chick."

"Casey!" his mom spurts out. But then equally curious, she asks, "You race cars in that wheelchair?"

The flush of her cheeks gives away the fact that even she's surprised herself with the boldness of her question.

Clearly, she isn't quite comfortable with the elephant in the room, aka, my wheelchair. But she is intrigued.

"Well, I get out of the chair and into the driver's seat, but yes, I can control a race car using my hands."

"What's the fastest you've ever driven?"

"Oh, I guess right about 120 on a straightaway."

"Dang! That's cool."

While Casey is utterly unfazed by my chair, and totally into my racing, it's obvious that the rest of the family is sufficiently confused.

Brian finally finds the words to give his family a summary of my story. "Rainey was injured in a car accident when she was fifteen. She's used a wheelchair ever since. Now she teaches elementary school and recently retired from competitive skiing. And, she is the woman I have been telling you all about since we met online back in August."

"You're paralyzed, like me, Rainey?"

"Yes, I'm paralyzed from my belly button down. A little lower than your injury, but not too far different. Either way, you learn to get around."

"You must. Uncle Brian told me how you whupped him in the ski race. Said it was emasculating to be killed so bad by a girl."

Brian turns three shades of red and continues, "Remember, Casey, what I say to you in the car about my love life stays in the car. Or else I'll tell everyone about your crush on Rachel."

Now it's Casey's turn to go red, but he neither confirms nor denies the statement.

Suddenly the weirdest thing happens. A room that was thick with tension visibly softens. I watch as shoulders literally relax and eyes become brighter.

Brian and I stay in the room for a good hour, while I go into more depth about my accident and my experiences adapting to the chair. I can tell that in those minutes, I give his family hope. Much more than they could grasp before Brian and I came through the door.

After a while, Brian says, "Excuse us," and leads me outside the room. "Rainey, I can't thank you enough for coming over here. I can tell they needed that boost. And the reassurance that everything is going to be all right."

"I'm glad I could do that for you and your family," I say. "Brian?"

"Yeah?"

"I want to stay here and be with you, but you know I need to get back to my father's wedding celebration."

"I know you do. But I appreciate you taking the time to come over here."

"Yeah, but Brian?"

"Yes," he says, trying to figure out where this conversation is going.

"There's a whole group of people in there who are not

going to leave Casey's side for the next handful of hours. Why don't you stay for a while, then come meet me for dinner at six? My family would love to meet you … and it would mean the world to me. Then you can come back and do the overnight shift at the hospital when everyone else is tired and could use a break to go home and rest. I'll even come and spend the night with you and Casey if you want. We'll watch movies until he falls asleep, and then you and I can curl up together on that pull out couch, which looks mighty comfortable.

"Uh, that couch is far from comfortable."

"I know. Those hospital couches never are, but with you, I think I could be comfortable anywhere."

He pauses for a moment and then smiles. "I'd like that."

Then he shakes his head, as if in disbelief.

"What?" I ask.

"All circumstances of this relationship have been completely out of the ordinary, and now we're having our first kiss, first, shall I say, relations, and meeting each other's families—one in a hospital and one at a wedding. All within twenty-four hours. Could it get any more bizarre?"

"Well, we are going to spend our second date night sleeping in a hospital," I respond. "But, in case you didn't notice, I don't do normal. I much prefer to be unique." And for the first time in my life, I truly believe it. And actually, appreciate it. I even realize I've finally learned to love myself for it.

EPILOGUE

IT'S DAD AND SARA'S ONE-YEAR ANNIVERSARY, and Natalie and I are sitting in the bridal suite. Well, it's not an actual suite, but a fancy room at the Alpine House Bed and Breakfast where Brian and I have chosen to have our wedding. I wring my fingers as she puts the final touches on my hair and veil. As she fusses over the placement of tendrils of hair that hang down in wisps on either side of my face, I have to continue to pinch myself. This is truly happening. I. Am. Getting. Married. I was beginning to think I would never see this day come to pass, but at this point, I can't imagine a life without Brian. I am overjoyed to become Mrs. Rainey May Matthews.

We've chosen to have a small wedding—mostly family, a few longtime friends, and some fellow ski teammates. Of course, I haven't forgotten Jake and Amber, but I consider them family. Natalie is my matron of honor, and my dad will walk me down the aisle. Casey is Brian's best man.

Christine asked me today if I felt badly taking the spotlight off Dad and Sara since it is *their* special day, but neither Dad nor I see it that way. This wedding was planned to take place on this day for a reason. Since my father and I lost the loves of our lives on the same day, so too shall our new loves join our worlds on the same day. That way we have a time to celebrate Mom and Sunny and a day to celebrate finally moving on and reigniting our hearts. We both have a lot of life yet to live, and it's about time we embrace it.

When the bride's wedding music begins, my heart starts to pound. I'm glad that I am beside my dad with his arm around me for support. I look at the brightly colored pink and orange tulips that light up our open-air wedding at the top of a ridge in the Colorado mountains. I told Brian that because the mountains have become such a part of me, I couldn't get married anywhere else. Fortunately, he wholeheartedly agreed.

We had to put down a special aisle runner to provide a sturdy surface for both Casey and me to be able to push along in our wheelchairs through the tall grassy field. Not all the world is built with easy accessibility, but we've made it work.

As I push down the aisle toward Natalie and Casey and Brian, I can hear Taylor, Natalie and Seth's five-month-old son, who is sitting on Cecile's lap in the front row and babbling. The sound is music to my ears. Seth swears he already sees signs of Taylor becoming a quarterback one day. "He has the build for it," he says.

Natalie is anxious for Brian and me to start having kids so our offspring will be best friends, just like she and I, but I keep telling her to give me a minute. "One thing at a time," I say. Although I've already talked it over with my doctor and gotten the green light to go ahead, I think it'll still be some time before we expand our family. Brian and I are anxious to enjoy our married life for a while first.

Although he's still trying to gain his footing, figuratively speaking, in his new life, Casey is taking the one-year mark of his accident remarkably well. He went to a camp in California in the spring where he learned that even with his disability, rock climbing is still a viable sport. He enjoyed learning the new skills required to get back up and going. But, interestingly enough, what he really wants now is to become a race car driver. Says it'll be a better way to pick up chicks. And what better role model could he have than Jake, who is already giving him mechanics lessons and teaching him driving skills and strategy.

I thought Brian's family might not understand him falling for a woman with a disability who lives her life from a wheelchair, but, in fact, I think they feel blessed by my presence. I am overjoyed that I have been able to contribute, even in a small way, toward helping his family heal, as he has helped my family to heal.

It's astounding how lives can be so purposefully intertwined that we end up somehow navigating toward the people who will fill our hearts and help guide us through our ups and downs. In my thirty-four years, I have learned how short and delicate life is. We may not always get things right, our paths might not follow what we imagine for ourselves, but it's up to us to hold on and find our life's meaning; to take what we're given and accept it. And, most especially, to open our hearts to love—to love ourselves and to be loved by others. Because in the end, that's all we truly have—love and our ability to pull others to us and embrace them.

THE END

INTERVIEW WITH THE AUTHOR

What was your inspiration in writing *Chance for Rain?*

In the fall of 2000, I was a competitive cyclist, but was hit by a car while training and suffered a spinal cord injury. I was in my early 30's, and it was a time in my life when I felt I was supposed to be finding the "man of my dreams," getting married, settling into my career, thinking about children and moving forward on the "typical" path of life (does that even exist?). Suddenly, my life was upended and I had to become accustomed to a new normal. I knew I still wanted a relationship, but I wasn't sure how my disability was going to change the dating scene. I met my husband while participating in wheelchair sports, and as I have met more women with disabilities, whether through peer counseling of newly injured women or through the non-profit I founded to teach women with disabilities sports and fitness (www.thecycleofhope.org), inevitably, the topic of relationships comes up and around it is a lot of uncertainty, anxiety, and worry that acceptance will be hard to find in a companion. Rainey is not created specifically out of my experiences nor any one person's experience, but around the stories of many women with disabilities, molded into one character.

You chose a romance for your first novel—do you plan on writing additional novels in this genre?

When I think of the genre of romance, I don't feel it completely describes *Chance for Rain*. To me, this novel is more about life experience and how we adapt to the situations that catch us off guard or for which we are unprepared—specifically the disability experience.

With that said, a big part of life is the relationships with which we surround ourselves and often the search for the unconditional love and adoration that comes with the childhood promise of "happily ever after." It doesn't always work that way and relationships can get complicated, hurtful or come to an end, but I admit, I am a fan of thoughtful stories about love, and am never disappointed by a happy ending. I am drawn to the expansive, intricate and quirky aspects of this emotion. And yes, I plan on continuing to write, bringing more stories to life which include characters with disabilities.

What is the importance of having a character with a disability as your central character?

One of the greatest challenges of having a disability is being viewed with sorrow or pity. I wanted to create a character who is not portrayed as "tragic" but could be viewed and appreciated for both her struggles and triumphs. Life with a disability can be every bit as fulfilling or rewarding as life without. And while it can seem difficult or tedious when viewed from the outside, it's not unlike any other life. I wanted to create a character where the reader could perhaps see a life different than their own, yet recognize her challenges as universal, and frankly, quite ordinary. At one time or another we are all insecure, concerned with body image, desperate to feel love both internally and externally; and of course, we all have areas of strength and confidence too.

There were many references to everyday life with a disability—the wheelchair-isms, the "inspiration" label and Brian's reference to May being "confined" to a wheelchair. Were these purposeful inclusions?

Yes. I think I would be doing a disservice to the inclusion of a character with a disability without giving a snapshot of what life can be like when people view you differently or see a disability before seeing the person. Just google "what never to say to a person who uses a wheelchair," "inspiration porn" or "person-first language" and you can learn a lot about the way disabilities are perceived and portrayed, daily obstacles those with a disability face, and some simple tips on disability etiquette.

Rainey is a Paralympic skier as well as a race car driver. Why did you choose to add those two aspects of her character?

Although some will criticize Rainey's character for being portrayed as a "super crip"—that she has a disability, yet has "overcome" it to become a Paralympic athlete, my goal is to show that some people have disabilities and, are simultaneously gifted athletes. Her athleticism was not meant as a characteristic to overshadow her disability. As a Paralympian myself, I want people to view me as an athlete first. I want my disability or "inspirational" nature to be secondary; perhaps not even at issue, as it relates to competing in sports. Paralympians train their bodies and minds just as Olympians do, and my hope is that Rainey will show readers that even with a disability, all things are possible.

BOOK CLUB QUESTIONS

- Describe Rainey's character as it relates to her disability. How does Rainey's character change over the course of the novel in coming to terms with her disability?

- What assumptions do you make about individuals with visible disabilities? Mobility disabilities? Does Rainey reinforce those assumptions or does she make you believe differently? What about Jake? In what ways do those characters change your lens?

- On their first "date" at Bittersweet Restaurant, was Rainey justified in making her quick exit? Why or why not?

- Imagine yourself in Rainey's situation and entering into an online relationship. Would you disclose a disability immediately, or give it some time, as Rainey did? When is the right time to share something like a disability?

- Would you feel comfortable dating someone who was "different" or had a disability? How much do you identify with Rainey's, Brian's, Natalie's and Jake's attitudes toward disability and difference? What influences attitudes about the prospects of relationships with people with disabilities?

- There is a thread running through the story about the other men in Rainey's world, including her dad, that Rainey admired for a variety of reasons. Rainey and her dad both experienced the significant loss of her mom and Sunny and experienced new relationships with their "improvised family unit." How did those experiences help shape Rainey's definition of love and relationships that would be worthy of trust and vulnerability?

- Do you feel that Rainey was a victim of her insecurities, or was she justified in her concerns around dating? How does her disability define her or affect her self-worth?

- What has been your exposure to Paralympic sports? Do you see it as "parallel" to Olympic sport, as its name suggests?

- What message does this book ultimately send about overcoming self-doubt and/or learning self-acceptance?

BOOK CLUB

INVITE TRICIA TO YOUR BOOK CLUB!

As a special offer to Chance for Rain readers, Tricia has offered to visit your book club either by Skype or in person.

Please contact Tricia directly to schedule an appearance at your book club.

Tricia@triciadowning.com

ACKNOWLEDGMENTS

Since the time I was seven years old and part of my first sports team, I have always appreciated that the greatest personal accomplishments aren't solo ventures. It truly does take a village. And, I have to admit, embarking on my first fiction novel was a daunting task, but knowing I had a team of knowledge behind me to help and support me in this experience was just what I needed to take it and run. Having support from all angles gave me the courage to give life to my characters, explore new ways to share the experience of disability and to let my mind wander through the unfolding relationship of Rainey and Brian, showing not only their vulnerabilities, but mine.

I am eternally grateful for the people who have helped me through the journey that is *Chance for Rain*. I so appreciate the help of my talented editors, Donna Mazzitelli who taught me about story and character development and Bobby Haas who nudged me out of my comfort zone as a writer and always threw in a kind and encouraging word, even when pushing me to grow and be better at my craft.

I am thankful for my longtime friend Sheila Kaehny for her excellent ideas and writing knowledge and spending hours with me helping me sharpen my descriptions and stories and to Damon Brown for getting me out of the many corners I found myself writing myself into. For all of the late-night emails you answered in ten minutes or less, with just the right words when I didn't have them, thank you.

I appreciate being able to turn to fellow Paralympian Sandy Dukat for help with my skiing knowledge, Michael Johnson for his car racing guidance, Ryan Harbuck for sharing her vulnerable high school years following a tragic accident, Valerie Schoolcraft at James Madison University for her disability studies lens and April Coughlin for reading the very first draft, years before the final would come to fruition. I thank all the friends who read drafts, sections and listened as I fleshed out characters and story and who listened with patience to my cycle of highs and lows as I went from confidence in my writing to uncertainty and back again. Writing a novel can certainly make you question yourself in so many ways during the journey from initial idea to completion.

I could not have navigated the publishing process without the generous guidance of my phenomenal friend and mentor, Polly Letofsky at My Word Publishing and her team of: Andrea Costantine, Victoria Wolf, Jennifer Bisbing, Donna Mazzitelli and Bobby Haas.

Lastly—to live with a writer is a truly arduous experience. Thank you to my husband Steve, who has demonstrated endless amounts of patience as he journeyed with me through the stages of writing a novel and offered solace every time I wanted to chuck the whole thing. And, as always I am grateful to have the little furry feet of my two cats Jack and Charlie, even when they walked across my keyboard, altering completely the meaning of a sentence I had perfected only seconds before.

To all those I have mentioned and the handfuls of others who are always on my team, my complete gratitude goes to you for helping me bring this novel to fruition.

ABOUT THE AUTHOR

Tricia Downing is recognized as a pioneer in the sport of women's paratriathlon, as the first female paraplegic to finish an Iron distance triathlon. She has competed in that sport both nationally and internationally, in addition to competing in road racing and other endurance events. She has represented the United States in international competition in five different sport disciplines—cycling (as a tandem pilot prior to her 2000 accident), triathlon, duathlon, rowing and Olympic style shooting, in which she was a member of Team USA at the 2016 Paralympic Games in Rio de Janeiro, Brazil.

She was featured in the Warren Miller documentary *Superior Beings* and on the lifestyle TV magazine show *Life Moments*. She has been featured in *Muscle and Fitness Hers*, *Mile High Sports* and *Rocky Mountain Sports* magazines.

Additionally, she is founder of The Cycle of Hope (www.thecycleofhope.org), a non-profit organization designed for female wheelchair users to promote health and healing on all levels—mind, body and spirit.

Tricia studied Journalism as an undergraduate at the University of Maryland and holds Masters degrees in both Sports Management (Eastern Illinois University) and Disability Studies (Regis University).

She lives in Denver, Colorado with her husband Steve and two cats, Jack and Charlie. Visit Tricia at triciadowning.com

88345082R00220

Made in the USA
Middletown, DE
08 September 2018